THEIR FOREVER
MELODY

**The Matched to Perfection Series
by Priscilla Oliveras**

His Perfect Partner

Her Perfect Affair

"Holiday Home Run" in *A Season to Celebrate*

Their Perfect Melody

Published by Kensington Publishing Corporation

THEIR PERFECT MELODY

Priscilla Oliveras

ZEBRA BOOKS
KENSINGTON PUBLISHING CORP.
http://www.kensingtonbooks.com

ZEBRA BOOKS are published by

Kensington Publishing Corp.
119 West 40th Street
New York, NY 10018

All Kensington titles, imprints, and distributed lines are available at special quantity discounts for bulk purchases for sales promotion, premiums, fundraising, educational, or institutional use.

Special book excerpts or customized printings can also be created to fit specific needs. For details, write or phone the office of the Kensington Sales Manager: Attn.: Sales Department. Kensington Publishing Corp., 119 West 40th Street, New York, NY 10018. Phone: 1-800-221-2647.

Zebra and the Z logo Reg. U.S. Pat. & TM Off.

First Printing: December 2018
ISBN-13: 978-1-4201-4430-7
ISBN-10: 1-4201-4430-8

eISBN-13: 978-1-4201-4433-8
eISBN-10: 1-4201-4433-2

10 9 8 7 6 5 4 3 2 1

Printed in the United States of America

It takes a village (at least for me) to inspire, brainstorm, write, revise, proofread, and send a book out into the world. This one came to fruition in large part thanks to the influence of . . .

Ines—a dear friend, dedicated victim's advocate, true rock star, and one of the strongest women I know . . . any errors are all mine, but Lilí's heart was created in your image; gracias mi amiga!

My #4ChicasChat hermanas (sisters)—Mia Sosa, Sabrina Sol, and Alexis Daria—You've made this scary, thrilling, frustrating, uplifting wild ride of published author life so much better; gracias por ser parte de lo que es bueno en mi vida!

The small, but growing Latinx romance author community—Here's to more of our voices being heard and our stories being shared with the world! Check us out via #LatinxRom!

My zumba familia—¡Mi gente! Our classes and Latin Nights kept me sane and helped work off my writing snacks during the looming deadlines! #GoGators #Wepa ¿Qué, qué? ¡Muchísimas gracias por su amistad, apoyo y amor!

Groups such as I Always Get Consent, It's On Us, and others striving to raise awareness and stop sexual assault, on campuses and beyond—your hard work and efforts are vitally important! Thank you! www.itsonus.org www.ialwaysgetconsent.tumblr.com

Mi familia . . . my Mami, Papi, sister, brother, and three amazing daughters—all good in my life starts with you; los quiero un montón!

Chapter One

"Look, lady, you need to calm down and step back. I really don't want to have to arrest you."

"Arrest? Are you freaking kidding me?" Lilí Fernandez slapped her envelope purse against her thigh and gaped at the muscular cop blocking her way up the ratty apartment building's cracked front stoop.

Dios mío, what the hell was this guy's problem?

It had taken her a good thirty prayer-filled and frantic minutes to cab it from the art museum downtown over to the Humboldt Park area on Chicago's West Side. No way was one beefcake-looking cop going to stop her from getting inside. Not when Melba needed her.

Feet spread in a wide stance, the cop cradled his gun holster with his right hand. He held his left arm out in front of his muscular chest, fingers splayed in a no-nonsense stop sign. The way he'd planted himself like a towering oak at the top of the third step, it was obvious this guy wasn't kidding.

"Look, Officer . . ." Lilí squinted in the waning sunlight glinting off the cop's name tag. ". . . Reyes, Melba González called me. Freaked out. Afraid for her life and begging me to come help her. I'm going in there whether you like it or not."

The officer gave another firm shake of his head. "Don't push your luck, okay? No one goes inside without clearance first."

Annoyed, Lilí rolled her eyes at his hard-line stance. "The victim *cleared* me when she called, asking me to come. Look, there she is!"

Lilí jabbed her hand toward the first-floor window on the right, pointing at a shadowy figure behind the filmy cream curtain. It could be Melba, though Lilí wasn't really sure.

Melba could also be lying on the floor in pain. Or worse.

The terrible thought had Lilí's heart thundering in her chest. Her skin prickled with unease at the idea of what might have happened since their call had been disconnected. *Dios mío*, she prayed it hadn't taken Chicago's finest as long as her to get here and that Melba was safe. Unhurt.

When Melba had first called earlier, Lilí hadn't answered. Normally when she didn't recognize a number she let it click over to voice mail. Besides, she'd been waiting in line at the fundraising event's open bar, her gaze perusing the mix of beautiful artwork and the elegance of some of Chicago's wealthiest society members. Marveling that she, one of the "little people" from the nearby suburb of Oakton, was rubbing elbows with them all.

That was her brother-in-law Jeremy Taylor's influence. Since his marriage to her middle sister, Rosa, four years ago, Jeremy's parents had welcomed all three Fernandez sisters into their home and social circle. Last Christmas, when the girls' cousin Julia had visited from Puerto Rico, Mrs. Taylor had hired Julia as an event planner. A move that ultimately led Julia to stay in Chicago, thanks to a job offer and a new relationship.

But, when the second call in as many minutes from the same Chicago area code had set Lilí's phone vibrating, something inside her pushed her to answer. Warily, she'd slid her thumb across the phone screen.

Her stomach dropped to her feet when she recognized Melba González's frantic voice. Between Melba's sobs and the thunderous pounding on the bathroom door behind which the woman hid, Lilí could hear Melba's husband's threatening voice. Tito was drunk. On an angry rampage. Again.

Sure, Lilí didn't typically share her private number with someone who came into the assault victims' clinic. Not that there was an actual policy against it, but Lilí figured the director might frown upon it if she knew. Forget how pissed Lilí's two older sisters would be.

Rosa and Yazmine were already worried about her living alone in the city, constantly harping on her to be safe and aware of her surroundings. As if she didn't teach community education classes on that very subject.

The thing was, Melba's dire situation had been rapidly declining over the past few months. Tito had been laid off and was drinking more, relying on buddies for odd jobs. Legal or illegal, it didn't seem to matter to him.

Lilí had tried everything she could think of to convince the thirty-year-old woman that she could truly count on her and the staff at the shelter to be by her side, guiding her through the ropes that would get Melba out of her toxic situation. Melba was *thiiiiis* close to having the confidence to pack up and leave her degenerate husband. Fear, borne from years of mental and physical abuse, kept the poor woman from gathering enough courage.

Two days ago, as a last-ditch effort, Lilí had scrawled her cell number on the back of her official business card when Melba had stopped by for what had become a fairly regular Wednesday midmorning visit on her way to work at a nearby laundromat. Lilí had pressed the card into Melba's hand, counseling her to keep it in a safe place, hidden from Tito, for emergencies.

When your drunk, and probably high, brute of a husband descended on you with a knife, it definitely counted as an emergency.

Lilí had promised to help. That meant, no cop, no matter how adamant, would stop her.

"Come on!" she pressed, her exasperation rising. "You have to let me in there."

"Sorry. No dice." The cop's exasperated frown belied his apology. "Until I can verify who you are, I can't let you go into the crime scene."

"Crime scene?" The words scraped her throat as she said them. Her thoughts instantly jumped to worst-case scenarios.

Tito breaking down the door, stabbing Melba as she cowered in the bathroom corner.

Melba lying on the floor in pain, wondering why Lilí hadn't come to her rescue.

Fear arced through her and Lilí squeezed her black evening clutch purse to her chest with both hands.

Even if the police had arrived in time to scare off Tito, Melba needed someone she trusted to better deal with the aftermath. Not a bunch of cops more than likely ill-equipped to console a battered woman, especially if they were as hard-assed as this guy. Melba needed *her*.

Screw this.

Anger galvanized Lilí's efforts and she lunged to the right onto the first step.

"Hey, what do you think you're doing?" Officer Reyes sputtered.

She quickly veered left and up another step in an evasive move, more determined than ever to get by.

Unfortunately, her stilettos slowed her down and he moved faster, deftly sliding to his right. She slammed into his broad chest, her breath coming out in a *whoosh*.

Lilí teetered on her heels, her arms flailing as she fought for balance.

He grabbed on to her waist to keep her from stumbling down the two steps. Instinctively she grasped his firm biceps. Her arm muscles clenched, jerking her toward him, and her chest wound up pressed against his. She gaped up at him in surprise.

This close she caught a faint whiff of his earthy aftershave. The angular features of his tan face filled her vision before she shook off his hands and scurried back to the sidewalk, annoyed at her inability to get around him.

Arms crossed, Officer Reyes frowned down at her, the firm set of his jaw a sign of his irritation.

She itched to move up to the first step, take away some of his height advantage. Unfortunately, she'd gotten up close and personal enough to him already. Better she stay down here.

"Listen to me," she huffed. "My client is inside there and you can't stop me from seeing her."

"Client? Are you a lawyer or something?"

"If being her lawyer gets you outta my way, then yes, I'm her lawyer," she threw back at him.

The cretin narrowed his eyes. His lips pursed in obvious annoyance. *Pues*, that made two of them.

Lilí swallowed her scoff. If he expected his stern expression to intimidate her into acquiescing, Officer Reyes had another think coming.

When it came to her clients—*bueno*, pretty much anyone in need of assistance—she didn't back down easily. Even wearing a short cocktail dress and heels, she'd readily go toe to toe with anyone who got in her way.

Hands on her hips, Lilí returned Officer Reyes's glare with one of her own as she gave him the once-over. Too bad he'd resumed his hand-over-holster, shoulder-wide stance. The man looked about as unyielding as she felt. Damn, she'd bet her life savings, meager amount though it might be, that she hadn't swayed him in the least.

Maybe in-your-face wasn't the way to go with this guy.

Straightening her shoulders, Lilí smoothed her hands down the front of her favorite little black dress. She channeled the polite manners Mami and Papi had drilled into her. The same ones she'd had on display at the benefit tonight, especially as she thanked Jeremy's parents for the invitation to their swanky fundraiser and apologized for her abrupt departure.

"Okay, I get it, Reyes. I know you're simply trying to do your job. And it's not always an easy one." Lilí deliberately pitched her voice to calm and soothing. Agreeable even. "So am I. I'm Melba González's counselor, and, given what I heard in the background when she called me, I really believe she needs me right now. Don't you?"

Officer Reyes's brutish expression softened the tiniest bit.

Bingo!

Lilí offered up a silent prayer that he'd see reason.

After releasing a heavy sigh, Reyes opened his mouth to respond. At the same time the apartment's main door swung open behind him. A lumberjack-sized cop with reddish-blond hair leaned out to say, "Hey, Reyes, we're supposed to be on the lookout for a Lilí Fernandez. The victim is asking for her."

"That's me!" Lilí scampered up the three stairs, sidestepping Reyes, who had turned his back to her when the second cop had called his name.

"Wait!" he yelled.

But she didn't stop, especially since the big guy in the doorway stepped aside for her to enter.

"Check her identification, Stevens," she heard Reyes say.

Without missing a beat, Lilí snapped open her clutch and rifled through it for her driver's license.

Inside, the gloomy hallway smelled musty, the air dank. The linoleum floor was aged and discolored in places, the wallpaper peeling. She hurried past the row of metal mailboxes and stopped in front of apartment B.

"Miss, I need to see—"

"Here you go, Officer Stevens." On her best behavior, Lilí handed the cop her driver's license. "I'm a victim's advocate over at the Humboldt Park area clinic. I hate to say it, but Melba is one of my regulars."

Stevens studied her ID, his head slowly nodding. "I'm sorry to hear that."

"Yeah, well, there are far too many women—and kids—in her same position. My job is to do my best to get them out of it. So . . ."

Lilí's voice trailed off in a huff of adrenaline-reducing breath. After the hectic rush of racing through city traffic to get here, only to be blocked and bulldozed by the hunky yet intractable Officer Reyes, she needed to regroup before facing Melba. She'd be no good to the scared woman if she herself was rattled.

Eyes closed, she sucked in the dank air until her lungs were completely filled, then she slowly released it, counting backwards from twenty, focusing her attention on her job and regaining her professionalism.

"Okay, can you give me a rundown on what I'm walking into here?" she asked, her voice calm, her pulse no longer racing. "Officer Reyes called it a crime scene. What happened? Is Melba injured?"

Officer Stevens handed her back her ID. "We got a call reporting a domestic disturbance. My partner Reyes and I were a few blocks away, so we responded. When we arrived we found the front door open. The living room and kitchen were vacant, but left in shambles. The bathroom door looks like it took a real beating. Allegedly by Mr. González. But the door kept Mrs. González safe."

Sweet relief at hearing that Melba was okay pooled through Lilí, calming her rattled nerves. "Melba called me from inside the bathroom and I told her to stay put and not let Tito in for any reason. Where is he, by the way? Did another car already take him to the station?"

Dios mío, she sincerely hoped Melba would press charges this time.

Officer Stevens shook his head, his face scrunched as if in pain. "I'm not sure if the sirens spooked him, but he was gone when we arrived."

¡Ay carajo! Lilí swallowed the oath, but hell was exactly where Tito needed to be, if not behind bars. He was a menace to his wife, and anyone else who happened to cross his path.

"And Melba?" she asked.

"Inside. She's pretty shaken up. The EMTs are bandaging her arm now. Apparently her husband slashed at her with a knife before she could get herself into the bathroom."

Anger vibrated in Lilí's chest, radiating out, fueling her determination to make Tito pay. "Have they put out an APB for his sorry ass?"

Officer Stevens nodded. "If he's out on the streets, we'll find him."

"I hope so." Lilí punctuated the words with a brisk nod. "Let's go in then. If all goes well, Melba will finally press charges and agree to move into the women's shelter."

Without waiting for Officer Stevens to answer, Lilí turned the knob and stepped into the mess of overturned chairs and broken glass that decorated Melba's run-down apartment like a home invasion.

Diego leaned a hip against the faded Formica countertop separating the kitchen from the living room in Melba González's shabby first-floor apartment just off Division Street. Broken dishes, picture frames with shattered glass, and upended metal chairs from the dinette set littered the area. All evidence of the struggle and rage that had led to the 911 call that brought him and Stevens to the González residence.

The EMS team had wrapped the cut on Melba's arm and cleaned a few scrapes on her elbow and left cheek, but she had declined the offer of a ride to the hospital for a more thorough checkup. More than likely she'd also deny Stevens's attempts to talk her into pressing charges against her husband. Despite the lunatic coming at her with a freaking knife.

Experience had taught Diego that a person had to actually want their situation to change for it to happen. Someone else wanting it for them wasn't enough.

With a muttered curse, he eyed Miss Fancy Pants perched on the torn sofa cushions, her arm around Melba González's heaving shoulders.

In her black, figure-skimming cocktail dress and mile-high black stilettos, her small beaded purse that barely held her cell or much else of importance tossed on the broken remains of a coffee table, Lilí Fernandez looked as out of place as a White Sox fan in Wrigleyville on a Cubs game day. Diamond studs sparkled on her earlobes. A dainty silver necklace with a matching diamond pendant hung on her tanned chest, dangling above the edge of the scoop-necked material and the enticing cleavage he was trying like hell to ignore.

Damn if his mind didn't keep going back to the moment when she'd body-slammed him in a poor attempt to get by. Her soft curves had pressed against his chest, her eyes going wide with shock.

Desire had shot through him. Surprised, he deliberately squelched it, instinctively backing away from temptation. He was on the job, and ogling a concerned citizen, as interesting as she might be, wasn't protocol.

Moments later, he'd caught the flash of triumph in her eyes as she'd tossed him a smug grin over her slim shoulder and scurried through the door Stevens held open. Diego had been left standing on the front stoop like a dope, stunned he'd let his guard down. That never happened. On the job or off.

The sexy minx had him off his game.

Only, she was also a fancy minx, apparently having come straight from some swanky fundraiser at the art museum. Or so said the ticket she'd dropped onto the coffee table when she'd been digging in her purse for a tissue for Melba.

Despite her society trappings, which were warning signs he typically took heed of and stayed away from, there was something about the mix of Lilí Fernandez's long dark hair, light hazel-green eyes and kiss-my-ass attitude that appealed to him. Crazy as that sounded.

Hell, the last thing he needed was to get involved with some rich do-gooder slumming on Chicago's West Side. Forget the fact that she was somehow involved in a domestic case he and Stevens would have to file a report on. In the forty-five minutes or so he'd been around Lilí Fernandez he'd already deduced this *chica* was a handful, and right now, he had enough on his hands to keep him occupied.

Diego scratched his jaw, deciding to let Stevens continue taking the lead with the questioning. Better he keep his distance from this one. The situation hit too close to home, reminding him of his sister and the life she couldn't bring herself to change.

"Have they located Tito yet?" Lilí asked.

Stevens glanced at Diego for confirmation. Lilí's and Melba's gazes slid over to him as well.

He shook his head, feeling bad about the scared look his answer put back in Melba's dark eyes. A shaky breath wracked her plump body as she slumped over.

Lilí's eyes narrowed, the determined jut of her chin clueing him in to the fact that he may not like what she was about to say.

Sí, he could already read her face. It was a skill that had led the narcotics squad to come knocking on his door a few months back. He'd turned down the promotion, determined to stay on his neighborhood streets. That's where he planned to make a difference. One kid at a time.

"Have you put out a description? You never know who might be listening on a scanner or with an app and call in," Lilí pressed.

"We're working on it, miss," Stevens answered, ever the polite Illinois farmer's son.

"Yes, but—"

"It's a busy day," Diego interrupted, recognizing the pugnacious scowl on her expressive face. "The word is out on the streets. You may not know this area well, but if he's lying low, it could take a while to find him."

"*Tengo miedo,*" Melba murmured in a shaky voice.

Hell, he'd be afraid, too, if some drug-crazed lunatic had left with a warning that he'd be back to finish things.

"That's why you should agree to press charges and let us get you to a shelter," Diego said.

He took the four steps that led him from the kitchen into the living room, sidestepping a chair tipped on its side, one of the metal legs bent in the wrong direction.

Man, Tito González must have been crazed. The place looked like it'd been tossed by druggies desperate for something they could sell to get a fix. Based on Melba's description of her husband's behavior, that might not be far from the truth.

"He's right, Melba," Lilí agreed, rubbing a hand on the other woman's knee in a show of support. "You shouldn't stay here. I can get you into the shelter if you want."

Melba shook her head. "I don't want to be with a bunch of strangers I don't trust. *Me quedo aquí, en mi casa.*"

¡Coño! Diego barely bit back the "damn" that itched on the tip of his tongue. No way should Melba stay in her house, alone and defenseless. Odds were Tito González would make good on his threat. Next time, Melba might not be so lucky.

"Ma'am, we're trying to do our job to keep you safe," Stevens tried, his polite Midwest accent softening the statement. "There are resources that can assist you."

"But you need to help yourself," Diego threw in.

Lilí scowled at him. Her eyes flashed with aggravation . . . maybe even a hint of anger . . . though he had no idea why the latter.

He stepped toward them. "*Mira—*"

"No, *you* look," Lilí interrupted in a stern voice that

halted his progress. "The last thing Melba needs right now is another man being pushy. Back off."

Diego blinked in surprise. What the hell?

He could show this *chica* pushy if he wanted to. Which he didn't. If there was one thing his *mami* had drilled into him, it was respect for all women.

Hands on his hips, he glared back at Lilí Fernandez like they were two middle-schoolers playing a game of chicken.

She narrowed her eyes the tiniest bit. He mimicked her.

Stevens cleared his throat—once, twice—before Diego could bring himself to forfeit.

He slid his gaze away from her, acknowledging with a brusque nod Stevens's unspoken reminder to get his act together.

Lilí ducked her head to whisper with Melba.

Ay bendito, what was it about this woman that drove him to act like a rookie fresh out of the academy? First he turned his back and let her get around him to slip inside. Now he was losing his cool, making Stevens have to rein him in.

The radio on his shoulder squawked and Diego took advantage of the opportunity to step aside to call in his response.

Moments later, he clued back into the conversation between his partner and the two women in time to hear Lilí Fernandez saying, "We've both already said you can't stay here alone, Melba. It isn't safe. What about . . . what if I stay with you?"

"What?! *¿Estás loca?*" Diego barked.

Stevens and the two women jerked, swiveling their heads his way with varying shades of surprise on their faces. Melba's was tinted with fear. Stevens's with disbelief. But Lilí's, her surprise held an air of mutiny that warned him he'd crossed a line. Like he didn't know that already.

"No, I'm not crazy," she muttered. "I'm worried."

She clasped her hand with Melba's and the two shared a shaky smile.

"I think what my partner is trying to say"—Stevens frowned at Diego before smoothing his pale, freckled face into his normal calm expression—"is that neither of you two ladies should stay here tonight."

Diego caught the slight tremble in Lilí's free hand before she drove it through her long hair in agitation. The move ruffled her wispy bangs, giving her a mussy, just-out-of-bed look he had no business admiring.

She put up a good, brave front. He had to respect that about her.

Her shapely brows furrowed, Lilí worried her lower lip, deep in thought. Diego could practically see the wheels turning in her head and he expected no good to come of it. Or at least nothing he'd consider a good idea anyway.

So far she'd gone from Melba being her client to her friend. He was sure she'd at least bent, if not broken, some type of rule in her professional capacity as a victim's advocate.

"Okay then." Lilí nodded slowly, her expression pensive. "If we can't stay here, then you should come stay with me."

Diego slapped a palm to his forehead.

Dios mío, Miss Bleeding Heart . . . okay, sexy Miss Bleeding Heart, most definitely had to be crazy.

Forget crossing the line, this girl had just leaped the hell over it.

Before Diego even said a word, Stevens sent him a wide-eyed, pursed-mouth, back-the-hell-off look. Yeah, his partner knew him too well. Because of his background, even with their average domestic case, Diego usually had a hard time shaking it. This one, thanks to Lilí Fernandez and her save-the-day tendency, had taken a sharp turn away from "average." If she took Melba González home with her, knowing that a drug-crazed Tito remained on the loose, she'd potentially be putting herself in danger.

No way would Diego be able to walk away from this. No way could he simply file the report at the end of the night and let it go. Lilí might have no idea what she was getting herself into, but he did.

And he'd be damned if he'd let anything happen to someone else on his watch.

Chapter Two

Ave Maria purísima, her sisters were going to kill her. No prayers to blessed Mary were going to save her either.

No doubt about it. When they found out Lilí had brought home with her one of her clients from the Victims' Abuse Center, Yazmine and Rosa were going to flip. Especially since, at the moment, home was her brother-in-law Jeremy's posh condo in the Loop. He'd graciously allowed her to move into his place in downtown Chicago when she'd graduated from college three years ago and gotten her job in the city. The condo had been vacant in the year since Jeremy had married Rosa and moved into the Fernandez family home in the nearby suburb of Oakton, where she and her sisters had grown up.

Lilí paid a ridiculously low rent to Jeremy. Mostly because she refused to live for free, and partly because on her measly salary it was all she could afford.

Staying here was a compromise for her and her sisters.

They'd balked at the places she'd considered where the rent was in her price range, going all big-sister, bat-shit overprotective on her when she'd shown them some of the apartments she'd found online. Then Rosa had suggested Lilí move back home with her, Jeremy, and their daughter, Susana Marta. In the years since, their family had grown to include baby Nico.

Lilí loved her *familia*, but the offer to move in with her sister's brood had been answered with a resounding: *¡No gracias!*

Jeremy would forever be Lilí's hero for volunteering his place. The twenty-four-seven security guard at the front desk appeased her sisters' concerns. The downtown address appeased Lilí's desire to experience single-woman-in-the-city life. Plus, it beat the heck out of commuting into the city every day.

The toilet flushed in the guest bath down the hall, signaling that Melba might be out soon.

Lilí dumped some tortilla chips onto the plate with the ham sandwich she'd made for her guest. Grabbing the glass of water, she skirted the breakfast bar that separated the open kitchen from the dining and living room area. Along the far wall, the big glass windows opening to the balcony provided a calming view of the city lights sparkling like diamonds in the dark night.

She was heading back to grab her water from the kitchen when Melba appeared down the hall leading to the master and guest bedrooms. The woman tugged on the hem of her stained floral tank top, then adjusted the waistband of her faded ripped jeans. She had combed her black hair and pulled it back into a neat ponytail, making her appear younger than her nearly thirty years. Her face was now washed free of the mascara that had streaked down her cheeks due to her tears, though there was little to be done about the bruise forming on her right cheekbone from Tito's right hook.

The jerk!

"*Te agradezco esto*," Melba said, expressing her appreciation for the umpteenth time since the two of them had hailed a cab to Lilí's place.

Lilí waved off the words and offered a comforting smile.

"I'm glad you called me. Here, sit down and eat." She gestured toward the sleek black dining room table with its matching black chairs and gray cushions.

"You have a beautiful apartment," Melba said. "It's really nice."

Lilí glanced around the open living-dining area, taking in the black leather sofa, the silver-and-glass coffee table, and the decorative modern art pieces on the end table and bookshelves. Intermixed with the items Jeremy had left behind were several of her family photos in noodle-art frames, courtesy of her nieces, her favorite TV binge-watching fluffy blanket, and the few mementos she'd collected over the years.

It was a strange conglomeration of decorating by shoestring budget and fancy interior design firm.

"I'm actually renting from my brother-in-law," she admitted. "But it's home."

"Sure beats what I see in my neighborhood." Melba tucked a loose strand of hair behind her ear, wincing as she brushed her bruised cheek.

Lilí joined her at the table. She sipped her water, quietly watching while Melba dug into her sandwich.

"I know I can't stay here long," Melba said after a few moments. She wiped her mouth with the napkin Lilí had left next to the white ceramic plate, then set it down, nervously smoothing out the paper. "It's not fair of me to pull you into my mess. *Perdóname.*"

Melba's voice quavered on the last word and Lilí set her hand gently on her friend's forearm.

"You don't have to apologize," Lilí told her. "You've done nothing wrong."

"I shouldn't have called you. *Pero tenía miedo.*"

"Of course you were scared. It was a scary situation," Lilí assured her. "I would have felt the same way, too. But this is not on you at all. It's important for you to recognize that."

Melba nodded, swiping at the tears drowning her eyes. "I'm trying to. I remember everything you've said during our talks. And . . ." She took a deep, shuddering breath. "And I want to be in a healthier place. I want to change things."

¡Sí! Lilí barely contained her exclamation of triumph.

Hearing those words made the stress and worry over the drastic actions she'd taken tonight all worth it. This was the first time Melba had initiated the topic about changing her situation. Until today, the majority of her conversation had been peppered with empty platitudes along the lines of *Tito loves me* or *Tito didn't mean to.* Or worse, *What am I doing wrong?*

It was time Melba realized the danger inherent in her codependency. The problem was, with most of her family back in the Dominican Republic, the poor woman had admitted she felt alone, trapped.

But if she took advantage of the guidance Lilí and the other social service providers offered, she might come to feel differently.

"It's good to hear you say that you want to be in a better place, Melba. Really good." Lilí gave her friend's forearm a gentle squeeze in a show of support. "Saying that out loud is a big step. I'm proud of you."

Melba's round cheeks plumped a little more with

her wobbly smile. "You know, you were pretty kick-ass tonight. It was funny to see you standing up to that cop, Reyes. I don't think he expected it."

Lilí waved her hands through the air in frustration.

"*Ave Maria purísima*, that guy really got me worked up." In more ways than one, if she were honest with herself.

She flashed back to their tussle on the stairs when she'd pressed up against him. Even in that quick glance she'd noticed the tiny swirl of a cowlick barely off center in the front of his dark brown, closely cropped hair. Her gaze had slid past the slight crook on the bridge of his nose down to his full lips. Admittedly, had they met in a social situation, she probably would have been enticed to try and coax those lips into a grin.

But, neither then or now was the time for her to get sidetracked by some *papisongo* who looked far too hunky in a uniform that fit him snug in places she had no business noticing.

"What'd he do that got you so riled up?" Melba asked.

"He was being a bully."

"Nuh-uh. Tito's a bully. But Reyes?" Melba shook her head, then took a drink of water before she continued. "I've seen him around the neighborhood, talking to the kids, trying to convince them to stay outta trouble."

That wasn't the same picture Lilí had gotten of Officer Reyes. First name Diego, according to the card he'd shoved in her hand when she and Melba were ready to leave.

From the moment he'd first barred her entry into the apartment building, the guy had been throwing around his badge and his contentious attitude.

Friendly neighborhood cop was definitely not how she would describe him.

"I've heard he grew up in the Humboldt Park neighborhood. Stuck around trying to make a difference," Melba said. "Maybe he's *uno de los buenos.* You know? One of the good guys? Unlike . . . *pues,* unlike others who only, well . . ."

Melba's voice trailed off as she pushed the crumbs around her plate with a finger. She opened her mouth to say something, only to close it with another small shake of her head.

"What is it?" Lilí asked.

"I'm thinking Tito will be wondering where I am. He might worry when I'm not at home."

Lilí blew a breath between her lips. "You know what I say about that, don't you?"

"*Ese es su problema.*"

"Exactly." Lilí thumped a fist lightly on the table before repeating the mantra she'd been trying to get Melba to buy into. "That's *his* problem. Not yours."

Melba nodded slowly as she stared out the balcony doors at the darkened Chicago skyline. She picked absently at the edge of the bandage on her arm—the bandage needed to cover the wound Tito had given her when he'd slashed at her with a steak knife!

Though Melba didn't say anything, Lilí had a pretty good idea what might be going through the woman's head. The same fears and thoughts that plagued the countless other battered and abused women and children who'd come through the clinic's doors in the three years Lilí had worked there.

Dios mío, there were so many who needed counseling and intervention. So many she hadn't been able to reach. Those were the ones who haunted her at night. Like Karen had in college.

Lilí scrubbed her face with both hands, as if she could wipe away the memories inside her head.

You can only do so much, her coworkers and sisters all cautioned her to remember. At some point you have to let it go. Intellectually, she realized that. Yet, she found it exceedingly hard not to bring her work home with her.

Ha! Cutting a quick glance at Melba out of the corner of her eye, Lilí gave herself a mental slap on the back of the head. Like Julia would do if she still lived here. *Gracias a Dios* her cousin had recently moved in with her boyfriend, Ben.

Today was an anomaly, Lilí assured herself. Or, more like a necessity.

Closing her eyes, she sent a prayer up to her parents, asking for wisdom. If taking this drastic step was enough of an eye-opener for Melba, it'd be worth the risk.

"Will you go with me tomorrow?"

Melba's question brought Lilí's attention back to her. "Go where?"

"To the shelter."

Lilí waited a beat, letting Melba's words hang in the air with the weight of their importance. This was a huge decision.

"Are you sure you're ready?" Lilí asked, keeping her voice neutral.

Trust laced with uncertainty and a dash of hope swam in Melba's dark eyes. Not much older than Lilí's twenty-five years, the young woman had experienced a lifetime of pain and regret at Tito's hands. Lilí's heart ached for her.

Melba reached for Lilí's hand, giving it a tight squeeze. "You stood up to Reyes for me. You came even when you knew Tito was going *loco* trying to beat down the door. Not caring or afraid of what you were getting into. If I can't trust you, then who?"

Lilí's chest constricted with emotion at Melba's heartfelt words. She knew she shouldn't care so much. It was dangerous to become so invested in her clients' lives. But that was like asking her feet to stay still when salsa music started playing. She couldn't stop it. They were both ingrained in her DNA.

The day she stopped caring so much was the day she figured she needed to change her profession.

"*Bueno*, I'll get things set up for you," she told Melba.

"*Gracias.*"

"Anytime."

She and Melba shared a fierce hug, before Lilí moved to the kitchen counter, where she'd left her clutch purse.

"I'm going to change and make a few calls. Feel free to make yourself at home," she told Melba. "The TV remote is on the end table."

Unsnapping her purse, she pulled out her cell phone. Diego Reyes's card slid out along with it. The nondescript white rectangle with the dark Chicago PD logo practically blended in with the mottled marble counter. And yet, his name in vivid black lettering grabbed her attention. Bold and unyielding. Kind of like the man himself.

Only, based on what Melba had said, maybe he wasn't as hard-nosed and by-the-book as he came across. At least not all the time.

For a fraction of a second, Lilí wondered what he might be like, out of uniform, hanging with friends, his handsome face lit with a smile at something she—

Ay, what was she doing? She should not be letting her mind run away with silly thoughts about someone who was completely inappropriate for her. No way could she be interested in Diego Reyes. Not with that machismo he threw around like shade.

About a year into her job, she'd dated a cop for several months. Big mistake. Certainly not one to repeat.

Leaving Diego's business card on the counter, Lilí strode down the hall toward the bedrooms. She'd have to give the guy a call tomorrow. Update him on where Melba would be staying.

When she did, though, it'd be professionalism personified. No sense getting all gaga over some guy with a hot body that made her knees weaken. Not with that shiny badge he had pinned to his muscular chest.

Cradling his coffee mug in one hand, Diego stared out his kitchen window at the area behind his apartment. He scanned the parking spaces between his building and the one across from it. Peered down the thin alley separating the brick buildings, then moved his focus to the wooden stairs going up the three flights, squinting at the shadows created by the late-morning summer sun.

The streets had been quiet last night. Good. But that didn't mean he altered his habitual morning lookout for anything out of place. Even more so with Señora Felipe across the way off visiting family in Florida and him promising to keep watch over her place while she was gone. In this neighborhood, one block off of Division Street near the start of Paseo Boricua, much like many other neighborhoods in Chicago, you could never be too careful.

Satisfied that all outside his window appeared normal, Diego trudged back to the coffeepot.

He rubbed a kink in his neck with one hand and poured his second cup of coffee with the other. Something he rarely needed to get himself going in the mornings. This second cup was the product of a night spent tossing and turning, unable to get a particularly pesky situation out of his head.

Namely, the one involving Lilí Fernandez.

Just thinking her name made his pulse blip, for multiple reasons. None of them good.

He had no business hyper-focusing on the feisty do-gooder's smokin' body and expressive eyes. Picturing them in his mind, seeing them in his dreams.

Sure, he'd always been a sucker for a pair of eyes that spoke to him without any words being said. Exactly how her hazel-green ones had yesterday when she'd done her best to protect her friend.

Scratch that, not her friend. Rather, the woman who'd come to Lilí's clinic for professional advice about a situation that had gone from bad to worse. A situation he doubted the feisty do-gooder knew how to handle.

Now that he and his partner were involved, Diego felt a measure of responsibility for Lilí's safety. Only in the sense that she was a law-abiding citizen of his city.

At least, that's the reason he planned to stick with.

Muttering a curse borne from years of experience dealing with domestic violence, both personally and professionally, Diego pulled out one of the wooden chairs at his kitchen table.

Lilí Fernandez had no idea what the hell she'd gotten herself into.

That's why he hadn't slept, flipping from one side of the bed to the other like an unreliable informant changing his story. He'd seen and lived through what it was like when you cared for someone in a bad spot who didn't want to or couldn't see their way out of it. Very little good came of the stress and sorrow.

By taking Melba home with her, Lilí had gotten personally involved here. By stepping in between Melba and Tito González outside of her professional capacity, Lilí had served herself up a slew of trouble.

All night he'd run through the various scenarios that could arise from Lilí opening her home to Melba González. None of them were pleasant.

He frowned, annoyed that she'd brushed off his offer for him and Stevens to escort them to her house. Instead, she'd glared at him mutinously, pissed at his continued insistence that she reconsider her ill-fated plan.

Because ill-fated was the only way to describe it.

Bueno, estúpido was another word that had come to mind, but he'd figured if he used that one, she would have been even more pissed at him.

Diego took a sip of his black coffee, certain the conclusion he'd made while watching the two women drive away in the cab last night was right. *La chica estaba un poquito loca.*

Yep, no doubt about it. She *had* to be a little crazy. Why else would someone of her social status be working in a low-paying position like hers?

And he was pretty sure about her social status because, despite her belief that she could get home safely without his assistance, as soon as the cab had turned the corner, he'd motioned Stevens to hop in their squad car to follow. From a discreet distance, mind you. With Tito on the loose, Diego wasn't taking any chances.

No way could he live with himself if he hadn't watched out for the two women. Not only because of the badge he wore and the oath he'd sworn to protect. More because his *mami* had raised him to do what was right. Not to mention, the disillusion he carried thanks to the older sister he was still unable to reach.

That's how he now knew the downtown location of the high-rent building where Lilí resided. You didn't have to be a detective to understand that no one living on a modest income the likes of which a non-profit organization typically paid could afford a place like hers.

So why was someone of her social status making a house call in Melba's part of town? What did she hope to gain or prove by putting herself in such a precarious position?

His cell rang, bringing Diego up and out of his chair. He padded barefoot down the hall, past his apartment entry door and into the living room overlooking West Haddon Ave. He hitched up the basketball shorts riding low on his hips, thinking it might be one of the guys calling to see about shooting some hoops at the park before their shift later today.

A strange number flashed on his cell phone's display. About to let it go to voice mail to avoid a telemarketer, he registered the 312 area code indicating a local number, so he slid his thumb across the screen to answer.

"This is Reyes."

The slight pause on the other end had him gnashing his teeth. *¡Carajo!* A freaking telemarketer.

"Good morning, Officer Reyes."

Hell indeed, but not a telemarketer. He'd recognize that perky, slightly high-pitched voice anywhere now.

"*Buenos días*, Ms. Fernandez," he said, squashing

the tiny thrill trying to worm its way through him at her call. "You're sounding peppy. I take it the sleep-over was a success?"

"Despite your incessant nagging and complaints to the contrary, yes the 'sleepover' went well."

Diego grinned at her petulant tone. Needling her was simply too easy.

At the same time relief that nothing had gone wrong eased the tension in his shoulders. As much of a pain in the ass as she might be, he wouldn't have been able to live with himself had Tito González figured out where his wife was staying last night.

Eventually those rose-colored glasses Lilí Fernandez wore would be ripped off. He hoped to hell it wasn't on his watch.

"That's good to hear," he said.

Sinking down onto his microfiber sofa, he propped his feet up on the coffee table and allowed himself to push her buttons a bit. "So, to what do I owe the pleasure of hearing from you bright and early this morning? Not that I'm complaining."

He pictured the flash of exasperation in her hazel-green eyes at his teasing banter.

"Don't get any ideas, wise guy."

Her curt tone had probably shut down lesser men than him. For his part, he'd spent most of his night dreaming and worrying about this woman, and knowing she was safe made him feel like having a little fun.

"What ideas might that be?"

Lilí's exasperated huff blew through the phone's speaker, making his grin widen.

Man, she was so quick to get riled up. Her fiery nature piqued his interest. Made him wonder what that passion, in an entirely different setting and focused in an entirely different way, would be like to see. Feel. Experience.

"Where's your keen mind off to now, I wonder?" he teased.

"Whatever," she grumbled. "I'm simply doing my professional duty by informing you that Melba has agreed to enroll in the program at the women's shelter."

Diego sat up, dropping his bare feet to the hardwood floor. "She has?"

"*Sí*, try not to sound so surprised. I know what I'm doing here."

That had seemed debatable last night, but he wouldn't go there. Not right now anyway. There were more important matters to address. Melba moving to the shelter was a complete one-eighty from where she'd adamantly stood yesterday.

"What about pressing charges against her husband? Is she in?"

"*Bueno* . . ."

"Well, what? Is she filing for a restraining order at least?"

The beat of silence that met his question had Diego muttering a curse as he pushed off the couch. If Tito was out on the streets, free to roam unchecked because Melba didn't file charges, able to contact her once she moved from the shelter to the transition home, odds that she wound up back with him were good.

Or bad.

From his perspective, getting back with that scumbag would be the absolute worst. For both Melba and Lilí.

"Look, working with Melba to get her through this is a process. I'm sure you know that," Lilí argued.

He took an agitated step toward his guitar propped up in the corner, stopping when his gaze caught on his family photo hanging on the wall to the left of his big-screen TV.

The picture had been taken when he was in the seventh grade. A few months before the first time Lourdes left home and disappeared for several days.

Until she'd shown up on the front porch with a black eye and bloodied lip, asking Mami if she could come back.

"Yeah, I know it's a process," he grumbled. "One I've seen far too many battered women go through. Most falling back into old habits."

"Being negative doesn't do any good," Lilí countered.

Again, he didn't have to see her to picture the scowl no doubt scrunching her cute face at his negativity. More like, reality.

"I'm telling it like it is." He dropped back down onto the couch and reached for his mug. "It's almost inevitable. And if she doesn't—"

"Enough!"

Her brusque command made him start. Hot coffee splashed out of his cup onto his thigh, leaving a large dark blue spot on the material of his basketball shorts.

"I don't have time for your attitude this morning," Lilí continued, her no-nonsense tone surprising him. "Melba's showering and gathering up the few things she brought over so I can drive her to the shelter."

He heard some type of rustling through the phone followed by the sound of a sliding glass door opening.

"Look," Lilí went on, her frustration with him loud and clear in that one word, "I figured you'd want to know where to find her in the event you actually pick up Tito. Or in case you have any more questions. Though, I caution you to have Stevens do the talking if you reach out to Melba. If you come at her like this, she'll shut down."

Por favor. Like he needed a lecture on interrogation and witness questioning techniques. Especially from someone with as little experience as Lilí Fernandez seemed to possess.

He started to argue, but in the short time he'd spent with Lilí he'd learned that when she got on a roll like this, any disagreement from him wouldn't sway her. Besides, while he might hate to admit it, she was right. He wasn't approaching Melba and this situation the correct way.

This call—hell, if he was honest it was also Lilí herself—had somehow managed to hit personal hot spots he normally marked off-limits with yellow caution tape.

Maybe he didn't understand how women like Melba and his sister couldn't seem to get away from these abusive, toxic relationships. But if someone like Lilí could teach them how to get to a healthier place, it'd be ludicrous for him to jeopardize those efforts. Even if the way Lilí went about it made him leery.

"You're right," he grudgingly admitted. "It's good you convinced her to go to the shelter. *No podía ser fácil.*"

There was a pause before Lilí's hesitant answer came through his phone. "Actually, it was easier than I thought. She brought it up all on her own."

"I'm sure you had some influence, in a good way," he said, and he meant it. "Last night she was lucky. Had Tito broken down that door before we got there . . ."

Dios, he didn't even want to think about that.

His gaze caught on the old family picture of his mom, his older sister, and him. Lourdes had been a junior in high school when she got sidetracked. Thanks to so-called friends.

Because of her, as a kid he'd personally witnessed the physical trauma a person in a drug-induced rage could inflict on another. One of the many times she'd gotten involved with the wrong guy, Lourdes had barely survived.

For his mom, dealing with the heartbreak of finding her daughter so badly beaten, clinging to life, had ultimately taken a toll. He hadn't been there to alleviate her stress, and by the time he'd flown home from the military base in South Carolina, his mom had suffered a catastrophic heart attack. He never even got the chance to say good-bye.

Diego rubbed at the ever-present ache in his heart when he thought back to those days. "Tito sounds like countless men I've seen in similar situations. Melba's safer, better off, without him."

"I think deep down she knows that." Lilí's softly spoken words dragged him away from his terrible memories.

"She's lucky to have you."

Another pause. "Um, well, I hope so. Thanks. Oh! She just stepped into my living room, I better go."

"Hey!" he said, hoping he caught Lilí before she disconnected.

"Yeah?"

Suddenly he found himself reluctant to hang up. Reluctant to break the fragile connection he felt they'd made just now. He shook off the silly notion.

"Be safe out there," he told her, stepping back into

the more comfortable role of protective cop. "As far as we know, Tito is still in the neighborhood."

"We will be."

Her strong, firm statement both appeased and worried him. Sure, she was confident, but he didn't think she knew exactly what she was up against.

Diego did. That's why he planned to be extra vigilant. Take to his neighborhood streets before his shift started. Poke around. Rattle some cages. Get the word out that he was looking for Tito. No doubt about it, he'd put a stop to any threat against Melba. And Lilí.

If a small part of him wondered why he felt this sudden need to save the day for her, he'd chalk it up to doing the right thing. Another lesson Mami had taught him.

As for why he found himself saving her phone number in his list of contacts once she'd hung up . . .

Bueno, he'd deal with answering that question later.

Chapter Three

"Are you sure it's okay for us to be doing this, *nena*?"

Lilí barely kept herself from rolling her eyes at Velma's question. The same one the older woman had repeated at least five times during their walk from their office to Melba González's house.

Out of respect for the hardworking, dedicated volunteer, Lilí kept the sigh out of her voice as she repeated, "*Sí*, Velma, I checked with several people at work."

"*Pues*, I only want to be sure. And I certainly do not mind keeping you company so you are not alone."

"*Gracias*," Lilí answered. Mindful of keeping her strides shortened so the older woman could keep up, she offered Velma a smile of thanks.

"*Pero hace un calor brutal!*" Velma complained, her right hand moving in short jerky motions as she worked her black lace fan in an attempt to combat what she'd aptly called the brutal heat.

The strong July sun beat down on them without mercy. It rose off the sidewalks and paved streets in waves that blasted pedestrians. Like it hadn't already baked their bodies on its way down from the sky.

Lilí dabbed at the perspiration dotting her forehead. Too bad she hadn't thought to grab the Spanish fan she kept in her purse. They'd only walked a few blocks and already sweat trickled down the center of her back, making the thin rayon material of her multicolored sundress stick to her skin.

These dog days of summer were meant for lazy-day picnicking on the shores of Lake Michigan or sitting in the bleacher seats at Wrigley Field watching her Cubs play baseball.

Not traipsing through the mean streets of west Chicago, eyes peeled for potential danger, on their way to Melba's place.

They passed a group of teens hanging out in front of a *mercado*. The corner store was a popular hangout for the street kids, their pants hanging low, bandannas wrapped around their heads or wrists showing their gang colors. Thin tank tops revealed the tattooed artwork snaking up their arms and necks, across their chests. Even the youngest, who couldn't have been older than fourteen, sported a tattoo of the Puerto Rican flag waving across the tanned biceps of one arm.

Their tough-guy, stoic expressions normally didn't bother her. Today she was grateful for Velma's company. Not because she felt threatened or afraid to be in this rough neighborhood. Some of those who lived here had visited her office, or were regulars at the youth center nearby, where she was scheduled to start teaching a self-defense course next week. She honestly believed some could be reached. That there was enough good in her city, in the people she hoped to positively influence, to make a difference.

No, her unease stemmed more from the idea of

going back to the scene of the crime. So to speak. Yesterday she'd been operating in victim's-advocate mode. Focused on Melba. On what needed to be said or done to aid Melba's ability to cope in the aftermath of a scary, life-threatening situation.

Today, Melba's frightening, tear-laced description of Tito's rampage ran through Lilí's head like a recording on automatic replay. Standing in the midst of the aftermath like she was about to do, unable to stop picturing the violent episode that had occurred within the confines of the home . . . that was never easy.

A chill shimmied her shoulders despite the heat.

They reached Melba's building and Lilí's gaze caught on the top step of the front stoop. Right where Diego Reyes had stood like an immovable oak. Large hand on his holster, his dark brown eyes unsmiling and his tanned muscular body unyielding. Practically daring her to try and get past him. Making her pulse race when she accidentally bumped into him.

Ave Maria purísima, that man was too hunky for his own good. Or hers.

But he was also equally hardheaded. The epitome of Latino machismo, certain he knew what was best for her.

Ay, no thank you. The last thing she wanted to deal with was someone else thinking she needed babysitting. Her two sisters had that covered.

Still, the rumble of his husky chuckle over the phone this morning had sent her belly flip-flopping. His playful side had surprised her. Pleasantly so. It made her wonder what it would have been like had they run into each other at a club or a bar out with friends. To have those intense brown eyes focused on her in a totally different way. The male-female kind of way.

Had they been at a club and she noticed him, she would have asked him to dance. You know, take the opportunity to run her palms over his muscular arms. Maybe eventually get a chance to see what those kissable lips of his could do other than frown.

Diantre, the heat spreading over her now had nothing whatsoever to do with the July sun.

This morning, Reyes had shocked the hell out of her when he'd admitted she was right about how to approach Melba.

Of course, the big lug hadn't said he was wrong. Frankly, few men, few cops, hell, even fewer Latino men who were cops, would admit that.

"¿*Vienes, nena?*"

Velma's call from the top of the stairs knocked Lilí out of her Diego Reyes mental side trip.

"Yeah, I'm coming. Just . . . just thinking about something." Or someone.

Pushing Diego Reyes to the back of her mind, she hurried up the three steps and tugged open the entryway door.

Inside the dingy hall, the same musty, moldy smell from yesterday greeted them.

"*Ay, huele mal.*" Velma covered her nose and mouth with one hand, her thick brows drawn together in a deep frown at the stench.

Lilí did the same, nodding at Velma's complaint. The place *did* smell bad.

It was another indication of why Melba needed to stay away from here. Never come back to the rancid life she had lived with Tito. Which was why Velma and Lilí were here to pick up some personal items for Melba to have with her at the shelter. They'd deal with packing her other belongings another day.

Lilí's tan sandals slapped against the aged linoleum

floor as they approached the first-floor apartment. She knocked on the door, breath trapped in her lungs as they waited, praying Tito hadn't come home. Velma's face scrunched with worry, deepening the grooves around her mouth and across her forehead.

When no one answered, they both breathed sighs of relief. Lilí pulled Melba's key ring from her brown and black messenger bag, then slid the key into the slot. The dead bolt unlocked with a heavy *click*. Lilí paused. She'd never get used to seeing what she knew awaited inside.

With her client tucked away in a safe place, no longer her immediate focus, there was always the danger of Lilí's emotions overwhelming her now. Sometimes she tried detaching herself and looking at the place as if it were a movie set. Props staged for a scene. Instead of the broken, shattered, ugly reality the room or home represented.

"*¿Estás bien?*" Velma asked. She wrapped a comforting hand under Lilí's elbow, the wrinkles in her pudgy, mole-speckled face more prominent with her concerned frown.

"*Sí*, I'm okay," Lilí reassured her. She had to be. This was part of her job.

The tones of a popular salsa song trilled from the dark purple sack-purse slung over Velma's shoulder. The one that matched the dark floral muumuu dress flowing over her round figure. That also matched the black and purple sneakers on her childlike size-five feet. The older woman was a fashion style unto her own. Lilí had total respect for her flair.

While Velma dug around in her purse, Lilí concentrated on calming her twitchy anxiety. She waited a beat, then twisted the scratched gunmetal knob and pushed the apartment door open.

The stench of stale beer, spilled and left to dry on the same cracked, faded linoleum as the building's entry, assailed her.

Behind her, the salsa music stopped, replaced by Velma's "*¿Hola, Frances, qué pasa?*"

Frances was Velma's oldest daughter. Mom of the two grandkids Velma often babysat. She was always keen to share a new pic she'd snapped of them on her phone. Cute kids whose silly photos made Lilí smile but not want any of her own quite yet.

Velma continued her conversation, her voice fading as, on wobbly knees, Lilí stepped into the shambles.

The pieces of the broken coffee table were butted up against each other in front of the sofa. Funny, she hadn't remembered the cushions being ripped, stuffing tumbling out of a gaping hole in one. Picture frames and shattered glass littered the floor. Crushed beer cans and an empty bottle of tequila along with the mangled backrest from one of the metal breakfast-table chairs lay scattered across the kitchen.

A chill shivered across Lilí's shoulders. *Dios mío*, a freaking tornado would have done less damage than Tito.

She picked her way through the debris, sidestepping the glass to avoid cutting her foot in her open sandals. Her eye caught on a photograph Melba had described to her. A young Melba, high school age she'd said, standing with her *mamá* at the beach in the Dominican Republic. Lilí stooped to pick up the frame, carefully dislodging a large shard of glass so it wouldn't scratch the picture.

The happiness beaming in Melba's young face, shining in her eyes as she posed with one arm around her *mamá*'s waist, sent a sharp pang deep in Lilí's chest. She'd never seen Melba smile like that before—relaxed, hopeful, almost excited.

Sadness for the difficulties Melba had faced spread through Lilí like thick molasses, leaking into the nooks and crannies of her soul. Unfortunately, Melba would continue to face those same difficulties, worse maybe, if she couldn't bring herself to completely cut ties with her degenerate husband.

Lilí clutched the photograph to her chest, vowing to do whatever she could to facilitate that process. Praying the young woman would finally agree to press charges and move on with her life.

"*Ay, nena, perdón pero me tengo que ir.*"

Velma's apology drew Lilí's attention.

"You have to leave?" she asked, turning to look over her shoulder at Velma, who remained in the open doorway.

"*Sí.* My daughter is sick and her husband is working a double shift at the hospital. I have to go pick up Pepito from school." Velma's gaze trailed around the chaos in the tiny apartment. Her frown darkened and she made a quick sign of the cross, ending with a kiss to her fingertips. "You should not stay here alone. We can come back tomorrow. *Vámonos.*"

"No, you go. I'll be okay. This won't take me long."

Lips pursed, Velma eyed Lilí like the stern *abuela* she could be when her grandkids weren't respectful or they misbehaved.

"Honestly, it's fine," Lilí reassured the older woman. "It'll make Melba feel more comfortable if she has a few personal items. Like this one."

She turned the picture of Melba and her *mamá* around so Velma could see it.

Velma's expression softened. Lilí knew the volunteer understood. Their shared empathy for the women and children who came through the Victim Abuse Center's doors bonded them.

"I'll grab everything and leave quickly," Lilí promised. She wasn't too keen on sticking around here anyway. Especially alone.

"*¿Me prometes?*" Velma demanded, her pointed finger and narrowed gaze brooking no arguments.

"Yes, I promise."

The mother hen routine didn't bug Lilí. Velma acted that way out of love. The woman might be tough as nails now, but according to her, that hadn't always been the case. She'd spent too many years in an abusive relationship before finding the strength to get out, so coming here couldn't have been easy for her. She had though, for Lilí's sake.

"*Bueno*, do your business. Then immediately leave. Okay?"

Lilí nodded solemnly.

"Remember, Tito is out there. *¡Cuídate!*"

With her final warning for Lilí to take care of herself, Velma moved back into the hallway. The *click* of the door shutting behind her resounded through the silent apartment with finality.

Lilí flinched.

Closing her eyes, she focused on her training. On why she needed to be here. On the fact that she was one of the lucky ones who'd never lived through a situation like Melba or Velma, so she had to be strong. For them, for others who would come behind them.

After taking a deep, calming breath, Lilí quickly got to work.

She dug through her messenger bag in search of the piece of notebook paper Melba had used to jot down the items she'd requested.

Picture with her mamá. Check.

Picture of her extended family, taken the day before she'd left for the US nearly eight years ago as a young bride, unaware of the despair and pain she'd face at the hands of the man who had pledged to love and protect her.

Rosary and prayer book. Should be in her nightstand.

A few more outfits, a pair of sneakers, another pair of chanclas. Melba had worn a brown pair of sandals when they'd left last night, so she'd asked for a black pair from her closet.

Baby blanket. Folded in her bottom drawer.

Reading this item the first time had made Lilí start with alarm. She'd met Melba's sad eyes, then listened with her heart in her throat as Melba shared the halting story about the night one of Tito's beatings had caused her to miscarry their child.

Disgust for the man rose like bile in Lilí's throat. It hardened her resolve to do whatever it took to save Melba.

Moving quickly, she stepped to the end table closest to the window overlooking the front of the building. Melba had said the family photo should be there. Odds were good it wouldn't be, seeing as how half the items in the living room were strewn all over the damn place.

Spotting the picture, surprisingly upright on the square spindle-legged table, Lilí bent to reach for it. A shadow passed by the front window. Paused. The large figure dodged from side to side as if trying to see if someone might be inside the apartment, partially hidden behind the filmy curtains.

The hair on the back of Lilí's neck stood on end.

It was hard to tell for sure, but . . .

The man put his hands on the window and pressed his face closer. Lilí gasped at his likeness to Tito.

Spinning around, she raced toward the front door, shards of glass cracking under her sandaled feet. Heart pounding, she turned the dead bolt, then slid the security chain in place for good measure.

Outside a car honked. Lilí flinched, but the hulking figure didn't move. Voices called out and blessedly the man turned toward the street. She held her breath, pulse pounding in her ears, as she pressed back against the door.

Terrified to move, she waited.

One. Two. Three seconds that felt like an eternity before the man finally edged away. Through the filmy curtains she watched him approach the idling car.

She couldn't be 100 percent sure, but . . . what if it *was* Tito. Ready to pounce on Melba if she came back. Ready to pounce on Lilí if he'd heard she'd taken Melba home with her last night.

Fear turned Lilí's legs into wet noodles, incapable of holding her up.

She slid down the length of the door until her butt hit the floor. Panic flared, ricocheting around her chest like dried beans inside a maraca.

Gracias a Dios Velma wasn't here. Lilí would never forgive herself if she put the older woman in danger.

The squeal of tires peeling away grated her rattled nerves and she stared at the window, breath trapped in her lungs, to see if the figure returned.

Seconds ticked by. No one appeared, but what if he'd stuck around, casing the place? *Ay Dios mío*, she'd messed up by staying alone. She needed to get the hell out of here, but was scared to go outside. Maybe if . . .

Lilí dug her cell phone out of her dress pocket. It took a couple nervous swipes to unlock her screen, a few more to bring up her contacts.

Without letting herself second-guess the idea, she tapped the name, then cleared the fear from her throat as the call went through.

"This is Reyes."

"Hi, um, Officer Reyes?" Lilí pressed a hand to her racing heart, willing a calm she was far from feeling into her voice. "Any chance you, um, might be nearby? And could, uhhh, meet me at Melba González's house?"

He didn't answer right away and chagrin heated her cheeks. This was a mistake. She shouldn't have called him.

In the background she heard male voices yelling. Some kind of rhythmic pounding followed by cheers.

"Hold on a second. It's kind of loud." The sounds faded slightly and Diego spoke again. "Sorry about that. I'm at the youth center playing basketball. What did you say?"

Lilí's shoulders sagged with relief as the breath she'd been holding rushed out on a whoosh of air. The idea of people carrying on with their daily lives, doing something normal like shooting hoops rather than hiding from a drug-crazed cretin, settled her.

She closed her eyes and counted to ten, concentrating on relaxing the muscles she'd unconsciously tensed in fear.

Everything was fine. She'd simply overreacted.

"Lilí, what's going on?" Diego's voice had slipped into cop mode. Brusque, demanding.

She shook her head, then realized he couldn't see her. "Nothing. Never mind. I think I spooked myself."

"Where are you?"

"I stopped by Melba's house to pick up a few things and—"

"You did what?"

"It's nothing. I just thought . . ." She trailed off,

embarrassed by her overreaction. "Someone was peeking in the window. I thought it might be Tito and I freaked. But he's gone. Or, whoever it was is gone. Probably. Forget I called."

"Keep the door bolted and don't let anyone in."

"I'm fine."

"Just do it. I'll be right over."

Diego disconnected the call before she could argue more.

Leaning back against the door, Lilí stared at the "call ended" flashing on her cell phone screen. Any other time his curt command would have irritated her. Right now, as much as she considered herself a strong, independent woman, there was no denying her relief that Diego Reyes was on his way.

"What the hell were you thinking, coming over here alone?"

The angry words slipped out before Diego could stop them.

Okay, so that wasn't exactly how he'd intended to greet Lilí when she opened the apartment door. But damn, it was a valid question.

Her hazel-green eyes narrowed, her chin jutting up at a pugnacious angle. Funny, he was coming to recognize that expression. It both annoyed and enticed him.

Annoyed because he knew she was about to fire back her own retort. Enticed because her kiss-my-ass attitude made him want to do exactly that. Amongst other places on her sexy, athletic body.

"I wasn't alone when I arrived," she answered, her voice tart. "Do you think I'm an idiot?"

Her mouth twisted in a grimace as she swiped a

hand through the air to silence any response he might have been foolish enough to attempt.

"Never mind," she grumbled. "Don't answer that."

Despite the fear for her safety that had fueled the fastest pace he'd run in ages, Diego found himself smothering a grin. Seeing that she was safe and unharmed made his breath come easier. If his pulse still raced, he chalked it up to running the seven or so blocks in the heat of the day, his gym bag slung over his shoulder.

He swiped his palm across his forehead, wiping away the sweat.

Lilí edged back into the apartment, leaving him to follow. "Sorry about interrupting your play time. I shouldn't have called."

"You shouldn't be *here* is more like it."

She shrugged, the motion drawing his attention to the way the material of her sundress flowed over her curves. Bold strokes of color brushed across the dark background, the vibrancy matching her personality. The thin straps left her tan shoulders bare while the tie at her waist accented her slender hips. The dress stopped a modest inch or two above her knees, but the smooth skin of her shapely calves left him wanting a peek at the rest of her legs.

"We left so fast last night, and at that point I think Melba was still in shock, thinking she'd be back soon. Anyway"—she paused, stooping down to pick up a broken picture frame—"now that she's at the shelter, she's allowed to bring items from home."

Diego closed and bolted the door behind him. "So why didn't she come herself?"

Lilí shook her head. "That's not the best idea."

"Oh, but it's a good idea for you to be here." He

flung an arm out to indicate the space and its battered contents. "By yourself."

Hands on his hips, Diego glared at her. A fat lot of good it did since she remained crouched down, peering at the picture she held, ignoring him.

Annoyed, he tugged open the zipper on his bag so he could grab a hand towel to wipe his face. He didn't stop to think about *why* her lack of regard for her own well-being bothered him so much. Bottom line, he'd be worried about anyone who put themselves in a potentially dangerous situation.

With a heavy sigh, Lilí pushed up to her feet. She brushed at her black wispy bangs, eyeing him with a mix of frustrated resignation.

"Look, I didn't call asking for a lecture. My sisters can do that all day. I had a volunteer from the clinic with me, but she wound up having to leave. I'm sure whoever that was outside is long gone." She waved a hand toward the window, like the situation was no big deal. "I probably freaked out more than I needed to and I regret having bothered you."

"I'd say you haven't freaked out enough. This neighborhood can be dangerous. And with Tito running around, itching for a score any way he can get it . . ."

He left the sentence to hang in the air between them. Hopefully the ruined mess scattered about the place painted a clear enough picture of the meaning behind his words.

Lilí's gaze traveled the length of him, taking in his sneakers, gray-and-blue basketball shorts, and sweat-stained Chicago Bears tank. His footrace through the streets after her call had added to the sweat on his skin after an hour of hoop time with the teens at the center. Right now he probably looked more like a gym rat from the hood than a trusty cop.

He noticed her attention caught on the thorny vine tattoo circling his right biceps, high enough that it didn't show when he was in uniform. Her gaze flicked up to meet his for a hot second before she turned away, but he coulda sworn he saw a flash of interest in her eyes.

Or was that merely his own awareness of her? The same awareness he was doggedly trying to ignore.

Based on where she lived, if his guess was right, she had no business hanging around in this neighborhood. And he . . . *pues*, he'd been born and raised and figured he'd die here. It's where he belonged. Where he was determined to make a difference.

Lilí stepped gingerly toward the window, hugging the wall to stay out of view. Broken glass crunched under her sandals and she winced.

Diego swallowed a curse. Lilí Fernandez was a contradiction unto herself.

Sure, she knew enough not to saunter to the window, effectively announcing to anyone looking in from the outside that she was here. On the other hand, her strappy sandals weren't exactly appropriate footwear for traipsing around a place littered with broken glass.

Remembering the wood-handled broom he'd seen in the small pantry when he and Stevens had searched the premises yesterday, Diego dropped his gym duffel bag by the front door and strode to the tiny kitchen. He tugged the pantry door open to find the broom leaning against a box of trash bags in the corner.

"Did you happen to see anyone poking around when you came in?" Lilí asked. Pinching the edge of the thin curtain between her thumb and pointer finger, she peeked outside.

"No."

"See, it was probably nothing," she protested.

"Not necessarily. I wasn't necessarily scoping out the place. My focus was more on getting inside to check on you."

"Oh."

The hesitation in her soft response drew his attention.

She had pulled away from the window, her back against the faded floral wallpaper. Melba's pictures were pressed to her chest, her hands gripping the edges of the mangled frames. Eyes closed, Lilí took a deep breath, then slowly released it through her slightly open lips. She took another, repeating the same process.

"You okay?" he asked.

She nodded.

The gesture wasn't too convincing, but her slowed breathing led him to believe she was trying to pull herself together. As "fine" as she claimed to be, it was evident that she'd been spooked.

Hopefully it was enough to have knocked some sense into her. It didn't seem like she had any intention of listening to him.

Silently grumbling about hardheaded women, like Lilí and his sister, Diego set to work sweeping the floor. The empty beer cans and shards of glass rattled against each other in a cacophony reminiscent of the broken lives that had inhabited this apartment.

"What are you doing?"

He glanced up to find Lilí still leaning against the wall, her brows furrowed in a deep frown.

"I'm cleaning up before you hurt yourself." He jabbed the broom handle in her direction. "Those aren't the smartest shoes to be wearing here."

She rolled her eyes in a perfect imitation of the teens at the youth center when he called them out for pulling some dumb stunt. At least his jab had brought a little color back to her pale cheeks. She might not want to admit it, but the idea that Tito could have been coming up the walk had scared the fight out of her. At least momentarily.

Hell, he'd been scared for her.

If Tito had barged in on her . . .

Diego shuddered. He'd seen for himself firsthand— both on the job and with his sister—the damage a man like that could do.

He hadn't figured out Lilí's angle or what led someone of her social standing to work at, rather than simply fundraise for, the shelter. Much less to step in and fight Melba's fight alongside the battered woman. What he did know is that he found Lilí's determination, and so far unwavering commitment to make a difference, appealing. That made it impossible for him to *not* worry about her. Even if she argued that she could handle things.

Based on the nervous pulse beating in the smooth column of her neck, or the furtive glances she kept shooting at the front window, he'd bet she was beginning to figure out that she'd bit off more than she could potentially chew. Thankfully for her, his determination matched hers, and he resolved to make sure she did not become another statistic in his part of the city. Not on his watch anyway.

"Look, I'll pick up this mess," he offered. "You grab

whatever Melba needs from the other rooms so we can hurry up and get out of here."

"Why?"

"Why?" He tilted his head, confused by the skepticism in her question.

"Yeah." Lilí pushed off the wall and stepped toward him. Her narrowed gaze said she didn't trust his intentions. Though he'd done nothing to give her cause to doubt him. "Why would you stick around here with me when you don't agree with what I'm doing?"

"Maybe because I'm a nice guy." Who was also apparently a sucker for a pair of eyes that did nothing to hide her emotions. Like now, when they flashed with interest, quickly shaded by unease.

"Yeah, that's what Melba tried to tell me," she grumbled.

"Oh, so you and Melba talked about me?" Interesting.

"Only in the sense of you being a cop in her neighborhood."

"But she said I'm a nice guy, huh? What else did she have to say? All good, I'm sure." He winked, getting a kick out of Lilí's answering eye roll.

In the midst of their current situation, he should feel no desire to tease her. Or to see the edges of her full lips tilt with the hint of her grin, just like . . .

Bingo!

Lilí chuckled as she shook her head. "Don't get too excited, big guy. The conversation was short."

"But sweet, right?"

"*¡Ay, que egoísta!*" Chuckling, she brushed past him, her shoulder grazing his arm. The contact of bare skin to bare skin sent heat shooting low in his body.

Lilí didn't even pause. Like their electric touch hadn't affected her in the least.

Instead, she set the pictures on the scarred Formica counter, then turned to face him, arms crossed in front of her chest.

"Melba seems to think you're one of the good guys."

"And you?" Hands one on top of the other, he leaned on the end of the broomstick, intrigued to hear her answer. "What do you think?"

"I don't know." She gave him a slow, assessing look that had his body humming with pleasure at her attention. "The jury's still out."

Laughter rumbled up from his belly and into his chest. He liked that she didn't hold back. She wasn't going to make any play for her easy. Not that he was thinking of making one. But it was fun to pretend.

Lilí grinned, her spunky attitude from when they'd first met firmly back in place.

"So, now that Melba's getting settled at the shelter, has she reconsidered pressing charges?" he asked.

Lilí's smile faltered.

Any good feelings elicited by their shared laughter shriveled inside him. ¡Coño! It never failed.

Damn! Diego repeated, giving the floor an angry swipe with the broom. Why was it so hard for victims to aid the system with putting a stop to their abusers? His sister had done the same thing, letting the man who'd beat her up get off without even a slap on the wrist. Twice!

That second time, after their *mami*'s death, had forged a rift between Diego and Lourdes. Sure, he prayed every night that she was safe and off the streets. Did his best to check up on her. Mostly from a distance or via phone when she had a good number. Lourdes had a habit of falling off the radar.

She didn't want his help. Nor did she want to help herself. Even after all these years, he couldn't bring himself to accept her willingness to let her life waste away because of some worthless dude, or drugs, or both. Just like Melba González might be in danger of doing.

Annoyed all over again, Diego took another angry swipe at the debris littering the floor. Then another. And another.

"It's not that simple," Lilí said.

Yes, it was. Someone beats the crap out of you, or threatens you with a knife, you file a restraining order. Press charges. Let the cops do their job to protect you. Seemed pretty simple to him.

He didn't say all that though. He'd said it all last night. In this very apartment. With Lilí and Melba González sitting on the same sagging couch.

Something told him his argument would fall on deaf ears.

"Diego, *me estás escuchando?*"

Yes, he was listening. He just didn't agree with her. There was no "different angle" like she kept referring to. At least, he didn't see one.

Besides, right now, he needed to focus on getting them out of here and keeping *her* out of Tito's harmful way.

Chapter Four

Back in Melba's bedroom, Lilí heard the various shuffles, sweeps, and thuds of Diego moving around the main living area, doing his best to pick up the mess. Keeping his distance from her.

Good. She didn't want to be around him and his moodiness anyway.

Being here, surrounded by the ugliness, was hard enough for Lilí without Diego making it worse.

Except, having him here actually made it better. Made her feel safer.

Ave Maria purísima, the contradictions when it came to Diego Reyes were driving her crazy. Hail Mary, indeed. She needed to pray for clarity of mind.

As it was, she'd spent the past twenty minutes or so rifling through Melba's drawers, shoving aside Tito's crap in the closet in search of the various items on Melba's list. It might have taken less time if Lilí hadn't frittered some of it away mentally reviewing potential reasons why Diego would be so pissed that Melba wasn't ready to press charges.

Lilí tugged open a drawer, relieved the see the

"*Pura Dominicana*" T-shirt Melba asked for on top of the far right stack.

It was strange, really. She'd been around enough cops handling domestic violence cases in the past few years that she'd come to expect a lack of understanding on their part when it came to the psychological aspect of her role as a victim's advocate. At times she'd even witnessed the inability to truly grasp the emotional difficulties DV victims faced. With Diego, though, there was something different.

She couldn't quite put her finger on it . . . but something told her that this was personal for him. How or why that might be, she'd lost track of the number of guesses she'd tossed aside.

The *screech* of a metal chair leg against the linoleum floor out in the living room spurred her back to action.

She pulled out the T-shirt, along with several others and a few pairs of shorts. Her fingers itched to grab a trash bag and toss all of Tito's belongings, but she didn't. He wasn't worth the waste of her time.

Instead, she continued checking items off her list. Already Melba's *abuela*'s rosary and Bible, a purple terry-cloth robe, and several outfits from the closet were packed in the black duffel bag Lilí had found under the bed. All she needed now were a few items from the bathroom.

Stepping out into the hall, she caught sight of Diego blowing what was probably a few glass shards off a broken picture frame. He placed it on the kitchen table, inadvertently angling it so Lilí could see it was a close-up photo of Melba and a group of other Latina women smiling for the camera. His large hand gently brushed at the paper. Almost like a comforting caress.

That he'd taken the time to try and salvage the photo spoke of a softer side. One he hadn't shown her that often in the less than twenty-four hours she'd known him.

The thought brought her up short.

Wow, it really *had* been less than a day since she'd raced from the cab out front, ready to defend Melba, only to be blocked on the steps by Diego. So much had happened. With him and Melba consuming the majority of Lilí's thoughts.

"You almost done?"

His question brought her out of her stupor.

"Uh, yeah. I only have to grab a few toiletries."

He nodded, then got back to work straightening up.

Lilí didn't move toward the bathroom though.

Instead she watched the muscles along the back of his shoulders ripple as he took another swipe at the floor with the broom. The armholes of his gray Chicago Bears tank hung low on his sides, giving her a nice view of his six-pack abs when he bent to reach for the dustpan. A man cleaning the house was a glorious sight to see, especially when he was built like Diego Reyes.

That he'd come to her rescue and the gentle care he took with Melba's picture. Those gestures attracted Lilí more than his ripped body.

Pues, who was she kidding, his hunkiness was an added bonus. No use denying that. But the peek into the man underneath the badge intrigued her.

"Everything okay?" he asked. His dark brows furrowed, he moved to set the broom aside.

Embarrassed to have been caught staring at him, Lilí rattled off a "Yeah, I'm fine" and scurried into the bathroom.

A short while later the duffel was packed, the items

on Melba's list safely zipped inside. Lilí strolled out of the bedroom, ready to leave.

Diego sat on the sofa armrest, scrolling through something on his cell phone.

"Thanks for waiting," she said.

"No problem."

"I mean, I know you're off duty, so I appreciate you coming over," she added. "Even though I probably didn't need—"

"Yeah, you did." He stood up, snagging the strap of her messenger bag on the torn sofa cushion. "You never know who or what's lurking around this neighborhood. Here."

He held her messenger bag out to her, at the same time reaching to lift Melba's duffel off Lilí's shoulder with his other hand.

His warm fingers grazed her bare skin. Tingles of awareness skittered from her arm across her chest, moving swiftly to parts of her body that hadn't seen much action since her breakup with Gregorio over a year ago.

Diego's hand stilled, trapped between the duffel's strap and the front of her shoulder.

She cupped his elbow, a magnetic pull drawing her to touch him.

"I'm, *bueno*, I'm glad you came," she admitted.

"Me, too."

His eyes met hers. The gold flecks swimming in the brown depths of his irises burned brighter. Desire, swift and strong, infused her, inciting a hunger she'd never felt before.

His gaze dropped to her mouth. Instinctively she licked her lips. Longing to find out if he'd taste as sinful as he looked.

Her feet took a baby step closer.

His did the same.

Anticipation tightened her chest as his dark head slowly lowered and she—

A loud *thwack* resounded in the room, startling her.

Diego threw his arms around her in protection. Tucking her head down to his chest, he held her tightly against his body.

They huddled like that for a few tense seconds and she felt Diego craning his head to look around them. Then, with a muttered *damn*, he dropped his arms from around her.

"*¡Coño!*" he repeated, *"Que estúpido soy!"*

"What?" she asked, wondering why he could possibly feel stupid. She's the one who'd nearly jumped out of her skin.

She peered around his back to see what he pointed at.

A giggle pushed its way up her throat when she caught sight of the plastic broom, lying on the floor beside the flimsy kitchen table Diego had propped it up against.

The glare he gave her over his shoulder made her giggle morph into a laugh. Tinged with a slight touch of hysteria and laced with a thread of relief.

She really needed to get out of this apartment. Between the disturbing scenarios the destruction sparked in her imagination and the tantalizingly distracting man protecting her from wayward brooms, she was a mess of rattled nerves.

Diego bent to pick up the duffel bag and Lilí realized it must have dropped when they'd ducked for cover.

Without a word, she moved to put the broom away in the pantry. The interruption was actually more of a blessing. If not, who knew what foolish act she'd be engaged in right now.

Desire hummed traitorously in her body.

Her ability to make responsible decisions was decidedly off-kilter around this guy. That made it far too easy to give in to the insane urge to run her fingers along the tattoo circling his biceps. Press herself against his hunky body and rise up on her toes for a delicious kiss.

Ave Maria purísima. Lilí closed the pantry door, taking an extra moment to remind herself why getting involved with Diego Reyes, in all his sex-appealing, badge-carrying, machismo-wielding glory, would be absolutely wrong.

One bad breakup with a cop who didn't understand her commitment to those who sought assistance from her should be enough to warn her away.

"You ready?" Diego asked, standing with one hand on the dead bolt and the other on the security chain.

Ay, she was ready all right. Ready for something that might feel really, really good right now, but would inevitably end badly.

Motioning for Lilí to stay behind him, Diego peered into the first-floor hallway outside the González apartment. He didn't want to take any chances.

Once he was confident the area was clear, he gave a brisk nod.

They stepped out and she turned to lock up behind them. He stood facing the main door, his back to her, blocking Lilí from anyone who might enter the building.

He needed to stay on his guard. Unlike those few

moments inside when he'd let the wrong head take control.

All he'd meant to do was relieve her of the heavy duffel bag, but the warmth of her smooth skin had seared his hand. Her quick intake of breath seeming to suck the air out of him.

In a snap everything else faded. His gaze had zeroed in on the ripe plumpness of her lips. The flash of desire in her expressive eyes. Blood had pooled low in his body and all he could think about was taking her sassy mouth with his. Dragging her closer to press a moist kiss along the curve of her throat.

Diego's body tightened and—

¡Carajo! He was doing it again.

Behind him, the dead bolt clicked into place. Lilí moved to his side and he stuck out an arm to keep her from going ahead of him. She gave him the side-eye.

"Can't be too careful," he cautioned.

Her lips twisted with displeasure, but she nodded her understanding, keeping a step behind him as they walked toward the exit.

"Any chance Melba will be up for a conversation later today?" he asked, determined to keep his focus on business.

"Depends."

"On what?"

"On whether by 'conversation' you mean an interrogation or an exchange of pleasantries and open-minded questions."

He scoffed. "Give me a break, I know how to do my job without being an ass."

"You had a pretty decent he-man act going on yesterday."

They reached the main door and he stopped,

quirking a brow at her interpretation of how things had gone down after Melba had dialed 911.

"What?" she asked. "I call it like I see it."

"Maybe it's your Pollyanna do-gooder tendencies that bring out the protector in me, you think?"

She tilted her head, her eyes narrowing as if she actually considered his question.

"Nope," she finally answered. A self-satisfied smirk curved the corners of her mouth.

"Smart-ass," he grumbled.

Her chuckle followed him as he led the way out onto the front stoop.

His answering grin faded the moment he caught site of Tito González standing on the sidewalk across the street from them.

For a split second the two of them froze, then Tito took off running.

"Stop!" Diego yelled.

Dropping his sports bag and Melba's duffel, he jumped down the three steps and raced after Tito.

"What the hell—"

"Wait here!" Diego called back when he heard Lilí's cry. He dodged a sedan driving by, then looked up in time to see Tito turning the corner to head toward Division Street.

Man, Tito might be short and brutish, but the dude was pretty fast. Once he got on Division, there'd be way more people milling about, making it easier to lose the scumbag.

Anxious to keep that from happening, Diego picked up his pace. The afternoon heat had sweat quickly beading his brow. A drop slid into his left eye, burning, and he swiped at it. Rounding the curve he scanned the busy street for Tito's red T-shirt.

"Hey! Watch out!"

Up ahead, Tito barreled through two young moms walking with strollers. One teetered on its wheels, the toddler inside screeching in protest.

Diego reached the moms, bending to scoop a stuffed giraffe from the dirt around a tree planted near the curb.

"Everyone okay?" he asked. He handed the toy to the crying toddler, waiting for a nod from both women before racing off again.

"Stop! Police!" Diego called, catching sight of Tito sidestepping around honking cars along Division.

Diego followed him into the street.

Wheels screeched as cars braked. He smacked his palm on the hood of a low-rider Chevy, scowling at the young driver gunning his engine behind the wheel.

"Yo, back off!"

The cry had him swiveling his attention toward the far sidewalk where Tito shoved a teen in low-slung shorts and a black tank, sending the kid sprawling onto the cement. Wild-eyed, Tito grabbed the handlebars of the teen's bike and hopped onto the seat.

Diego made it across the road in time to see the boy scrambling back to his feet, cradling his left arm in pain and cursing Tito's mother in Spanish. Fat lot of good that did.

By now Tito had hopped the curb on the ten-speed and merged into the traffic. He swerved around a city bus, giving the finger to a driver who honked in protest when Tito veered into his lane.

Diego skidded to a stop at the kid's side.

"Chicago PD," he identified himself in response to the teen's mutinous glare. When he looked back up, Tito was gone.

Damn it! Diego smacked his fist into his other palm, pissed that the degenerate had gotten away. Again!

"Are you hurt?" he asked, huffing to catch his breath after the unsuccessful footrace.

"The jerk stole my bike!" the kid wailed. Blood oozed from a scrape on his elbow, but he wiped it with the edge of his shirt. "How the hell am I supposed to get my bike back? My mom's gonna kill me!"

Diego reached for his cell only to remember that his basketball shorts didn't have pockets, so his phone was tucked into the outside pocket on his sports bag.

"What's your name?" Diego asked.

"Gui. Guillermo." The boy added his full name at Diego's frown.

"You got a phone on you, Guillermo?" Diego asked. "I'll call the precinct to have dispatch send over a patrol. That way you can file a report."

"Shit, a report ain't gonna do me no good, man! My bike is gone!"

Footsteps slapping against the sidewalk drew closer and Diego glanced up to see Lilí racing toward him, her messenger purse, his sports bag, and Melba's duffel slung across her shoulders.

Fear blanketed her face. She drew to a stop, a hand slapped over her heart as she gasped for air.

"Are you crazy? Running after Tito like that? You could have gotten hurt!" she cried.

He nearly laughed at her ludicrous outburst. Probably would have if he wasn't annoyed that she hadn't followed his order to wait back at the apartment.

"Running after perps like Tito is my job," he reminded her. "Yours, on the other hand, is not."

Dropping the two heavy bags to the ground, Lilí jammed her hands onto her trim hips. The scowl she gave him rivaled Guillermo's.

So much for thinking Tito showing up might scare some sense into her.

Dios lo ayude, por favor. Though Diego wasn't sure how God could help him when it came to Lilí's penchant for heading toward danger rather than away from it. She was going to get herself into trouble. And probably drive him bonkers in the process.

A few hours later, Diego found himself canvassing a two-block radius around Lilí's condo off West Washington Street. Keeping his eyes peeled for any sign of Tito.

He wasn't sure if Melba's husband had figured out who Lilí was or where she lived, but Diego wasn't taking any chances.

After López and Charles had arrived, two cops Diego knew from the precinct softball team, they'd taken Guillermo's statement and called in Tito's description. Lilí had hopped a cab back to the shelter, promising to touch base with Diego to let him know she'd arrived safely.

He'd expected a phone call. A chance to hear her voice again.

Instead, she'd sent a smart-aleck text: Back at the ranch, surrounded by my posse. No bad guys lurking.

Cheeky girl.

In another of her signature moves, she'd rolled her eyes at his lecture about her propensity to dive head-first into trouble without thinking. His warning about why she shouldn't follow a cop in pursuit of a suspect had more than likely fallen on deaf ears.

Which led to his current situation: flashing Tito's last mug shot from his cell phone, asking if anyone had recently seen the short, bald-headed man with colorful tattoo sleeves and the Dominican Republic flag etched on the back of his neck, hanging around the area. So far, from the barista at the corner coffee shop, to the owner of the dry cleaners a block over, to the older couple walking their weiner dog, and anyone else Diego had run into on the street, the answer had been a resounding *no*.

His final stop was the security desk inside Lilí's building.

He definitely wanted to make sure Tito was on their radar. It might allow Diego to sleep better.

He approached the gleaming brownstone high-rise and tugged open the heavy beveled-glass door. Cool air greeted him as he stepped inside, the smell of fresh flowers and money in the air. The rubber soles of his sneakers squeaked softly as he crossed the green marble floor in the open vestibule.

He scanned the area, getting a lay of the land, barely containing his whistle of appreciation.

Lilí Fernandez certainly lived in style.

A few years back he'd mistakenly, and briefly, hooked up with a woman in Lilí's social stratosphere. Ilene had bid the highest in the charity auction he'd agreed to support as part of the precinct's community outreach. Of course, in his mind support had meant moving tables and chairs, heavy lifting behind the scenes. Not becoming an item up for bid in the "Win an Evening with . . ." beefcake auction.

Man, the jokes and catcalling from the guys in the locker room at work had been never-ending.

Thoughts of Ilene and her misguided attempt at using him to make an ex jealous, faded as Diego pictured Lilí here.

She'd probably blow in off the streets, her long hair up in a perky ponytail that matched her Sassy Sally–Positive Patty personality. Maybe she'd pause to chat with a neighbor in the small sitting area off to the right. Her trim legs tucked under her as she got comfy on the matching small settee or wingback chair. The elaborate glass and muted gold light fixture hanging from the tall ceiling casting a cozy glow on the space.

Or she'd assist an elderly neighbor fumbling for the right key to check the mail in one of the intricately carved wooden mailboxes lining the far left wall, numbers etched on their faces.

Knowing her, she'd greet the tall, gangly, middle-aged man dressed in a crisp white long-sleeved button-down with a black tie and slacks who now rose from behind a curved dark marble counter. The security desk partially blocked the walkway leading to the bank of elevators deeper into the lobby area. There was no getting by anyone posted here. Good.

"May I help you"—the older man's sharp gaze flicked to Diego's badge clipped to the waistband of his jeans—"Officer . . . ?"

"Reyes," Diego said, extending his hand to shake the older man's long-fingered one. The dude could probably palm a basketball. With his height and the ease with which he moved his long limbs, Diego would be surprised if the security guard hadn't played a little ball at some point.

Diego fished his cell out of his back jeans pocket, pressing his thumb onto the home pad to unlock the screen. "And you are?"

"Bill Ryan, chief security officer. Is there some kind of problem? I haven't been notified by any of our tenants."

"More like, trying to avoid a problem." Diego held his cell phone up so the security officer could get a good look. "Any chance you've seen this man hanging around? Poking his head in here, maybe asking about one of your tenants?"

Bill Ryan took the phone, using his thumb and pointer finger to zoom in on the tiny screen. The close scrutiny he gave the photograph told Diego the man took his job seriously. Perfect.

"No one like that has been through my door. Believe me, I'd remember."

Relief eased the pinch in Diego's shoulder blades.

Ryan handed the phone back, then crossed his arms in front of him. "I'm here Monday through Friday from eight to five, but if you send me that, I can check with the other guys. At least one person is at this desk twenty-four-seven, with two men on every shift."

Ryan leaned back around the counter to snag a business card. "Anything we should be aware of? Or alert our tenants about?"

"I don't want to alarm anyone else. Just keeping an eye out for one of your tenants. Lilí Fernandez, you happen to know her?"

A grin spread the guard's lips, lighting his gray eyes and deepening the grooves on the sides of his mouth. "Friendly girl. Grew up in the suburbs, comes from a modest background, so I make sure to ask how city life's treatin' her. She's always asking about my family, checking if I'm doing my PT exercises to ease this ol' knee pain. Old basketball injury. Loves to talk baseball, that one."

Of course Lilí had charmed the guy. Diego would bet she had that effect on most people.

"Has she lived here long?" he asked.

"She moved into Jeremy Taylor's place about, let's see." Ryan's features scrunched into a pensive frown and he brought a knuckle up to his chin as he thought. "Hmm . . . I'd say not quite four years now. Yeah, the summer my youngest headed down to college at U of I."

"Jeremy Taylor, as in—?" Diego worked to hide his surprise at the name Ryan mentioned.

"Yeah, same Taylor family you're probably thinking of. Most folks in this city have heard the name. Good people, and believe me, I don't say that about everyone. Even the younger one the papers like to gossip about. Michael probably plays hard like the papers say, but he's a good kid. Always respectful and genuine when I run into him."

Ryan was right. You didn't hear much about the older brother, Jeremy, he kept out of the spotlight. But Michael Taylor was young, single, and rich. The perfect combination to sweep a pretty girl off her feet.

If Lilí had grown up in the Chicago suburbs and didn't come from money, maybe her connection to the Taylor family was a romantic one. She didn't have to worry about not being able to afford the rent here if she'd moved in with her boyfriend. And if she was dating a Taylor, no way would Diego stand a chance with her.

Whoa! He put the brakes on that line of thinking so fast it left skid marks on his brain.

It didn't matter who Lilí was or was not dating.

What mattered was that she not be in harm's way.

Bill Ryan's frown deepened as if he'd read Diego's last thought. "What's that punk with the mug shot have to do with Ms. Fernandez? This about her job down at the abuse clinic? Maybe the guest she had last night?"

The fact that Ryan knew where Lilí worked and the situations that could arise from it, that he was aware Melba had stayed over—they were all signs of the close tabs the security team kept on the comings and goings in their building. Very reassuring.

Diego nodded at the older man. "He was involved

in a domestic violence case that could have been uglier than it was. Though, with DV cases like this, there's always the potential for it to go sideways."

Ryan's jaw tensed. The wrinkles in his face deepened with his fierce scowl.

"It's not certain if he knows where Lilí lives," Diego continued, "but I don't want to take any chances. Especially since I'm not completely convinced that she understands the severity of the situation."

"Sees the good in everyone, doesn't she?" Ryan shook his head slowly from side to side.

Well, she didn't seem to have trouble finding fault in him, Diego noted. He kept that thought to himself. Instead, he reached for his wallet to swap out one of his business cards with Ryan's.

"I'll shoot you an email with Tito González's mug shot for you to share with the security staff. If anyone hears something, if you see anything out of the ordinary, call me ASAP. Whether I'm on duty or not, I'll be here."

"Will do," Bill Ryan assured him. "And thanks for looking out for her. Ms. Fernandez is a special lady. I'd hate for anything to happen to her."

Determination straightened Diego's shoulders like a steel rod sliding down the center of his back. "That's not gonna happen. Not as long as I have anything to say about it."

The older man gave a brisk jerk of his head. Diego reiterated his promise to send the picture, then headed out.

As he stepped onto the sidewalk in front of Lilí's building he shot a quick glance up at the cloudless July sky. He said a silent hello to his mom, a reminder to himself that once he hadn't been there for another "special lady"—one who wanted only good for those she cared about.

Just like Lilí Fernandez.

He wasn't dumb enough to think he could save everyone. Hell, there were countless times he felt like trying to get through to his sister was the same as beating his head against the cement walls on Lower Wacker Drive. But he could damn well do his best to save some.

Even if that meant saving them from themselves.

Chapter Five

"So where's your class located again?"

Lilí rolled her eyes at Rosa's nagging question. A response which, had they been chatting in person rather than over the phone, would have garnered her a frown of disapproval from her worrywart middle sister.

"It's probably going to be dark when your class finishes," Rosa's henpecking continued. "I'm always worried when you tell me you've stayed late at work as it is."

"The center's a safe place," Yazmine chimed in. "It's where I started the first dance program. Maria's even volunteering with the summer session this year."

Lilí mentally high-fived her older sister as she stopped several feet away from the Humboldt Park Area Youth Center's entrance.

"*Bueno*, you just can't be too careful."

Rosa's worried sigh came through the cell and Lilí pictured her two sisters sitting on the family's living room couch together. Yaz probably wearing leggings and a blouse, her long dancer's legs folded underneath her. Her black satiny hair more than likely pulled back in a high ponytail or sleek bun. Rosa, battling baby bulge since the birth of her son six months ago, wearing one of her trademark loose-fitting summer dresses, her wavy hair loose around her shoulders. Little Nico liked to play with it when he was nursing.

Apparently with Yazmine's husband Tomás out of town on a business trip, Yaz had come over to Rosa's for dinner with her daughter and young son, who were planning to stay for a cousins' summer sleepover. Jeremy, brave soul, was upstairs playing a game with his and Rosa's oldest and Yaz's two. Knowing her nieces, the poor man was up to his elbows in miniature doll clothes and tiny plastic heels that didn't stay on.

Usually their sister chats were via a three-way conference call, each sister headed in a different direction. Yaz to an after-school activity with Maria or some mother-toddler class with Rey, if not to the dance studio. Rosa running to keep up with her four-year-old while juggling caring for a new baby. Lilí at the clinic or the shelter, teaching classes in the evenings.

With her two *hermanas* together, Lilí was on speakerphone so both sisters could hear. That meant she was privy to the occasional shouts from the older kids upstairs. Or her sweet nephew's baby babble from his perch in a bouncer nearby.

A pang of regret that she'd missed out on the impromptu family get-together burned in her chest.

Then the metal front door of the youth center banged open and she caught sight of the spacious main lobby area. Teens and younger kids milled about. Hopefully some were here to take advantage of her free self-defense class.

Determination to do better for them, like she hadn't

been able to do in college with Karen, swept aside any lingering familial homesickness.

"I'll be fine," she assured her sisters. "This is exactly where I'm supposed to be."

"Mami, can we have *mantecado*?" Yaz's oldest, Maria yelled in the background. "Uncle Jeremy said we had to ask your permission if we wanted ice cream."

Lilí pictured her niece's brown eyes, earnest and pleading, the expression on her round face hopeful. At eleven, and the official leader of the cousins, she could bargain better than Lilí had at that age.

A car drove by on the busy street, the exhaust from city buses and other vehicles adding to the July heat and humidity weighing down the air. Propping the super-sized zippered bag, which held the protective gear needed during the physical portion of the class, onto its wheels, Lilí dabbed at the sweat dotting her upper lip. Ice cream sounded pretty good right now if you asked her.

Diantre, it was equator-hot tonight!

In preparation for the hands-on self-defense demonstration, she'd worn black capri yoga leggings and a black "Respect" Cubs T-shirt from the team's recent World Series Championship run. Lugging the self-defense class supplies from the clinic several blocks away might not have been her smartest move this time of year. Perspiration had the cotton material of her shirt sticking to her back.

While Yaz let her ten-year-old explain why she and her cousins deserved the treat, Lilí checked the time on the pace-counter strapped on her wrist: 6:40.

She'd better get inside. Class started in twenty minutes. If she was lucky, there might be a few early arrivers she could break the ice with.

"Come on, give the kid a break," Lilí said into her phone. "It's summer. Time for lots of junk food, staying up late, and having fun."

"*¡Sí!* Tía Lilí understands. I think we should listen to her. *Por favor,* Mami," Maria pleaded. "We haven't had dessert with dinner all week. I'll clean up the dishes after. Deal?"

Lilí grinned at her niece's smart negotiation skills. "My vote is yes. But I gotta go."

"Wait!" Rosa called. "Will we see you this weekend? Maybe Sunday morning mass and family breakfast? Or we can go Sunday early evening and you stay for dinner. You didn't come last weekend."

Because she'd been hanging at the women's shelter. Filling in where needed. Being a source of support to anyone, another pair of ears to listen. Letting others talk and share when they were ready. Especially with Melba, who was still adjusting.

But Lilí didn't say that. Her sisters didn't know about what had gone down with Melba, in part due to client confidentiality, in part because they'd freak out if they found out about Tito, who remained on the street nearly a week later.

"Hello? Are you still there?" Rosa asked.

"Yeah, I'll try," Lilí answered.

"Aww, I hope you make it, Tía." María's little-girl voice grew louder, like she'd leaned close to the phone to make sure Lilí heard her. "I'm taking hip-hop this summer and wanna show you some of my new moves."

No way could she disappoint any of her nieces or little Rey. And baby Nico already had her wrapped around his pudgy pinky finger.

"For you, *chiquita,* I wouldn't miss it. We'll have a dance-off in the basement, okay?"

"Yesss!" Maria's cheer had Lilí laughing, picturing the young girl doing a salsa step on the floral area rug in their living room.

After hurried cries of *adios* with *besos* and *abrazos* from everyone, Lilí disconnected the call. The good-byes, kisses, and hugs always lifted her spirits, love for her rowdy, if sometimes busybody *familia* filling her.

As she turned to face the two-story redbrick build-ing with the thin bars of protection crisscrossing its arched windows, the blessing that was her family hit her like one of the rubber dodgeballs the kids tossed at each other in the gym at the back of the building.

Many of these kids struggled while dealing with broken homes, parents trying to make a living on low incomes that often left them without enough food in the pantry, and the ever-enticing lure of the spider's web that was gang life.

She strived every day to make a difference for those she came into contact with in her role as an advocate.

Years ago, as a young resident advisor her junior year of college at Southern Illinois University in Carbondale, she'd made a vow to do better. In the days and weeks after Karen Fowler had knocked on Lilí's dorm room door, tears streaking down the fresh-man's pale, makeup-smeared face, Lilí had tried, but failed.

Hindsight had shown her that no amount of basic RA training could have prepared her for how to properly assist a co-ed who'd been drugged and date raped at an off-campus party. As if the act itself hadn't been horrendous enough, the legal process, the he said–she said tug of war, had dragged Karen through reliving the events, facing her assailant, and ultimately watching him walk away without a single consequence.

The pain Karen had gone through was more than physical. The damage to her psyche had been inconceivable. Despite Lilí's attempts to reach her, supporting her through campus calls to action against sexual assault and violence, sitting quietly with her late at night when Karen couldn't sleep . . . everything Lilí had tried that spring semester to help Karen work through her pain had failed.

At the end of the semester, Karen had taken a leave of absence, returned home to the central Illinois area, and eventually transferred to another university.

In the years since, Lilí remained in touch with her. Karen had moved on, was now a nurse in St. Louis. Dating a guy who sounded like he might be the one.

But the ways in which the system had failed in the aftermath of Karen's ordeal had fed something within Lilí. Her own inability as a young RA, ill-equipped to provide more support, had been like Miracle-Gro sprinkled on a seed that had planted itself deep inside her after Mami's death when Lilí was a preteen. When Papi and her sisters had been walking zombies of emotional hurt and she had sought a way to ease their sorrow. That seed had sprouted those last two years of college, leading to her focus on women and gender studies followed by the decision to serve as a victim's advocate. And now, it led her to this sidewalk in front of the youth center.

Like she'd told her sisters, this was exactly where she was meant to be.

Grabbing the equipment bag's stiff handle, she marched toward the gray metal door, ready to do her best to teach these girls how to defend themselves.

Because in a world where the bad might win a few battles, she was determined to not let it win the war.

"Okay, so now that we've spent some time discussing the importance of safety measures and security, both online and in your daily lives, does anyone have any questions?"

Lilí trailed her gaze over the twelve girls sitting at the school desks lined up in rows in the first-floor classroom. Half of them had walked in together, quickly claiming desks in the center rows. A sort of queen bee marking of the territory.

Based on their artfully ripped skinny jeans, figure-skimming blouses, and the inches-high wedges some wore on their feet, it was obvious they hadn't paid attention to the note about proper class attire. Although, maybe practicing self-defense moves in the clothes they normally wore wasn't such a bad idea.

The other half of the students had either paired off or sat alone. Of those, only three had dressed appropriately in exercise clothes.

Lucky for them, tonight she'd only demonstrate. Next class the girls would put on the pads themselves and try their hand at several scenarios.

"So, you're saying we shouldn't tag our location when we're out having fun?" one of the queen bees asked. Her gum smacking picked up speed as the rest of her hive looked askance at Lilí.

Dios save her from the social media age, Lilí grumbled to herself.

This need to see and be seen, to broadcast to the world what you were doing and with whom, twenty-four-seven, had its drawbacks. But these girls didn't want to hear a lecture. Ha, at their age she wouldn't have listened to one either. Though Papi would have made her spit her gum out had she smacked it like that. She could hear him now: *¡Es una falta de respeto, nena!*

The fact that she found herself agreeing with Papi's claim that it *was* a lack of respect made her feel old.

"Here's the thing, Omara. I'm not here to tell you what to do." Lilí spoke slowly, measuring her words to better walk that line between teacher-mentor and friend. If she had to come down on one side or the other, mentor won hands down. Often there were enough adults in these kids' lives who acted more like friends than authority figures. Lilí refused to be another one. That'd be doing them a disservice.

"The stories—the police cases—I've shared tonight are true events. That college girl who was stalked by her ex did figure out that he knew where she'd be, and with whom, based on her social media updates and location tagging. Does that mean you have to stop altogether?"

Twelve pairs of eyes widened.

A mix of Spanish and English protests rumbled from several girls. In the back row Juanita and Kendra shook their heads, lips puckered in derisive pouts, their expressions screaming, "No way, lady!" loud and clear.

"I would say . . ." Lilí waited for the room to quiet down before continuing. "I would say that's up to you. Use your judgment. Be aware of who's around you. Ask yourself if you really need to post that pic or call out where you're hanging. It's about situational awareness."

She came out from behind the small podium where she'd kept her notes. Moving closer to the girls, she leaned her left hip against the top of a desk in the front row.

"Look, I am all for keeping our own power. It's why I teach this class. To empower you. Tonight it's mostly been with information. After the break, for the last thirty minutes I'll show you some of the moves you'll be learning when we meet again on Thursday and next Tuesday."

Lilí looked around the room, stopping to make eye contact with each one of the teens. "I want all of you to be safe. To make smart decisions. And after this class, to be confident that, should you find yourself needing them, you'll have tools that could increase your odds of getting away from a bad situation."

Silence met her when she finished.

The sullen looks Omara and some of the girls in her posse had arrived with had faded.

Progress.

"Empower, huh?" the group leader asked, a keen sparkle in her dark eyes.

"¿*Como* Wonder Woman, *verdad*?" Juanita called out from the back.

Chuckles and giggles erupted, along with a little muscle flexing by a few.

Lilí grinned back at them. Definitely progress made.

"So, take a bathroom break, then let's meet in the lobby to head to the gym." Lilí checked the time on her Fitbit. "I'll meet you there in ten minutes."

That gave her some time to call Kent, the cop who typically assisted her with the physical portion of the class. He should have been here by now.

The girls crowded toward the door to head out.

Lilí turned to gather up her supplies as the room quieted. Lifting the strap of her messenger bag over her head and across her shoulder, she stepped toward the left front corner of the room where she'd propped up the supply bag.

"Hey, how's it going?"

Her pulse blipped at the greeting. Or rather, at the deep voice she'd recognize anywhere.

Craning her neck to look over her shoulder, she slowly spun around to find Diego Reyes lounging in the doorway.

Dressed in dark jeans and a pec-hugging red tee that complemented his olive skin, a pair of white Nike Dunk sneakers with a red swoosh capping off his look, he flashed her that sexy smirk of his. If the guy was going for casual yet mouthwateringly gorgeous, he'd hit a bull's-eye.

Diego crooked an arm to lean against the door frame, his biceps pulling his sleeve taught.

She hadn't seen him in five days. Not that she'd been counting.

Nor had she made note of the fact that the last few times she'd swung by the shelter to touch base with Melba, the woman mentioned that he'd been by earlier. Lilí had come insanely close to asking if he'd said anything about her. *Gracias a Dios* she had enough self-respect to keep the question to herself.

"It's going good. You?" she asked, determined to keep their exchange low-key.

He'd been radio silent since their eventful visit to Melba's house and his footrace with Tito. In fact, the one phone call she'd received from the cops to verify some info had been from Diego's partner, Officer Stevens.

That told her she was the only one who hadn't been

able to stop thinking about their "moment" in Melba's living room. Whatever the "moment" had been.

Maybe she'd imagined the electricity zinging between them.

The golden flecks in his eyes sparking with desire.

Knowing him, it'd been with annoyance.

"I hear you're in need of an assistant," Diego answered.

"Uh, not that I'm aware of. Officer Smith, Kent, usually assists. He should be—"

She broke off when Diego shook his head.

"What do you mean, no?" A sense of foreboding settled onto her shoulders.

"Apparently Kent can't make it. I was on my way out and David stopped me at the front desk. Looks like you're stuck with me for tonight."

Diego watched Lilí's mouth open, then close. Her expression quickly moved from blank surprise to a scandalized frown.

Hell, even irritated she looked cute. A fact his simmering attraction had already noted. Which is why, after learning from the head of security at her place that she might be romantically involved with one of the Taylor brothers, he'd kept his distance.

He wasn't one to poach another man's woman.

Yet, he wasn't going to leave her in the lurch if she needed his assistance tonight.

"I'm surprised Kent didn't let me know," Lilí finally answered.

"I guess his wife's out of town and his kid got sick right before your class started. He said he'd left you a voice message, then called the front desk just in case."

"That's strange." Lilí unzipped her brown bag,

then reached inside to pull out her cell phone. "I didn't get a . . . *ay Dios mío.*"

She stared down at the device as she muttered. A beat later she turned the phone to show him the screen.

"Darn thing died. I meant to plug it in to charge when I got to the classroom, but one of the girls was already hanging out by the door when I arrived. We started talking, the other girls began filtering in and, *bueno,* I forgot."

"It happens."

Lilí scoffed. "Yeah, tell that to Rosa. She's always on my case about having my phone charged in case of an emergency."

"I take it Rosa is . . ."

"My middle sister," she answered. "AKA, the worrier."

"Ahh, got it. I've heard of those. I only have one older sister. 'Worrier' is not the word I'd use to describe her."

He mentally kicked himself. Why the hell had he brought up Lourdes? He had a strict rule, no talking about his family.

"So, what do you need?" he asked, changing the subject.

Lilí hesitated, then dropped her phone back in her bag with a resigned sigh.

"Are you sure you don't mind? It's only for about thirty minutes. Demonstrating what we'll be doing in Thursday's class." She swiped at her wispy bangs in a nervous gesture he'd caught her doing the other day. "I have a video, but, um, after two-plus hours of sitting and listening to me, I've found the kids are more engaged, more apt to return for the next class, if I give them a taste of what we'll be doing."

Diego pushed off the doorjamb. "I wouldn't be here if I minded. I'm all yours."

Something flared in her eyes in the seconds before she turned to snag the plastic handle on a super-sized black rolling bag at the front of the room. He figured it held the sparring pads they'd need to demonstrate the self-defense moves.

Her back to him, he let his gaze caress the length of her. From the long, dark braid that fell nearly to her waist, down the fitted black Cubs T-shirt, to the capri leggings hugging the curve of her firm butt.

She was enticing, but taken. Which meant he had no business being this excited to step in as her assistant. And he definitely had no business checking her out.

Her shoulders rose and fell as if she'd taken a deep breath to brace herself before facing him again.

"Okay, then," she said, her chipper, I-can-handle-it attitude firmly in place. "Let's go meet the girls in the main entrance area and head to the gym."

He stepped back out of the doorway, bending to pick up his guitar case.

"Hey, do you play?" She waved a hand at the battered case plastered with stickers from various places he'd vacationed. Mostly beaches where he stuck his toes in the sand, stared out at the infinite ocean, and strummed away the stress and guilt.

"Yeah. Since I was a kid."

He'd actually learned here, at the center. Meeting Carlos Nieves and taking up the guitar was a big part of what had kept Diego off the streets. That and witnessing the pain his sister's bad decisions had caused his mom.

"You any good?" Head tucked, Lilí slanted him a playful, challenging glance.

"I can hold my own."

She chuckled, a husky sound that laved his attraction like a cat's warm tongue.

"You surprise me," she finally said.

"Why?"

Again with the swiping at her bangs move. Was it habit or nerves? It would be interesting to find out.

"I don't know," she hedged. "I guess humility isn't a trait I would have expected."

Diego slapped his free hand to his chest. "*Ay, mujer,* you wound me!"

Her second low chuckle stirred his body.

"Oh, I'm sure it takes much more than that to wound your ego."

"Not ego. Confidence."

Her arched brow encouraged him to elaborate.

"Nothing wrong with being proud of who you are and where you come from," he said. The army might have taken him far from home, but home had never been far from his thoughts. Or his heart. "It's something I tell the kids I work with. Here, and on the job."

"It's important for them to have positive role models."

"Yeah, it is. Like what you're doing with these girls."

"I try." A mix of hopeful determination stamped her beautiful features as she gazed ahead of them toward the main lobby at the end of the hall.

They walked in silence beside each other, passing the other three classrooms that comprised the first floor of this wing. In the seventeen years since he'd taken his first guitar lesson at the age of ten, the center had aged.

Money from a fundraiser last Christmas had gone to gym renovations, a high-use area that desperately needed it. But in this wing, the original white and gray linoleum flooring was now yellowed. Deep scrapes marked several areas. Based on his expanding handyman skills from remodeling his place, he'd say the center would be better off replacing the linoleum with vinyl composition tile. However, expenses were probably an issue.

Even the corkboards papered with flyers and displays of artwork lining the walls sported splotchy areas where some of the cork had flaked off from overuse. The metal and wood desks inside the classrooms were the same, some a little worse for wear. Odds were, if he knelt down to check, names on top of names were carved or scrawled on the underside of the laminate wood desktops.

But while the building might benefit from a makeover, one thing remained the same. The familiar scent of the floral cleaning liquid the people in his community preferred, mixed with the smell of teen bodies in all their sweaty, perfumed or male body-sprayed glory, permeated the air. It reminded him of home and the place where he'd found the one gift that calmed him. Music.

"So you happen to be at the youth center, carrying a guitar, ready to fill in for Kent because, why?" Lilí asked.

The rumble of voices grew louder as they neared the lobby area.

"Because on Tuesdays I teach two guitar classes."

"You do?" She drew to a stop.

"Hey, now, don't look so shocked. Melba already told you, I'm a nice guy."

Her mouth twitched, like she was fighting a smile.

Sucker that he was, he wanted her to give in to it.

Who was he kidding?

What he *really* wanted was to sneak into one of these darkened classrooms with her for a make-out session like two horny teens.

He'd run his hands along her sexy hips. Skim past her slim waist to cup the weight of her shapely breasts. Bend down to taste the smooth column of her throat. Feel her pulse beating against his lips.

Turn that playful smile of hers into a moan of pleasure that sent them both over the edge.

His body stirred at the images invading his head.

She was off-limits, he reminded himself. Spoken for by a guy playing in a different league than Diego. Though whether it was a better one depended on your perspective.

As for him, he was fine here, in his neighborhood. Fighting the good fight.

"Cool," she murmured, almost as if agreeing with his thoughts.

They arrived at the lobby, crammed with kids either in constant motion or lounging on the couches squared off near a large bookshelf and a magazine rack.

"Okay, ladies, let's go," Lilí called out. She circled an arm in the air, signaling for her group to follow her toward the center hallway leading to the gym in back.

Diego noticed that Omara and a few of the girls she hung with were in the mix. As soon as the teen saw him she waved, shooting him a real smile that softened the edges of her typical tough-girl façade. One of her friends nudged her to get her attention and the mask slipped back into place.

Lilí must have caught the exchange because she tilted her head in question. "You know the queen bee?"

He smirked at the apt moniker. Omara and her group definitely had the we-rule-the-school attitude.

"She's not all bad. Underneath that crusty exterior is a kid looking out for her younger brother, worried about a mom who's working two jobs. Pissed at a dad who's in and out of the picture." Like his had been.

"Sounds like a lot of kids who come here," Lilí answered. "It's not easy for them."

"No, but that's not an excuse to turn to drugs or gang life."

"It's not always that simple."

"I get that. But, few things that are worthwhile are simple," he told her.

She started to say something, probably to debate her point, but one of the girls sidled up to ask Lilí a question and the opportunity was lost.

Reaching the metal gym doors, Diego pushed the left side in, moving to prop it open with his foot so the class could enter.

Inside the gym a game of full-court basketball was in play. Had to be a shirts versus skins match-up as half the boys were shirtless, their young bodies wet with sweat. The air rang with the sound of sneakers squeaking on the court floor, voices yelling in support or complaint or a cheer over a dope move someone made to the basket. The damp, earthy smell of bodies in motion filled the air.

On the far right corner, the last two rows of bleachers hadn't been pulled out, leaving an empty space for Lilí's class to congregate. She led the way there, rolling the supplies bag behind her. The girls followed her along the edge of the court, under the basket to the other side, like ducklings trailing the mama duck.

Diego brought up the rear, the better to admire the

shake, shake, shake of Lilí's shapely hips. He grinned. Watching her work was gonna be fun.

Twenty minutes into his job as Lilí's assistant, he realized his miscalculation.

Playing the role of the aggressor in a self-defense demo meant having up-close-and-personal contact with the one woman he shouldn't.

So much for *look but don't touch.*

Lilí demonstrated the initial stance the students were taught to assume when they felt danger approaching. Right foot back. Both knees slightly bent to better move and twist into action. Left arm outstretched, palm facing forward in the universal "stop" signal. Right arm bent at her waist, biceps flexing as she curled her hand in a tight fist, ready to punch forward with a jab if needed.

She reminded the girls to make eye contact, letting the aggressor, in this case Diego, know she meant business. Then she signaled him over.

He moved to join her in front of the class, standing about twenty feet away.

"Diego's going to come at me in some way I find offensive," Lilí explained to the girls.

Suddenly, the idea of being the bad guy in her eyes, even if pretending, didn't sit well with him. He thought of Tito and any other scumbags she'd had to deal with, chafing at the idea that she'd associate him with any of them.

"Come on." Lilí bounced on the balls of her black Nikes. Excited energy personified.

No way he could back out now.

He pushed his mind into role-play mode just like any other training scenario. Rolling his shoulders, he shook out his arms, loosening his muscles in preparation for his "attack."

Diego took a few steps to his left, pretending to leisurely amble away while craning his neck to keep Lilí in his sights. A guy checking out a girl who's on her own. Weighing the situation, considering his chances.

Lilí eyed him while she spoke to the girls. "See how I'm looking straight at him. Letting him know I'm aware he's there. I can give him an opportunity to do the right thing, and shake my head no. Indicating he should move on."

She followed her own instructions as she gave them. But a real bad guy wouldn't be dissuaded so easily.

Pivoting, he sauntered toward her, his upper body swaying in a loose, homeboy swag. "Yo, baby, whatcha got goin' on?"

"Not interested," she answered. Her head shaking grew more firm.

"Come on, girl, I got what you want," he singsonged.

"Get back!" Her firm voice echoed through the gym as she crouched in the defensive position.

Heads swiveled in their direction. A few basketball players stumbled to a halt at her cry.

The girls tittered nervously, but Lilí had gotten their attention.

And his.

Her expression fierce, the muscles in her firm thighs strained under her black leggings. Power emanated from her slight figure like a caged force ready to pounce.

A carnal desire to feel her power in a completely different, far more positive role-play situation, coursed through him. Surprised by its intensity, Diego froze. He blinked, taken aback by his inappropriate response to their situation.

"Well, I doubt the guy's gonna back off so quickly." Lilí straightened, turning to face the girls. "I didn't think Officer Reyes would be such a pushover."

He huffed in complaint and she shot him a teasing grin.

"He's probably taking it easy on me 'cause this is our first time working together. But"—her grin faded as she looked from one girl to the next—"a real creep on the street won't do that."

Several girls murmured their agreement.

Diego stuffed his hands in his back jeans pockets. Feeling a bit like a chump, he waited to see Lilí's next move.

She answered a few questions, referring by name to each girl who spoke up. Encouraging them. The upfront, honest way she handled the difficult topic impressed him. Her voice filled with strength and conviction as she spoke of empowerment and self-confidence. Not as some authority figure, but as someone who listened when the girls talked, showing them she really cared about what they had to say.

If only his sister had had someone like Lilí Fernandez to rely on when she'd been in high school. Straddling the line between child and young adult, she hadn't wanted to listen to their mom. Maybe she would have listened to another woman closer to her age. One who was passionate about teaching others to make smart choices.

It was too late now for Lourdes. But Lilí could make a difference for girls like Omara.

"On Thursday, you'll put on protective pads. Then we'll work together so you can learn and practice the actual moves. We might even get to simulations by the last half."

Lilí paused, nodding yes in response to several "No way!" murmurs.

"Officer Smith and his partner will be here to serve as aggressors. But I'll be verbally guiding everyone through the scenarios and I'll have a whistle to signal an immediate halt for any reason."

Diego wondered if Kent's partner might welcome a night off. Not that he had any business thinking about volunteering.

"Can you show us some of those moves now?" a tall, skinny girl Diego had seen with Omara asked.

"Sure, we have some time. First, you've seen the protective gear we'll all wear on Thursday." Lilí motioned toward the red upper and lower body, arm, groin, leg, and feet pads laid out by the rolling duffel she'd dragged with her from the classroom. "We'll have full sets for everyone at the next class. For tonight, Officer Reyes and I won't wear any since we're only simulating, not going through the full motions. Now, to start with . . ."

She took the girls through a brief explanation of the various self-defense moves, then segued into the scenarios. "You've just seen when someone comes at you directly. We'll go through what to do should the defensive pose and verbalizations not be enough to make the person back off. Unlike with Officer Reyes a few moments ago. Another scenario puts you at an ATM or waiting in an area like the bus stop. Finally you'll be approached with your eyes closed to simulate nighttime, when it's harder to see. Keep in mind, through all of these, the idea is to get away. Not stay and fight, but flee to safety."

"So, with the ATM." She turned her back to Diego, but glanced over her shoulder as she spoke. "Officer Reyes will come at me from behind. As he draws near, the first thing I do is verbalize my desire for him to back off." She wiggled her fingers at him, signaling for him to proceed.

Diego knew the drill, having volunteered with similar classes in the past. Only, the instructor hadn't been Lilí, who had him getting all kinds of completely inappropriate ideas when she asked him to "come at me from behind."

Dios, ayudalo por favor.

Uh, yeah, he could use a little assistance keeping his thoughts in check right now.

Trying to focus on the scenario Lilí described to the girls, he approached her, rolling through his steps and swaying his shoulders in the same tough-guy stroll as before.

"Hey, sweetness. What up?"

"Get back," she warned.

He ignored her, moving closer to brush up against her back.

Electricity sparked in his chest, swiftly arcing through him at their contact.

Lilí stepped to the side, her firm butt inadvertently swiping across his groin. He sucked in a sharp breath.

"I said back off!" she ordered, continuing to act like she was tapping buttons on a teller machine.

Undeterred, he crowded her space once more.

"Come on, let's have some fun." Snaking an arm around her waist, he pulled her firmly against him. Her body spooned with his, the front of his thighs nestled along the back of hers.

Muffled gasps came from the students.

"On Thursday," Lilí said, her voice raised so the girls could hear her, "you'll learn several options to try and get out of a situation like this."

Damn if she didn't sound perfectly normal. As if

being pressed chest-to-back like this didn't affect her in the least. While all he could think about was the urge to slide his hand up to cup her breast. Ducking his head to take a bigger whiff of her coconutty-lemon scent. Blowing gently in her ear. Get her pulse racing to match his.

"You can release me now," she mumbled under her breath.

She put her hand over his on her waist and he swore her heat seeped into him. Her fingers brushed softly over his for a pleasure-sparking moment before she dropped her hand.

He followed suit, releasing her to back up a step, then another. Distancing himself.

Slanting a glance her way he caught the faint blush darkening her olive-toned cheeks. Maybe he wasn't the only one wondering what might happen if they were someplace else. Somewhere way more private.

Rather than continue the demos, Lilí stepped toward the girls, gathering them in a semicircle around her. She explained how the last two classes would proceed, stressing their importance. Not once did she look in his direction. Even when she asked the class to thank him for his time before she dismissed them.

"You need any help packing up?" he asked once the students had wandered away.

Lilí crouched near the black bag, gathering the protective pads.

"That's okay, I got it. Thanks for sticking around to help."

Still no eye contact from her.

She had to sense the attraction sizzling between them. Either she was embarrassed or trying to ignore it out of respect for her boyfriend.

The polite thing for him to do was ignore it, too.

"Okay then," he said, reaching for his guitar case. "Guess I'll see you around."

"Yeah, maybe. Thanks again."

He wanted her to look at him, give him one last glimpse of her sassy grin.

Because he wanted it more than was wise, he made himself walk away.

Even so, that didn't make him stop hoping he'd run into her again. Soon.

Chapter Six

"*Adios, Velma, nos vemos mañana*," Lilí called on her way out the clinic front door Wednesday evening.

"Yes, I will see you tomorrow," Velma answered. She poked her head out of the break room to wave good-bye, her multicolored bangles jangling on her wrist.

They were the last two people in the building, having stayed late to review plans for an upcoming survivors' leadership luncheon. Most of the staff had left over an hour ago and now dusk loomed.

Lilí stepped onto the sidewalk out front, stopping to admire the early evening watercolor sky. The sun hid behind the city skyline, reaching around the skyscrapers with orange and red fingers. Wispy dark purple clouds billowed behind them. The heat from the day lingered, humidity hanging in the air, heavy and thick.

With rain predicted off and on throughout the day, she'd driven to the clinic rather than walk to the "L" station to grab the train this morning. Head bowed, she dug in her messenger bag for her car keys.

The street lamps lining the road had flicked on already, casting shadows along the walkway ahead of her. The darkened alley between the clinic and the vacant redbrick building beside it made her unusually nervous tonight. Her pace quickened. Instinctively she tucked her house key between her pointer and middle fingers. The end could easily become a weapon if need be.

Until the run-in with Tito last week, she'd never been uncomfortable in this neighborhood. Tonight, she was relieved that teaching the self-defense course at the center had led her to brush up on her own skills.

With her navy-blue Corolla a few cars away, she clicked the driver's-side door open. A nervous ripple skittered between her shoulder blades. Footsteps sounded to her right and she glanced over her shoulder in time to catch a figure slithering out of the alley shadows. An overhead street lamp illuminated part of the face.

Lilí gasped when she recognized Tito.

One of his shirtsleeves was torn, his faded jeans spattered with mud or dirt.

"I heard you know where my wife is." He spit on the ground, then swiped at his mouth with the back of his tattooed hand.

"Stay away from me!" she cried, racing toward her car.

Tito gave chase.

He body-slammed her against the right side of the vehicle nearby, knocking the wind out of her.

"Where's Melba?" he growled, his foul breath making her gag.

"Let me go!" Lilí yelled.

His dark eyes were wild. His fierce scowl menacing.

She struggled to push him off her, trying to jab him with her key, but her right arm was trapped between their bodies.

Tito shoved her against the car again. She yelped as pain shot through her shoulder blade.

Fear grabbed hold of her with icy fingers, squeezing her chest.

Years of training, dating back to college after Karen's attack, kicked in. Hiking up her knee, she got a swift jab to his crotch before bringing her foot down to stomp on his instep.

Tito howled in anger, but he didn't back away. He shoved a forearm against her throat, choking her, and grabbed her arm in a viselike grip, pinning her to the car.

"*¡Dime! ¿Donde está Melba?*" he demanded.

"I'm not telling you where she is," Lilí rasped. "Melba's safe. Away from you!"

She punctuated the last word with another attempt at a kick to the balls followed by a quick jab to his ribs when he hunched over in pain.

"Lilí! *¿Qué pasa?*"

Velma's cry brought a rush of relief, along with a renewed sense of fear. Lilí didn't want Tito to hurt her or anyone else.

"*Ching*—" Tito growled, biting off the curse word as Velma hurried down the clinic's front steps.

"Leave her alone!" Velma cried.

"I'm watching you," Tito threatened. After one final push against her windpipe along with another bone-crunching squeeze of her arm, he ran into the alley, disappearing in the darkness.

Lilí sank to her knees on the curb, gasping for breath.

The sound of Velma's gold sneakers pounding on the sidewalk was punctuated by a car honking somewhere down the street.

"*¿Nena, qué pasó?* Who was that?"

"It's nothing," Lilí answered, her pulse pounding in her ears.

"*Qué* nothing. Who was that man? I am calling the police."

"Wait!" Lilí held up a hand. "Just give me, give me a minute to think."

Head bowed, palms pressed to the rough cement, she struggled to pull her thoughts together. *Dios mío*, what if Velma hadn't come out when she did? Worse, what if Tito had turned on her? Fear and anger fueled the adrenaline racing through Lilí.

The good news was that Tito had just added to his list of charges. He would definitely pay now. She vowed to make sure of it.

Sitting back on her heels, Lilí unzipped her messenger purse, digging through it for her cell.

Before dialing 911, there was one person she felt compelled to call. One person she was convinced she could trust on this. A cop who went above and beyond, like speaking to Bill Ryan and enlisting her condo's security office to ensure Tito wasn't lurking around. Finding out about that from Bill had given more credence to her suspicions that Diego Reyes might indeed be a good guy.

Her fingers shaky, Lilí tapped her cell screen.

She waited for the call to go through, recognizing she was beginning to form a pattern that might not be too healthy. In need of rescuing, call 1-800-Diego-Reyes.

Right now, she was too freaked out to care.

"*Hola*, Lilí, what's up?"

"Tito was here," she rasped, relief knocking her back on her heels as soon as she heard Diego's deep voice. Then, despite her best intentions, Lilí burst into tears.

"Please, I'm fine. There's no need to call EMS." Lilí waved off Velma and Diego, turning instead to plead with the two cops who'd arrived on the scene shortly after Diego.

The female cop nodded. The tall, skinny guy looked to Diego for confirmation. Like he had a say in what she did.

Dios mío, she should never have called him.

Chalk it up to lack of normal brain function in the aftermath of Tito's manhandling.

Diego had pulled up in the street next to her car, tires squealing as he braked. His emergency lights flashing, he'd left his car double-parked in the middle of the road and raced over to where she sat on the steps of the vacant building next to the clinic.

Velma had taken one look at him and practically swooned.

If she hadn't felt like such a wimp for bawling on the phone with him, Lilí would have laughed. Or probably swooned herself.

He was a delectable man in black tonight. Wearing snug jeans, a form-fitting tee, and a pair of vintage Air Jordan sneakers in black, he looked rugged and ready to kick some ass.

Unfortunately, with Tito out of sight, Diego had zeroed in on lecturing her on the folly of leaving her office alone. After checking to make sure she wasn't critically hurt, of course.

"It's okay," he told Jordan and Shapiro, two cops it turned out he'd worked with before. "I'll stick with her for a bit longer and follow up when I'm on shift tomorrow."

"We'll put out the description," Shapiro said. "Make sure everyone's keeping an eye out for him. Maybe we'll get lucky and finally nab the scumbag."

Handshakes were exchanged along with thanks from Lilí and Velma. Shortly after, the two cops left, headed to another call a few blocks over.

Velma sat beside Lilí, patting her knee in a maternal gesture.

"I'm sorry you had to stay," Lilí told her coworker.

"*¿Qué?* And miss meeting your young man?"

Lilí winced. Thank goodness Diego was moving his car into an open parking space across the street.

"He's not my young man," she insisted.

"*Bueno,* he could be, *no?*" Velma gave her sly grin.

"No. I don't date cops, remember? One bad experience was enough for me."

"*Por favor.* Don't be like that. One man is not the other. And this one, *ay, esta súper sexy.*"

Lilí slapped a hand over her eyes and shook her head at Velma's Spanglish. "Please, stop. I can't even . . ."

Any other time and she might have laughed at Velma's teasing.

As it was, she'd spent most of last night thinking about Diego. Remembering the feel of his strong arm wrapped around her waist when they'd role-played during the self-defense class. Recalling how perfectly her body fit, molded to his.

Never, not in the two years since she'd been certified as an instructor, had she experienced any physical response to a fellow instructor getting so up close and personal like they did in class. Until Diego Reyes.

The man had been wreaking havoc on her senses

since he'd blocked her way into Melba's apartment last week. She'd been mortified by her reaction last night, unable to even look at him after class. Afraid he'd see how turned on she'd been during a mock scenario in which she had absolutely no business being turned on.

Diego jogged back to her and Velma. A tantalizing devil in black.

"How are you two doing?" he asked, for the millionth time.

"I'm good, *mijo*. More worried about her," Velma answered. "She's a tough one, our girl. But this has her shaken up."

"Please, I'm sitting right here. And I'm good, too."

"*Sí*, I know. You're always good. Always taking care of everyone else." Velma rose to her feet, her brightly colored muumuu floating around her plump figure. "*Bueno*, I need to be going. I promised my grandson I would be there to read him a bedtime story tonight. Will you see to it that she gets home safely?"

"Sure thing," Diego answered.

"I'm—"

"Fine, we know." Diego shared a grin with Velma, who patted his arm affectionately. Probably so she could cop a feel of his muscles, wily woman that she was. After a quick peck on his cheek and Lilí's, the older woman headed to her car at the end of the block.

Diego watched Velma until she was safely inside and her car had started. Only then did he sink down to sit next to Lilí.

"Okay, now that she's gone, lay it on me. How are you really doing?"

Lilí picked at her short nails. The dregs of the paralyzing fear that had gripped her when Tito rammed into her felt like a million army ants marching across her skin, threatening to bite. It had all happened so fast. A blur of motions and pain. Anxiety rising like bile in her throat.

She liked to think she could have shaken the creep off. That her defensive moves would've done the trick. But he'd been strong. Fueled by drugs or desperation. Or both.

Gracias a Dios nothing had happened to Velma. The situation could have been so much worse. Yet, as scared as she'd been, Lilí thought of Melba and how the poor woman had lived with a similar fear every day because of Tito.

She thought back to when Karen had come to her RA dorm room in the middle of the night, fall of Lilí's junior year in college. Tears had smeared the young freshman's makeup. Her expression dazed and confused due to the aftereffects of the Rohypnol some jerk had slipped into her drink at a party. Her memory of the assault was fuzzy. But those few details and the aftermath were enough to haunt the traumatized girl.

Lilí had stood beside so many others like Karen in the years since then, but despite all her schooling and hands-on training, tonight had been frighteningly eye-opening. Until this moment, she'd never truly understood what it felt like to be a victim. And still, what she had experienced was nothing compared to what most of her clients went through.

Her whole body trembled, a mix of emotions coalescing inside her. Anger, empathy, remorse, fear.

"Hey, you're safe now." Diego covered her hands with one of his. "I'm here."

Her chest heaved as she sucked in a shuddering breath. She caught a faint whiff of his musky aftershave and found it oddly comforting. Instinctively she leaned toward him, letting her head fall against his shoulder.

He squeezed her hands gently. "How 'bout we get out of here. Go grab some coffee."

"I've already interrupted your night long enough," she objected.

"I was home, practicing the guitar, getting ready to order takeout from the Chinese place around the corner. You're not interrupting anything."

She concentrated on the soothing sound of his deep baritone. The strength and sense of security she felt sitting next to him. The comfort of his larger hand enveloping both of hers.

"Chinese food does sound good." Too late she realized she'd spoken the words out loud. Like she was inviting herself to join him. "I mean, well . . ."

"Come on. We'll call in the order and pick it up on the way to my place. I don't live far from here." He stood up, reaching out to pull her to her feet.

She winced at an ache searing across her back.

"What's wrong?" Diego ducked down to look at her face in the streetlight.

"Nothing. A little sore from ramming into the car, but I'll be okay."

He put his arm around her, gently guiding her toward his vehicle. "I'll drive. We'll swing by later to pick up your car and I'll follow you home to make sure you're safe."

"I don't know," she hedged, still embarrassed by her self-invite.

"It's dinnertime. We're both hungry. Plus, I promised Velma I'd take care of you. She doesn't seem like an *abuela* I want to cross. So you're coming with me, okay?"

"You're pretty bossy, you know that?"

"Ah, there's that sassy mouth of yours," he teased.

For the first time since she'd recognized Tito, her world righted itself. Thanks to this man who excited, annoyed, and, strange as it might sound, calmed her.

Diego opened the passenger door of his silver Dodge Charger and she lowered herself into the seat.

Maybe giving him an SOS call hadn't been a mistake after all.

Bringing Lilí to his house for dinner had been a mistake.

Seated in a chair he'd dragged over from his kitchen table and angled next to his couch, Diego watched Lilí working her chopsticks like a pro as she dug into her bowl of kung pao chicken. She snagged a piece of meat dripping with sauce and brought it to her mouth. Her lips closed over the chopsticks and he had to force himself to look away.

Who knew a woman could make eating Chinese takeout look so damn seductive.

He did now. Thanks to Lilí.

His intent had been to be with her as she eased through the aftermath and the adrenaline letdown. He knew what it was like. On the job, it wasn't always easy to shake off a stressful, intense situation afterwards.

Getting that call from her, listening to her struggle to get the words out, to explain where she was while hiccuping around tears. Damn if he hadn't time-warped back to the number of times he'd gotten a similar call from his sister.

Some guy had roughed her up. She'd been left stranded, no purse, no money. No way to get someplace safe. Could he come bail her out.

Similar, yet different.

Lilí had been roughed up for doing her job. Not for making a poor life choice like leaving home to move in with a loser. Or ditching rehab to go back to the guy who got you hooked in the first place.

He'd heard Lilí's distress, sensed her fear and disillusion through the phone, and he hadn't thought twice. As soon as Velma had taken the phone and told him they were in front of the clinic, he'd grabbed his keys, jumped in his Charger and roared off. Ready to save the day.

Only, his job was done the minute Jordan and Shapiro had arrived on the scene. They could have handled it from there. Instead, he'd stuck around. Unable to bring himself to leave until he was absolutely certain Lilí was okay.

Driving her to his place might not have been his smartest move. Not when she had a boyfriend probably waiting for her at their condo.

"Do you, uh, need to call anyone? Let them know where you are?" he asked.

"Uh-uh." Lilí spoke around a bite of food. She chewed, swallowed. Licked a drop of sauce off the corner of her lip.

Dios sálvame, he prayed. 'Cause saving was what he needed all right. Saving from the inappropriate thoughts being around this woman had him contemplating. He shifted on his chair, adjusting his jeans.

"I can't tell my sisters about this over the phone," she explained. "They'll freak. Rosa'd probably demand I move back home until Tito is caught or dealt with."

She shook her head and dipped her chopsticks back into her bowl.

Okay, he hadn't been thinking about her sisters

when he'd asked the question. More like, her rich boyfriend.

One ankle propped on his other knee, Diego forked a bite of beef and broccoli, contemplating how to ask without really asking why she'd called him, again, instead of whichever Taylor brother she was dating.

Maybe the guy was out of town.

Maybe the relationship was on the skids.

Maybe he needed to quit being a punk and simply ask.

Lilí had toed off her gold strappy sandals, leaving them on the hardwood floor between his sofa and the dark-stained crate table he'd recently bought. With her legs tucked to the side, her pink painted toes a stark contrast to the deep green microfiber sofa cushion, she leaned her left elbow on the furniture arm and cradled the bowl of food in her hand.

Today she'd swapped her sundress for a pair of skinny jeans. Emphasis on the skinny. Meaning, they hugged her body like a second skin. The wide neckline of her loose-fitting orange top slid down to reveal her tan shoulder. Teasing him.

At first glance she seemed casually comfortable. Completely misleading unless you peered closely.

Only then did he catch the nervous energy that had her hands fidgeting, her feet tap-tapping against the cushion. Her eyes darted around his apartment, from his front door to the window overlooking West Haddon Avenue to all parts in between. Occasionally stopping on his guitar, nestled on its stand in the corner.

The aftereffects of an adrenaline rush had her on edge.

Earlier, in the kitchen, while he'd gotten bowls and

drinks, she'd paced the floor, only stopping to peek out of the blinds at his back porch and the town houses behind his.

With the lighting inside far better than the street lamp in front of the clinic, he'd noticed the bruises forming on her right upper arm. Evidence of Tito's finger marks marring her soft flesh.

Anger had flashed through Diego like an emergency road flare, swift and bright, when he thought about that punk hurting Lilí.

She'd brushed it off. Saying it looked worse than it felt.

Diego had insisted on wrapping a gel ice pack around her arm and started a timer. She was now on her second round of twenty minutes on, twenty off.

Lilí jabbed her chopsticks into her rice, then leaned forward to grab her glass of ice water. Her shirt dipped lower in front, giving him a quick peek at what lay underneath. He looked down at his food, trying to be a gentleman. Or save his own sanity.

"So we've determined your sisters are on the do-not-call list. Anyone else you should inform of your safe whereabouts?" Diego asked, dancing around the real question he wanted to pose.

He took a sip of his beer and waited.

A tiny V formed between her brows as she thought about it. "Probably the clinic's director. There's a protocol when a client's family member is involved in an incident. Paperwork to be filed."

True, but not the person he was thinking of. Time to bite the bullet.

"What about your boyfriend?"

"My what?" Lilí gaped at him in obvious surprise, eyeing him like he was crazy.

"Your boyfriend, one of the Taylor brothers?"

Her eyes widened even bigger.

"I'm thinking he'd probably want to know what went down. I mean, I would." Diego lifted a shoulder in a noncommittal shrug. "Is he not home tonight?"

Suddenly a laugh burst from her and she doubled over.

"Wai-wai-wait a minute. Let me get this straight." Chuckling, she plunked her bowl of food along with her drink onto his coffee table. Swiveling on the couch, she changed positions to sit cross-legged as she faced him. "You think Michael Taylor and I are . . . what, dating?"

Amusement danced across her face.

"*Que cómico*," she murmured, her lips curving in what he'd definitely call a bemused smirk.

"What's so funny?" he asked. "If not Michael, maybe Jeremy. There's some connection, right?"

The "duh" expression she gave him was classic middle school caliber.

He returned it with a blank look of his own.

"Yes, there's a connection. Jeremy is my *brother-in-law*." Her brows arched, wrinkling her forehead as she leaned toward him to make her point. "Married to my sister Rosa. Father of my niece and nephew, Susana Marta and Nico. The same brother-in-law who's living in our family home in Oakton. And subletting his place in the city to me."

With each revelation she dropped, another piece of the puzzle that was her personal life snapped into place. Problem was, the image being created was not the one he'd pictured on the front of the puzzle box labeled Lilí Fernandez.

Lilí sat back, arms crossed in front of her chest. Her shirt slipped down again, her right shoulder teasing him with the burning desire to know if her tanned skin felt as smooth as it looked.

He knew better than to move closer and find out. Even if she might not be quite as off-limits as he'd once thought.

"You and Michael Taylor, the younger brother, you're not . . . you know?" He jiggled the bottom of his beer bottle back and forth, allowing her to fill in the blank.

Lips pressed together in a temperamental pout that rivaled one he'd seen on Omara's face more than a time or two, Lilí shook her head slowly back and forth.

Talk about faulty detective work on his part. He'd made assumptions based on partial information shared by one informant, the head of her condo's security office. Rookie mistake.

Coño, he couldn't remember the last time he'd acted like this much of a chump. Had he made a gaffe like this on the job, "damn" woulda been the nicest word coming out of his mouth.

"So, you gonna tell me what gave you the impression I'm dating one of the brothers?" Head tilted at a saucy angle, she stared back at him, her hazel-green eyes sparking with a challenge.

He took another long pull of his beer. Weighing his options.

Something told him that in this instance, he'd be better off relying on his right to remain silent.

Lilí narrowed her eyes, pinning him to his seat.

He swallowed. "Faulty intel."

Mostly his inability to think clearly when it came to her.

"That's all you have to say?" she countered.

Diego tipped his head to the side in a noncommittal concession.

With a frustrated huff she fell back against the sofa cushions. She winced and he remembered her mentioning the pain from her shoulder blade striking the car when Tito shoved her.

One way or another that *idiota* would pay. He'd get nabbed by the cops soon. If Tito was lucky, someone other than Diego would find him first.

"I don't know why I'm shocked by your non-apology," Lilí complained.

"What am I supposed to be sorry for?"

The unladylike snort paired with her prickly moodiness should be unattractive. Not appealing. More evidence of his lack of clarity when it came to this woman.

Tucking her heels on the edge of the sofa cushion, Lilí wrapped her arms around her bent knees. "For thinking I'm the type of girl who'd come over here when she has a boyfriend waiting for her at home."

"Maybe he's outta town and you were scared. How was I supposed to know? I'm just trying to be a good guy here," he argued, even though he knew it was a lame excuse.

"Whatever," Lilí muttered, her eyes closed.

Despite her crankiness, which he deserved, the way she curled up in a ball in the corner of his sofa emphasized her petite frame. The blue gel ice pack Velcroed to her arm called his attention to her frailty, as strong as she might come across when she was in a snit. Her spiky eyelashes, high cheekbones, and full lips meshed with her long tresses to give her an exotic vibe that drew him to her.

Put it all together and the entire appealing package

that was Lilí Fernandez made him want to scoop her up in his arms and carry her off to his bed.

"Okay, I'll accept a song in the way of an apology."

"Excuse me?"

Stuck trying to decide whether or not he was crazy enough to make a move, if Lilí was even interested, Diego didn't catch her meaning.

She rolled her head along the back of the sofa to pierce him with her hazel-green eyes. The moody attitude she'd given him moments ago had vanished, replaced by a sadness that tugged at his need to soothe her pain.

"When I was little, and I had a bad dream, my *papi* used to sing me to sleep to ease my fear." Her voice was hushed, a wistful melancholy lacing her words. "Would you play for me? *¿Por favor?*"

He didn't need her whispered "please" to get him moving. Not when at the foundation of all he did lay his determination to make others feel safe, protected. Something he'd always wanted for his mother and sister. Something he found himself wanting for Lilí in the short time they'd known each other.

Lilí's lips curved in a tender smile when he set down his empty beer bottle, then rose to retrieve his guitar.

The alarm on her phone beeped, signaling the twenty-minute timer. He heard the scraping sound of the Velcro straps being pulled apart and turned in time to see her lay the gel pack on the kitchen towel he'd given her earlier.

"Any special requests?" he asked.

"I'm not picky."

He dragged out a small padded footstool he kept under the end table next to the couch to prop up his foot. His left hand cradled the classical guitar's neck as he settled back on the kitchen chair. Resting the bottom edge of the guitar on top of his right thigh, he leaned the top curve of the instrument's body on his left knee, raised higher by the footstool.

Lilí scooted over on the couch to sit closer to him.

Knees bent on the sofa, she clasped her hands as if in prayer, tucking them between her cheek and the back cushion. "How about playing your favorite song. I'm sure it's beautiful."

He stared at her, taken by the incredible mix of strong woman and gentle soul. She saw good in everyone. Her rose-colored glasses firmly in place.

Tonight, that good had been challenged. Her glasses ripped off in a brutal way. If he could comfort her by playing his music, she didn't have to ask twice.

"How about 'Leyendas.' It's a classic Isaac Albéniz. Pepe Romero plays the hell out of it. But I can get by."

She smiled at him, a wistful impersonation of her trademark cheeky grin that hit him like a smack upside the back of his head every time.

"I knew your ego-laced humility was hiding in there," she teased. "Blow me away, music man. Let's see what you got."

Chapter Seven

Lilí watched Diego underneath her lashes as he played his classical Spanish guitar in a private concert, for her.

His handsome face was a study in concentration and relaxation. As if the music demanded his attention while easing his stress. The fingers of his right hand deftly strummed and plucked the six nylon strings. At the same time, the fingers on his left fluctuated between pressure and release as they crawled along the strings running up the guitar's fretboard. The muscles in his forearms danced and shifted with the motions.

The strong rhythmic tones of the flamenco music alternated between wild-mustang fast and languidly slow. Exciting and lulling. Frantic and calm.

Exactly how she felt around him.

Eyes closed, Diego strummed as if the music moved through him. The same way it had with Papi when he'd played with his *trío* group, Los Paisanos.

The mix of notes and chords flowed over her. Reassuring in its familiarity.

Music had always been a huge part of her family life

when she was growing up. Whether she'd been down in the basement studying during Los Paisanos rehearsals, heading to a gig with her father, or joining him at the mic for a song or two if the venue allowed it.

In the four years since Papi's death, she hadn't sat like this, sharing the intimacy of listening to someone play who physically relished the beauty and wonder of live music as much as she did.

Longing and pain clogged her throat. Tears burned her eyes.

Tears evoked by the memory of losing Papi, the devastation cancer had inflicted on her and her sisters. Tears for Karen. And Melba. For all the women who came into the clinic seeking assistance. And tears of awe, for this shared love of music and the connections it brought to life.

With each chord Diego played, her tension ebbed. The anxiety caused by the what-ifs she hadn't been able to purge after Tito's attack finally drifted away. The passion in Diego's movements, the muscles in his arms and hands flexing, straining as he caressed and commanded the music from his guitar, melted all the negativity away.

The tempo picked up its pace. The notes raced to a powerful crescendo, only for him to tease her with several languid, final plucks of the guitar's strings, drawing the tune to a melancholy close.

Silence descended. She watched as his upper body relaxéd, the music working its magic on him, the same as it did with her.

Diego's eyes drifted open. He shot her a sheepish smile, his eyes crinkling at the corners when he caught her watching him.

"You said play my favorite." His left hand slid up and down the guitar's neck in a loving gesture that made her envious. "I can't seem to play that song without falling into the notes. Losing myself a bit."

"That was beautiful," she whispered, reaching up to swipe a tear trailing down her cheek. "Thank you for sharing it with me."

"Hey, you're crying?" He lowered his guitar like he meant to set it aside. "I didn't realize I was that bad."

She chuckled. "Keep playing. You know you're good."

He winked at her, the playful gesture making her belly flip-flop.

"You said you started at the youth center. How old were you?" she asked.

"Ten. Stumbled into an empty classroom and there sat Carlos Nieves. Retired music teacher and accomplished guitarist. Taught me everything I know. *Bueno*, first Carlos, then years later, when the beaches of Florida lured him south and I joined the army, I turned to videos on the internet."

"I'll have to thank Carlos if he ever makes it back up here for a visit."

Sadness descended over Diego's face before he shook it away. "I wish you could. He died a few years ago."

"I'm sorry."

"Pancreatic cancer. He went quickly. But not before we made one last trip to the beach together." He stared straight ahead, a faraway look in his brown eyes as if he was picturing the memory. "Feet in the sand, rum and cokes chilling beside us, we played till our fingers ached. Then played a little more."

He strummed his guitar, emitting a doleful chord.

"Cancer took my dad a little over four years ago," she shared, lured by Diego's own reminiscing. "He would have loved listening to you play."

"Oh yeah? Was he into music?"

She nodded, snuggling deeper into the back sofa cushion, feeling content for the first time all evening. "He played guitar and was the lead singer in a *trío* group. Los Paisanos."

"Hold on!" Diego's fingers ceased their strumming. Surprise widened his eyes. "Did they play a few times at the Fiestas Puertorriqueñas in Humboldt Park?"

Lilí nodded, her heart swelling with pride that Diego remembered Los Paisanos and the several times they'd been invited to perform at Chicago's Puerto Rican Festival. Papi would have been so proud. After his family and his religion, Papi's devotion had been to music and the other two men in the trío, Pablo and André.

"I remember hearing them. Ten, twelve years ago, maybe?"

"Yeah, it's been a while," she agreed.

Nostalgia wrapped her in its warm embrace and she snuggled into it, remembering the gigs Papi and Los Paisanos had played.

"I can't believe that was your dad. They were great!" Diego's awe eased the ever-present sorrow when Lilí thought of Papi and how he'd been taken from them much too soon.

"My mom used to make me get up and dance to one of their *romances* with her." He jabbed a hand through his short hair, sliding it down to knead the muscles in the back of his neck. "Said it took her back to the Island and brought great memories of her childhood in Puerto Rico."

"It did the same for my parents."

They shared a soft smile, the unbreakable bonds of music tying them together. First years ago with their respective parents. Now with each other.

"I haven't thought about those times in a while," Diego said, more to himself than her.

Lilí followed his line of sight to a framed family portrait hanging on the wall to the left of his big-screen TV. A middle school–aged Diego flashed that cocky grin of his. On one side of him stood an older woman who shared his same nose and eyes. On the other, her arm wrapped around Diego's shoulder, stood a teen-aged girl Lilí assumed was the sister he had mentioned once, before quickly changing the subject.

"I don't play standards very often, but I've learned quite a few over time," Diego said. Regret stamped his features as his gaze remained glued to his family's picture. His throat bobbed as he swallowed.

Empathy welled within her as she watched him struggle with whatever memory their conversation had unburied.

When he spoke, his voice was gruff with emotion. "This song, ah man, how my *mamá* loved it."

The fingers of his left hand curled around the fretboard. He swiveled his right wrist as if to loosen it, then strummed the first notes.

Love, regret, and grief crested like a tidal wave in Lilí's chest when she recognized Mami and Papi's wedding song. The one her father had sung to her mom every year on their anniversary. Or when he had pissed her off and was trying to get back in her good graces.

Lilí had known the words to "Somos Novios" probably long before she could sing her ABCs. When she'd gotten older, she'd even performed it with Los Paisanos a time or two.

But she hadn't listened to this song since Papi's passing.

Now, the words were pulled from her as if Papi had

reached down from heaven, handed her a microphone, and asked her to sing for him.

Eyes squeezed shut to ward off the threat of impending tears, Lilí took a deep breath. With the vision of Mami and Papi's love giving her strength, Lilí joined in, midway through the first verse.

The music halted abruptly. Lilí slanted a questioning glance at Diego.

He gazed back at her, his face colored by surprise.

"You mind if I sing while you play?" she asked softly.

He gave a mute shake of his head, so she motioned for him to continue.

When Diego started back up, Lilí closed her eyes again and sang from her heart.

Diego watched, mesmerized by the sight and sound of Lilí Fernandez crooning his mom's favorite love song. The one she'd begged him to learn. Then once he did, she'd made him play it for her. Every single day.

Man, she would have loved listening to Lilí sing.

Strong and pure, rich and soulful, soft and sincere when the lyrics called for it, Lilí's voice filled his living room, wormed its way into his heart. The words spoke of a profound love shared by two sweethearts. Of stolen kisses and desire kindled. Of occasional spats, as lovers have, and stolen moments in the dark.

He'd heard the lyrics thousands of times before. Never had they meant as much to him as they did in this moment.

Lilí held him spellbound. Head thrown back, veins straining in her throat. Fists clenched in her lap as if she fought to rein in the power of the song and its control over her.

Others had joined him in singing plenty of times in the past. Bored in the barracks when he was in the army, sing-alongs had helped pass the time. Sometimes guys asked him to play simply to ease the lonely quiet. He'd been happy to oblige.

As a kid, the more he improved, the more he'd been hired to play at church and community events. He'd even landed a job at a tapas restaurant in high school. Strumming his guitar sure beat the hell out of washing dishes or waiting tables like he did on the nights the restaurant didn't offer live music. Not to mention the tips were way better.

But never, in all his years and all his gigs, had he experienced this weird sense of connection with someone singing to his accompaniment. This sense of certainty that the way music made him come alive was reciprocated in her. As if together, they could re-create the emotions, the sensuality. Bringing the lyrics to life.

Gracias a Dios he could play this song in his sleep. He was so mesmerized by Lilí he barely remembered playing the chords.

"'. . . *somos novios. Siempre novios.*'"

Lilí's husky voice drew out the final words as his fingers strummed the last notes. The idea of the two of them always being lovers, as if the words she sang referred to something they shared, set his heart pounding faster.

Desire swooped over him with white-hot flames only she could extinguish.

The remnants of the music drifted over them, slowly fading until all that remained was its memory. Lilí sat perfectly still, eyes closed as if she wanted to hold on to the moment.

The air around them lay heavy and thick, charged with emotions. A single tear escaped from the corner of her eye to trail down her cheek. And still, she remained motionless.

Inexorably drawn to her, Diego laid his guitar on the floor next to his chair, then moved to join Lilí on the couch.

She startled when the cushion gave under his weight. Sadness tinged with gratitude shone in her beautiful eyes as he cupped her cheek and brushed her tear away with the pad of his thumb.

A corner of her luscious mouth curved as she told him, "I'm not usually this much of a sob fest."

"You keep this up, you're going to give me a complex. I swear I'm not that bad."

"No, you're not." She put her hand over his on her cheek, leaning into his touch. "You play beautifully. It's just, that song . . ."

Her voice cracked on the last word and she broke off. Her lids fluttered closed for a moment, then opened to reveal a look of such pure longing, she might as well have reached into his chest and squeezed his heart with her fist.

Their gazes locked, Diego slowly leaned toward her, allowing her the opportunity to back away, to let him know if he was misreading the signs and was completely off base.

Instead, she met him halfway.

Their lips touched in the lightest of kisses. Testing. Tasting. A brief sample of the pleasure they could give the other.

Lilí's free hand fisted in his T-shirt, pulling him closer. That was all the encouragement he needed.

With a groan Diego slid his palm from her cheek to

the back of her neck, cradling her head as his lips
devoured hers. He licked her bottom lip and she
opened for him. Her tongue brushed his, sensual
and seeking.

She tasted tangy and sweet and all he could think
of was more. He wanted more.

As if she'd read his mind, Lilí scooted closer.

Encouraged by her soft moan of pleasure, he
grabbed her waist, lifting her to sit on his lap.

She yelped in surprise. Then her arms were around
his shoulders, her fingers splaying into his hair as she
pulled his head to hers. She nipped at his lips. Tiny
teasing kisses, until he growled, desire driving him.
She answered by deepening the kiss.

He palmed her hip, his thumb sliding under her
blouse to brush the bare flesh along her jeans waist-
line. Warm and soft, it tempted him to explore the
rest of her tantalizing body.

Breaking their kiss, Diego trailed his lips across her
jaw, down the smooth column of her throat. He gave
in to the temptation to sneak a lick of her warm skin.

"Mmmm, you taste delicious," he murmured.

Lilí answered by arching back, giving him full
access to continue his exploration. Not one to be shy,
or pass up an invitation he'd been dreaming about for
nights, Diego obliged.

Her shirt slipped off her shoulder at the same time
his hand slid from her trim waist, up her rib cage to
cup her breast. The top edge of her cream-colored
lace bra peeked out of her wide shirt collar and he
tugged the cup down to reveal her breast's rosy peak.

She moaned again, arching back against the sofa
arm behind her.

Blood surged low in his body and he hardened, desperate for what she offered.

He took her into his mouth, his tongue laving her pert nipple. His palm held on to her back, pressing her closer to him as he suckled and teased, a man starving for the sweet satisfaction only she could give.

"Yes," she whispered, her body writhing with every flick of his tongue. "*Más*. I need more."

Her words echoed his thoughts and Diego tugged her collar lower, ready to lavish attention on her other breast. Lilí pushed at his shoulders and he glanced up, afraid he might be moving too fast. Prepared to stop if she said so.

Instead, she reached for the hem of her blouse, tugging it up and over her head. She tossed the orange material across the room, where it floated through the air to land in a heap near the front door.

Before he realized her intent, she twisted on his lap to straddle him, placing her knees on either side of his hips. With her lower body pressed intimately against his and the way he strained against his zipped jeans, no way she could not know how badly he wanted her.

Her gaze caught on his. Intense. Searching. Passion turning her eyes more green than hazel.

Silently she reached behind her back to unclasp her bra, freeing her breasts for him to feast on.

He sucked in a breath, desperate to control the over-powering urge to flip her onto the couch and bury himself deep inside her.

She was absolutely beautiful. Her silky black hair disheveled. Lips full and swollen from their kisses. Her neck and chest bloomed with color from the scratch of his late-day scruff.

His mark on her fired his blood. Made him strain for release.

Unable to resist anymore, he cupped her breasts with his hands, kneading and plucking as her nipples pebbled against his palms. Her whimper nearly undid him.

He bent his head to taste her again. Dragging in a breath, he filled his lungs with her tropical scent. An aphrodisiac that drove him to take a nipple in his mouth, sucking and laving until she bucked in his lap.

She ground against him, the material of their jeans a barrier between them that both frustrated and heightened his senses. His mouth moved from one breast to the other, a starving man, desperate to taste all that was being offered.

She bucked against him, over and over, the rhythm driven by their mutual desire. Her breaths came faster, her breathing ragged as she ground into him. Her pleasure-filled murmurs drove him. He craved more of her. Needed to give more to her.

"Yes, yes!" she moaned as he made love to her breasts.

Savoring, fondling, greedily accepting what she willingly gave him. He tugged a nipple into his mouth again, gently grazing it with his teeth and she cried out.

Suddenly her body tensed. She ground her crotch against his and cried out his name on a moan of ecstasy.

He felt her tense as the orgasm gripped her, the muscles in her thighs clenching his hips. Grabbing on to her waist, he held her as she rode the wave, head thrown back in abandon.

Her body melted with the last of its release and she bent toward him. Laying her head on his shoulder, she buried her face in his neck.

Her breathing slowed as Diego caressed her back, gently skimming his fingertips up and down her spine.

"*Dios mío*, I can't remember the last time I dry humped on a living room couch." Lilí mumbled the words against his throat, her lips tickling him.

He chuckled. "Was it as good for you as it was for me?"

"Stop it." She hit him lightly on the chest. "That could not have been anywhere near as good for you. I'm sorry."

"Hey." He tipped her chin up so she would look at him. "Being here like this suits me just fine."

She craned her head to kiss him. A slow, languid tease of her lips that fueled his lust for her. When she pulled back, she gifted him with a seductive smile. It morphed into an unexpected shyness seconds before she buried her face in his neck once more.

Diego looped his arms around her, savoring the warmth of her body nestled against him. She pressed a soft kiss to the sensitive spot behind his ear and he shifted slightly, trying to ease the pressure straining beneath his zipper.

"'Somos Novios' was my parents' wedding song," Lilí said, her voice husky with emotion. "Papi used to sing it to Mami every year on their anniversary."

"I'm sure she loved it."

"*Sí*, she did." Lilí rubbed her palm over his left pec, then slid her hand over to trace the crown of thorns tattoo wrapped around his biceps. Diego let his eyes drift closed, enjoying her touch. The desire she evoked pulsed through him.

"Mami would get teary-eyed by the end of the song," Lilí continued, no doubt unaware of the affect her featherlight touch had on him. Then again, the bulge pressing into her crotch might be a clue.

"So the tears are a family tradition, then, huh?" he teased.

She huffed out a gentle laugh. Her soft breath warm along his neck.

"Then Papi'd wrap her in his arms and they'd kiss. Sometimes enough to make my sisters and me groan at the PDA."

"Somehow I doubt their public display of affection ended like this," he teased. "At least, not in front of you girls."

They shared a laugh before settling into a comfortable silence. He, enjoying the rightness of holding her in his arms like this.

As if someone flicked on a flashlight, illuminating a dark corner in his heart, he realized he hadn't felt this relaxed with another person in a long, long time. Here he'd been trying to comfort her. And yet, she'd managed to touch him.

"You're pretty amazing, *sabes?*" he told her.

He felt her shake her head against his shoulder.

"I was scared tonight," she murmured. "I freaked out, and for a second, I forgot everything I know."

"Fear's natural. But your instincts kicked in and you fought back." Gently he rubbed his hand in small circles along her back. "What you're doing with the girls at the center, that's really good. I wish—"

He broke off, shocked he'd started to go there with her.

"You wish what?"

"Nothing. It doesn't matter now."

"Come on. Tell me." She nuzzled his neck. Worming her way deeper into his heart.

"It's not something I normally talk about with . . ."

She stiffened, then sat up to shoot him a frown. "With who? Women you bring home to fool around with?"

Too late he realized the way his words could be misinterpreted.

"Never mind. Forget I asked." Hurt flashed in her eyes as she leaned to the side to roll off his lap.

He grabbed on to her hips, holding her still. Lilí narrowed her eyes at him in a challenge.

"It's not something I normally talk about with anyone," he admitted. "It's a personal problem I'm handling. Sort of."

"Did you stop to think working through similar issues with individuals and families is what I do for a living? You know, working through their personal problems."

He pressed his lips together. Annoyed with himself for bringing this up. For even thinking about Lourdes when he'd found a few moments of peace with Lilí.

She moved to slide off his lap again and he tightened his grip. "Come on. Don't be mad at me."

"I'm not," she said. "This sounds like it's going to be a serious discussion, because you *are* going to tell me what's bugging you. But I feel at a slight disadvantage here. So either you're going to take off your shirt or I'm going to put on mine. And I have a feeling that if you take off your shirt, we won't do much talking."

"But that would be a lot more fun." He gave her a hopeful smile, looking to distract her.

"Nice try, Romeo. Now let me up." She patted his chest and he released her.

Lilí reached down to the floor to snag her bra strap with a finger, then slid off his lap to sit next to him. He watched her slip the straps over her shoulders, then rise to retrieve her orange blouse by the front door.

The fun was definitely over. Any conversation involving his sister was never pleasant. More like, stress-inducing.

Pissed at his inability to keep his trap shut when things had been progressing so well with Lilí, Diego scrubbed his hands over his face in frustration.

The sofa cushions dipped as Lilí sat beside him. "Okay, now talk. What do you wish?"

He gave an exasperated huff and fell back against the sofa. "No good comes of wishing. Not about the past anyway."

"But good comes from talking. Letting out whatever's eating you up inside."

"Says the counselor."

"I'll take that as a compliment."

Head resting against the back cushion, Diego gave her a sideways glance.

Lilí sat cross-legged, hands on top of her knees, her expression all calm patience. And determination.

He knew that look. Had stared it down in Melba's living room when he'd tried telling Lilí it wasn't wise to take the other woman home with her. Fat lot of good his arguing had done then.

She wasn't going to rest until he spit something out.

"I wish my sister, Lourdes, would have had someone like you in her life when she was the same age as Omara and her group."

"Thank you," Lilí answered. She tilted her head, considering him. "Why?"

He grimaced, certain "Because" wasn't an answer that would satisfy her curiosity.

Turning to stare up at the ceiling, he let his mind

go back to those years, and all the ones leading up to today. He avoided the years when he'd been away in the army, fraught with doubts about whether enlisting had been a smart decision on his part. His mom wanted him to go to college. The GI Bill had seemed like the best way to make that happen.

But the shit his sister had pulled while he was gone. The stress she'd caused their mom. It made his blood boil. That he hadn't been here to step in, ease some of his *mami*'s burden was a guilt he'd carry with him always. Something else to blame his sister for.

"The problem is, wishing won't change what happened back then. Or how messed up things are now," he muttered.

"So I take it things aren't good between you and your sister?"

Understatement of the year. He hadn't heard from her in a couple months and the last number she'd given him had been disconnected. The only reason he knew was because he'd tried calling in a weak moment last night after Lilí's self-defense class.

"Have you two ever tried counseling?" she asked. Her voice had taken on that smooth, reasonable tone you used when trying to rationalize with an unstable perp or a CI wavering on whether or not he wanted to spill the info you needed for a case.

That she'd so easily gone from sensual lover to cool clinician irked him.

"I'm not the one who needs therapy. She is. But as if dragging her ass to rehab isn't hard enough, getting her to stay in the program is a damn joke."

"You can't make her go. Or stay."

"You think I don't know that?" He lifted his arms like the solution might fall out of the sky and drop right into them. Instead he plopped his empty arms back onto his lap in disgust. "Here's what I know. There's a definite line between right and wrong. And for a long time now, my sister has chosen to live on the opposite side of where I stand."

"It's not always so black and white."

"Tell it to the judge when she gets hauled in."

"Diego—"

She broke off when he pushed up from the couch, exasperated with their conversation.

"Look, I get that you want to see the good in everything. In everyone," he said, stepping around the coffee table to pace toward the front windows.

A sense of inevitability ratcheted up inside him. A reminder of why it'd been a mistake to bring her here. To give in to temptation with her.

Lilí would never be able to understand him because she had never lived through what he had. What he still did. The heavy weight of guilt he couldn't shake when it came to his messed up family life made him weary. Pissed off.

A large part of him was thankful she hadn't experienced this type of disillusion. It hardened a person. Lilí's positivity was part of her essence. It drew him like the shore calls the tide.

It also scared the hell out of him because it sparked a tiny flame of hope in a quiet corner of his soul. One that had burned him in the past.

Refusing to go that route again, Diego spun back around to face Lilí. "But no matter what you say, there's no good in my situation."

"What if you—"

"Look, I understand why you think you can do

something here. But frankly, this isn't any of your concern."

Lilí flinched at his gruff words.

He dragged a hand through his hair, despising himself, but determined to protect her. *Carajo*, why did the problems with Lourdes have to poison everything? *Hell*, indeed.

Rather than back down, Lilí straightened her spine, her expression cool and distant. He preferred her hot and bothered.

"Maybe you're right. Maybe this isn't my business. But you're my friend, or . . ." She scowled, an embarrassed flush darkening her cheeks. "Or, whatever we are. So if I can help in some way, I'm here. As long as you don't act like an ass."

"Duly noted. I appreciate the offer." Though he wouldn't avail himself of her counseling services. Not when he'd much rather avail himself of her sexy body. Preferably in his bedroom. Naked. On his king-size bed.

She must have read his mind or understood the "not gonna happen" subtext of his response because her mouth twisted with derision.

"Forget it." Uncrossing her legs, she shoved her feet in her sandals. "Once again, I don't know why I expected something different. You're all the same."

"What does that mean?"

"Nothing." She bent down to buckle her shoe straps, dismissing his question.

Hands on his hips, he matched her glare with one of his own.

Before he could press her for an explanation, a popular salsa tune chimed from Lilí's messenger bag where she'd dropped it next to the sofa. At the same time, his cell vibrated in his back jeans pocket.

She reached for her bag and he pulled out his phone. When he saw the number scrolling on his screen, he slid his thumb across it to answer.

"Reyes here, what's up?" He listened to his buddy on the other end of the line while keeping an eye on Lilí, who was more than likely speaking to another cop on her cell. He knew the moment she heard the news.

She sucked in an audible breath. Fear, followed quickly by anger and grit, flashed across her delicate features.

Her gaze came up to meet his.

"Reyes, did you hear me?" his buddy asked.

"Yeah, I heard you," he answered. "I know where Lilí Fernandez is. We'll be down there shortly. She won't have any problem IDing Tito Gonzáles."

Chapter Eight

Diego sat next to Lilí at the table in one of the station's interrogation rooms. He'd wanted to handle the photo array identification process in the break room and make it a little less intimidating. But cops where milling about, grabbing late-night snacks and coffee, so he'd been stuck following protocol and bringing her here.

The stark room with its tan walls housed a sturdy table bolted to the floor, a small window with industrial blinds, and three plastic chairs with metal legs and no armrests. Purposely the opposite of warm and inviting.

Undeniably a place he despised Lilí's having to become acquainted with.

He'd dragged the third chair from the corner. Typically the second cop sat in it behind the alleged perpetrator or witness's side of the table. Out of view, giving the illusion of privacy between the cop asking the questions and the person giving the answers. But this wasn't a regular photo array ID. Not by a long shot.

So instead of sitting off to the side, behind her,

he'd set his chair right next to Lilí's. Leaving no doubt that she wasn't alone in this.

"You doing okay?" he asked, pitching his voice low for her ears only. Though odds were the microphone and surveillance camera were already live.

"Uh-huh."

No eye contact. Dull tone.

He watched her alternate between nervously picking at her cuticles with her thumbnail and smoothing it down with the pad of her finger. She clasped her hands and put them in her lap, only to bring them back up on the table seconds later to pick at her nails some more.

She hadn't said much on the drive over. Nor when they'd entered the building. Some young cop Diego didn't know had moved in to frisk her before she could head upstairs to the offices. Diego's glare had sent the rookie packing.

His hand on the small of her back, he'd gently guided her up the steps. Sure, he knew she'd been here before, but this situation was different. This time she was here as a victim.

She didn't deserve to be in this situation. All she wanted was to do what was right for her clients and the kids at the center.

As they'd walked up the steps, the need to protect her had engulfed him, tightening his chest.

Now, watching her nervous gestures, he had to tamp down his caveman urge to locate Tito González in the building and pummel him into the ground. Losing his shit on the man might hinder the case. That definitely wouldn't make things easier on her.

Feeling like a powder keg one flick of a match away from exploding, Diego leaned his elbow on the table and stared passed Lilí, pinpointing his focus on the doorknob directly in his line of sight. Relying on his TACT training, he concentrated on centering himself. Similar to what he'd learned in martial arts as a kid, the Tactical Arousal Control Technique of centering he'd studied at the academy allowed him to slowly breathe out his anger, leaving a calm awareness at his core. It radiated through him, banking his instinctive emotional reaction.

Years of practice had him back in control after a few deep breaths. Confident he would now be more help than hindrance, Diego snagged his water bottle and took a chug.

Lilí had declined the offer of coffee earlier, so he'd asked for a couple waters instead.

Together they waited while Jordan and Shapiro, who'd been on the scene earlier tonight, rounded up an independent administrator to videotape Lilí's photo array ID.

"It might help if you took a sip." He tapped her drink with the back of a finger.

"No thanks. I'm good."

He caught the tremble in her hand as she reached up to brush her wispy bangs out of her eyes. It took nearly everything inside him not to put his arms around her, tell her everything was going to be okay. But they weren't really a couple. Despite how hot and heavy they'd gotten at his place.

Plus, she was known here in her professional capacity. He'd do nothing to undermine her reputation by making her look weak in front of the cops she often butted heads with when it came to her clients and what she believed was right.

Just like she'd done with him at Melba's house that first night barely a week ago.

Through the window Diego watched cops carrying

on with their business. Typing reports, yammering into their phones about one problem or another, eating a sandwich in their chairs while they worked late into the night. At a nearby desk, a man in a dark suit and tie, his white shirt wrinkled and stained, shook his head in disagreement. Despite the light sound-proofing, the guy's raised voice could be heard inside the interrogation room.

The female cop speaking with him pushed back her chair to stand when the businessman did the same. Anger scrunched his craggy face and the cop held both hands up, palms facing him. Several other policemen abruptly stopped whatever they were working on. Sharp looks that gauged the situation shot their way.

Diego didn't have to hear the conversation to know the cop was trying to get the guy to calm down. Not make his situation, whatever it might be, even worse. So far, it wasn't working.

Sometimes, no matter how hard you tried to make something right, it didn't matter. Life, and the job, had taught him that much.

"How long do you think this is going to take?" Lilí asked, interrupting his musings.

She twisted her wrist, then double-tapped her Fitbit, making it light up and display the time: 9:45 PM shown in white electronic numerals.

"It shouldn't be much longer," he assured her.

He placed a hand on her back to offer comfort. She flinched at his touch.

Swallowing his disappointment, he drew back. "They'll bring in a set of pictures, usually about six. You'll look at them and point out the one with your assailant. Take your time, then indicate if you see him."

She slanted an annoyed glance at him out of the corner of her eye. "I know what Tito looks like. If they picked up the right guy, I'll ID him immediately."

"Okay, I'm only trying to give you a lay of the land. Not sure if you've been with a client during an ID or not."

"I have."

Lilí leaned back in the plastic seat with a huff, wincing slightly, no doubt from the injury to her shoulder blade. Arms folded across her chest, her brows furrowed in frustration. And probably unease. She flicked a quick glance at him before turning to stare out the window.

"You don't have to stay, you know," she grumbled. "I'm fine."

"I drove you here. I'm not leaving you."

"This is one of your simple right-versus-wrong situations. I either see his photo or I don't. When it's over, I'll call a cab to get back to my car. No big deal."

The nervous tap-tap-tap of her sandal on the vinyl flooring told him differently.

Her "right versus wrong" comment let him know she hadn't forgotten about their argument back at his place. Regret weighed on him.

"We're gonna have to agree to disagree when it comes to my sister."

Lilí's toe-tapping stalled. Chin tucked to her chest, she slowly shook her head.

"No, what?" he asked.

Like a witness pleading the fifth, she gave him the silent treatment.

Swiveling in his chair, Diego put one hand on the table in front of her, the other behind her on the back of her chair. His thumb snagged the material of her orange blouse and the image of it flying through the air earlier flashed in his mind.

If only they could go back to that moment. Before he'd been dumb enough to bring up his sister. Seeking that connection with Lilí again, Diego rubbed his thumb up and down her arm.

"You can't agree to disagree?" he pressed.

"Sure," she mumbled. "Whatever."

Petulant wasn't quite the reaction he'd wanted. "Then why the head shake?"

She heaved a sigh weighty with resignation, but finally turned to face him, her lips pursed in an exasperated pout. Her knees bumped his left one as she slid around to sit with her legs in between his.

"Because I have a habit of leaping without looking. Like tonight, in your living room. Rosa's always harping on me to 'think first, act later.'" She air-quoted her sister's advice with her fingers. "But I never seem to listen."

"Personally, that's a leap I'm happy you took with me."

She blew out a breath on a laugh. "Yeah, I'm sure you are. But the head shake? That's for me." Lilí pressed a hand to her chest, self-reproach filling her beautiful hazel-green eyes. "Because I should know better. No matter how hot you are, you're a cop. I've worked around enough of you for it to compute by now. It's like you said, everything's always black and white. And me? My bleeding heart, as some people around here call it, and I hang out a lot in the gray area. Where emotions intersect with actions. Where feelings are explored to find out the 'why' something happens so we come out stronger in the end. So this"—she waved a hand back and forth between them—"this can't go anywhere."

Talk about a thanks-but-no-thanks brush-off. And while lust pushed him to grab her knees, tug her toward him and show her exactly what she'd be missing, what *they'd* be missing together, he banked the carnal need. Because she was right.

He'd seen too much. Lived through too much to think differently.

Until Tito, maybe even despite him, she believed in good.

Lilí's lips wobbled in that sad version of her usual spunky grin. Even though she was pushing him away, or more like because he knew she was right to do so, he sought to lighten her mood before the others returned. Hoping to ease her turmoil.

"So you think I'm hot, huh?" he teased, arching a brow and giving her an exaggerated smoldering look.

Lilí's lips twitched seconds before she threw back her head and laughed. The low, throaty sound wrapped around him like a lover's caress, warming his blood.

"*Ay, que hombre,*" she murmured, staring up at the ceiling.

The delicate curve of her throat beckoned him to move closer. Diego tightened his fists, fighting the compulsion to press his lips against her smooth skin, breathe in her intoxicating scent.

It would be good between them. Hell, based on how turned-on he'd gotten simply dry humping in his living room, he bet it'd be amazing. The need to taste and touch all of her, lose himself in her passionate nature until the rest of the world and all its problems faded away, thrummed inside him.

Yet, she deserved better than a hookup that would only burn fast and bright. Right up till it exploded in the face of their ideological differences.

Her phone vibrated on the table next to her water. Lilí sat up in her seat, leaning forward to read the display.

"Speak of the devil."

Diego caught the name "Rosa" flashing across the screen. "She's called twice already, hasn't she?"

Lilí nodded. "I swear, it's like she has some sixth sense and can tell when I've got something going on." She reached for the phone, her hand hovering above it, as if afraid to grasp the device. "If I don't answer this time, she'll worry. I was supposed to touch base with her after work."

"Go for it. C'mon," he urged when Lilí slid him a nervous glance.

Setting one elbow on the table, she rested her forehead on her open palm as she snatched up the cell and tapped the screen.

"Hi, Rosa, how's it going?" she answered, her voice overly chirpy, even for her. "Uh-huh. *Bueno*, I'm . . . actually . . . don't freak out, okay?"

Diego pressed his lips together, barely containing his huff of disbelief. Hell, even he knew that wasn't the right thing to say to a woman. Especially one who, according to Lilí, had a mile-long worry streak.

Sure enough, Rosa's screech came through loud and clear. So loud Lilí pulled the phone away from her head. Rapid-fire Spanish blew from the speaker. It reminded him of his mom and the way she used to get on him or his sister. He smiled at the memory, picturing his *mamá* wagging her finger, or with her hands fisted on her round hips, as she lectured them about one thing or another. Always out of love.

The screeching eventually quieted and Lilí pressed the phone back to her ear. "Are you finished? Can I talk now?" She paused for a beat. "No, I'm not being disrespectful."

Diego grinned at the big sister–little sister banter. Despite the heavy topic and the scary news Lilí was about to share, he relished this peek at her family dynamics.

"*Bueno, la cosa es que* . . . um, well, the thing is . . ." She repeated the words, her voice shaking at the end, and he knew she was struggling with how to tell Rosa about Tito's attack. Earlier she'd admitted wanting to wait and tell her sisters face-to-face. That way they could see for themselves that she was fine. On the outside at least.

He placed a hand gently on the center of her back to offer comfort.

Lilí looked at him, unease turning the color of her eyes a tumultuous deep green.

No way could he ignore her need for reassurance. Not when she so willingly gave it to others. Holding his other hand out, palm up, he wiggled his fingers, indicating that she should give him the phone.

Tears filled her eyes as she whispered, "Yeah, I'm here. Hold on a sec, Rosa, okay?"

He nodded his encouragement, taking the phone when she gingerly extended it toward him.

"Hello, Rosa? This is Diego Reyes. I'm a . . . a friend of Lilí's."

"Where's my sister? What's going on?" The brusque questions were insistent, no nonsense, tinged by the same fear he'd seen on Lilí's face when he'd arrived at the clinic earlier.

"She's here with me." His gaze remained locked on

Lilí's, willing her to understand and believe that she could count on him.

"Like your sister said, she's physically fine," he told Rosa. "But there's been an incident, and we're down at the police station to ID the perpetrator."

"The police station?! *¿Ay Dios mío qué pasó?*"

"I think Lilí would prefer to tell you in person, or at least once I get her back home."

Lilí jerked her head up and down in agreement, her big eyes wide with apprehension.

"My husband is out of town. I can't leave my children or I'd drive into the city right now," Rosa answered. "Let me . . . let me call Yazmine. If Tomás is home maybe she can come here and I'll head to Rosa's."

"No, no, no, please," Lili murmured. She leaned toward him, panic blanketing her face.

He cupped her shoulder, trying to ease her worries while he did the same with her sister.

"Hey, it's late," Diego said into the phone. "You probably don't want to make that drive now. I'm a Chicago cop and I'm sticking with her, so she's safe."

There was a long beat of silence before he heard a heavy sigh on the other end of the line. "You promise?"

Two simple words that carried a load of responsibility.

"*Sí, te lo prometo,*" he answered. He squeezed Lilí's shoulder, silently making the same promise to her.

She covered his hand with her own and mouthed the words "Thank you."

"I don't know who you are, Diego Reyes," Rosa told him, her earlier fear replaced by a steely firmness, "but I am trusting you with my baby sister's care. If anything happens to her, you will answer to me. As well as our oldest sister, Yazmine. *¿Me entiendes?*"

"Yeah, I understand."

It wasn't anything he didn't already expect of himself. Keeping Lilí safe, that is. It had been his goal from the first night they'd met. When she'd been crazy enough to take Melba González home with her.

Sure, the reason might now be more personal. No longer simply because she was a citizen he'd sworn to protect. More because she was an incredibly sexy, giving, strong-willed woman who intrigued and enticed him. Made him yearn for good, even when he didn't deserve it.

The interrogation room door swung open and Officer Shapiro stepped inside.

"Look, Rosa, we have to go now. I'll have Lilí give you a call later, once we're done here."

"Diego, I am counting on you," Rosa warned.

"I know." And he didn't intend to let any of the Fernandez sisters down. Especially the dark-haired, feisty beauty staring at him with trust in her soulful eyes.

Lilí waited on the sidewalk next to Diego's car while he grabbed his cell from the center console.

His parking karma was great and he'd found an open spot about a block down from her condo, directly under a street lamp. Sure, it offered lighting for safety. What she also didn't mind was that it provided great lighting for her to admire the view of his black jeans stretching over his butt as he bent and leaned across the passenger seat in his car.

Pity, she'd not get a chance to feel that butt under her hands. Not now that, based on their non-conversation at his house, it was clear her initial impression of Diego that first night at Melba's was bull's-eye accurate.

He was a one-track-minded cop. Right and wrong, no room for in-between. Unwilling or unable to recognize the value of communication with others.

A sliver of guilt wedged in her chest at the brutal description.

He'd been supportive tonight throughout the whole identification ordeal. Patient. Reassuring. Gently reminding her that she could decline to be videotaped if she felt uncomfortable.

As nervous and out of sorts as she'd been, used to her role as a voice for the victim rather than the victim herself, she had agreed to the recording. No way would she leave any room for Tito and whichever public defender caught his case to weasel out of the assault charges.

"You ready?" Diego backed out of his car, pausing to click the lock.

Lilí quickly swung her gaze to the empty street ahead. No need to be caught admiring his goods. The man's ego was big enough without her inflating it more.

"Yeah," she answered. "I was ready to be home over an hour ago."

Reaching her side, Diego motioned for her to proceed with him down the sidewalk.

He checked the time on the black sports watch strapped to his left wrist. "I hadn't anticipated them asking Melba to come over from the women's shelter tonight."

"Me either. I figured it was late enough already so they'd wait until tomorrow."

"Smart move, though. Hearing what happened to you seemed to flip some kind of switch in her, don't you think?"

Lilí nodded. She added a yes when she realized he

may not have caught her nod in the shadows created by the street lamps.

After she had IDed Tito, Officers Jordan and Shapiro had snapped a couple pictures of the bruises Tito had left on her right arm. She'd even gone to the bathroom with Shapiro so the female cop could check out Lilí's achy shoulder blade. That had resulted in a few pics of the bruise coloring the upper half of her back.

Unbeknownst to her until later, the images had all been shown to Melba when they'd told her about Tito's attack on Lilí.

Protocol demanded the two of them be interviewed, go through the photo array ID process, and make their statements separately. Lilí hadn't even been aware that Melba was at the station until they'd met in the open office area a little while ago.

Melba had been forlorn and remorseful. Worried about Lilí and whether or not she'd refuse to see her. Lilí had opened her arms to hug her friend and the woman had burst into tears.

"I'm relieved to know she's pressing charges," Lilí admitted to Diego.

"That makes two of us."

A group of teens approached them, heading in the opposite direction. One kid shoved another playfully as they joked.

Sidestepping behind Lilí, Diego deftly moved to walk between her and the group. He swung his right arm behind her, looping it around her waist and angling his torso as if to shield her from the boys. She caught him placing his other hand on his hip, right by the five-pointed-star-shaped police badge he'd clipped to his jeans waistband.

One of the kids must have noticed Diego drawing

attention to his star because the teen elbowed the guy next to him. That kid mumbled something and swatted at the guy walking backwards, arms flailing through the air as he regaled them with some story. The third one craned his neck to see what his buddy indicated, spinning around as soon as he saw Lilí and Diego.

The group quieted, their expressions serious. As they passed by, the boys exchanged classic cool-guy chin juts of respect with Diego.

Like she'd taught the girls in the self-defense class last night, Lilí made eye contact with two of the boys. It let them know she was aware and unafraid of their presence. Not that she expected them to try something, but it leveled the playing field of power in her mind.

The teens moved on without incident, their chatter starting up again once they'd passed Lilí and Diego.

She expected Diego to step away from her once the boys were gone and the sidewalk leading to her building was clear again. Instead, he kept his arm around the small of her back, his large palm hugging her right hip. The same palm that had fondled and teased her breasts earlier. Her nipples puckered at the delicious memory.

Unnerved by his effect on her, Lilí veered to her right a step, aiming to put a little distance between them.

Diego's hand slid off her hip. It skimmed her butt, sending tingles to places in her body that had no business coming to life around him.

Glancing over her shoulder, she searched the shadows, making sure the boys had continued down the street before she said, "It's pretty amazing what the flash of your star can do."

"It's not something I take for granted."

She couldn't quite make out Diego's expression in the shadows, but she heard the conviction in his deep voice. Angling her head, she peeked at him from under her lashes. His dark hair, black clothes and sneakers gave him a stealthy aura. Like a thief in the night, capable of stealing her heart if she wasn't careful.

"With great power comes great responsibility," he said.

She chuckled. "A fan of Spider-Man comics, are you?"

"Uncle Ben was a wise man. And if the adage fits." Thumbs tucked in his front jeans pockets, Diego lifted a muscular shoulder.

"Not everyone thinks that way," she mused.

They reached the glass front door to her building and Diego reached to open it for her. "I can't speak for everyone, but I don't take any responsibility, any person, for granted."

Lilí paused in the entryway. Her gaze snagged on his. Intense. Certain. Like he really wanted her to know he meant what he said.

Diantre, she could totally fall for this guy. And wind up getting hurt.

All the more reason to let him walk her inside like he insisted, then wave good-bye. With Officers Shapiro and Jordan handling her case and Diego's partner a contact for anything having to do with Melba moving forward, she should delete his number from her contacts.

"Hey, Reyes!" Bill Ryan popped up from his seat behind the security desk in the lobby. The lanky older man hurried over, his black rubber soles soundless on the tile floor. "Thanks for texting me the news. I've been pulling a few extra shifts just to be safe. Happy to hear the guy's behind bars tonight."

They clasped hands in a hearty shake.

"I appreciate you and your team keeping an eye out in this area," Diego answered.

"Anything for Ms. Fernandez. She's a real gem, this one."

Lilí smiled at Bill, an embarrassed flush heating her cheeks. "Thanks. You doing okay tonight? Need me to bring down some coffee for you?"

"You see?" Bill gestured toward her with his thumb, but tilted his head at Diego. "Always looking out for someone else."

"That she is." Diego eyed her speculatively, making her squirm under his close scrutiny.

Before he could add a dig about how that's what had gotten her into this mess in the first place, Lilí said goodnight to Bill and hurried toward the bank of elevators.

The trip up to the sixteenth floor was fast and quiet. Lilí dug her keys out of her messenger bag and prepared her "thanks, see you around" speech in her head.

At her door, she slid her key in the dead bolt and turned to Diego.

"I appreciate everything you did tonight. Coming to Velma's and my rescue. Sitting through the long wait at the station."

She purposely left out the time at his place. Seemed kind of awkward to thank him for the make-out session on his couch. Regardless of how amazing it'd been.

Diego frowned, his dark brows angling down. "You don't want me to go in, check the place out?"

"For what? Bill's downstairs. Tito's in lockup. It's fine."

She twisted the bolt open, then did the same with the lock on the doorknob.

Diego stepped closer. So close she couldn't miss how the scruff on his face had thickened through the evening, giving his chiseled features a rugged, bad-boy appeal.

"I told your sister I'd make sure you were okay," he insisted.

"And you did. You have. I've taken up enough of your time. Your rescue is complete."

"Come on, Lilí. Don't be like that."

"Like what?"

She was trying hard to come off as nonchalant. In reality though, no way could he come inside. After everything that had happened today, her nerves were shot, her willpower low. If Diego Reyes in all his hunky glory followed her in, no telling what foolish thing she might do.

"Look, I know you're busy," she said. "If something comes up, I'll call Officer Shapiro. She gave me her card at the station."

Diego reared back. "Shapiro? Why would you call her and not—"

Lilí's front door swung open and they both jumped in surprise.

Yazmine stood on the other side, her tall, slender frame barring the entryway. One hand holding on to the edge of the door, the other fisted on her trim hip, she glared at both of them.

"*Bueno*, are you two going to hang out in the hallway arguing all night, or come inside so I can grill my baby sister?"

One dark brow arched for added emphasis, she pierced first Lilí, then Diego, with a don't-mess-with-me big sister stare.

Lilí gulped. This was the last thing she needed.

"Figure the odds," Diego murmured.

She watched, stunned, as he stepped toward Yazmine and wrapped his arms around her for a hug.

"It's good to see you again, Yaz," he said. "Lilí was just inviting me in."

Chapter Nine

Pleasantly surprised by this new turn of events, Diego strode into the foyer of Lilí's swanky digs, doing a quick scan of the open living area. He eyed the wall of glass leading out to a balcony overlooking the darkened Chicago skyline. Nice view.

Man, who would have thought that Yazmine Fernandez, the former Broadway performer who'd started the center's dance program a few years ago, was Lilí's big sister. He'd heard Rosa's name, the middle one, but now that he thought about it, he couldn't remember ever asking about the oldest.

Talk about fortuitous.

Without Yaz here, he'd be on the other side of Lilí's door, about to be shut out.

Swiveling to look back at the two sisters, he caught Yaz grabbing Lilí's wrist to drag her inside. Lilí's wide eyes and dropped jaw told him she was still trying to figure out how to connect the dots between him and Yaz. Obviously she kept coming up empty. After the heave-ho she'd been trying to give him a few minutes ago, he was inclined to leave her swinging in the Chicago wind a little longer.

"Come in, make yourself at home," Yaz told him, gesturing for him to head into the living area.

"Or not and feel free to go," Lilí added.

Yaz elbowed her. "*¡No seas mala!*"

"I'm not being mean." Lilí sidled away before her sister could jab her again. "The man's wasted enough time tonight. Let him go home."

"I'm good." Diego winked at Lilí when she threw him one of her trademark dirty looks.

"Whatever." She stomped past him with a huff.

"Don't mind her," Yaz said, ushering him in. "She knows she's in hot water. Especially with Rosa. Come, sit down."

When he'd first met Yaz, she'd been dressed pretty much the same: figure-hugging tank, black leggings, and a pair of canvas slip-on shoes. Even without knowing about her Broadway experience, based on the way she carried herself, it was obvious she'd been a dancer at some point. They'd hit it off when he'd stepped in to resolve a snag with the first dance recital, remaining in contact from time to time about events at the youth center.

Lilí made a beeline for the leather sofa squared off in front of a wall lined with bookshelves on either side of a flat-screen TV. Dropping her messenger bag on the glass coffee table, she plopped down onto the couch, her body slouched. She did a pretty good impression of a moody teen when she wanted to.

Yaz veered left to the kitchen, separated from the dining/living area by a high-top breakfast bar. "Can I get you something to drink?"

"I'll take a water," Lilí called over her shoulder.

"Yeah, right. Get in here and serve your guest."

"Hey, I didn't invite him in. You did."

Lilí's mutiny lasted all of a few seconds under Yaz's

evil eye before she pushed off the sofa to join her older sister in the kitchen.

Enjoying the big-little sister tug of war, Diego opted to take one of the brushed metal stools at the breakfast bar to stick close by the action. It was interesting to see Lilí with her family. First on the phone with Rosa. Now in person with Yaz.

Lilí was clearly the baby of the bunch, used to following her sisters' orders. This was a side of her he hadn't seen before, but it clarified a little more why she didn't back down in her professional life. An area where her family couldn't hold sway over her.

Standing across from him, Lilí placed her hands on the edge of the deep sink butted up against the high breakfast bar. She shot him a saccharine smile, dripping with sarcasm. "Diego, may I interest you in a cup of coffee, pulp-free orange juice, or water? My sincere apologies that it's not of the bottled variety."

Such a smart-ass, this woman. He was interested in a hell of a lot more from her than any of those options. Most of what he wanted was completely inappropriate, but ooh, it'd sure feel good.

"No sparkling water either, huh?" he teased.

Her kissable mouth pursed in a you've-got-to-be-kidding-me pout.

Behind Lilí, Yaz smirked at him. She opened the top right door on a stainless steel refrigerator with a large freezer drawer on the bottom.

Only because he'd spent longer than he'd wanted to, pricing items and budgeting when he'd remodeled his kitchen last year, he could appreciate the top-of-the-line, French-door appliance. Not to mention the sleek marble countertops, white tile backsplash, and state-of-the-art gas range with the center grill plate between the four burners.

He imagined *arroz con gandules* and *pollo a la parrilla* would taste delicious cooked on that bad boy. Ah man, he could practically taste the pigeon-pea rice and grilled chicken just thinking about it.

Yaz pulled out a filtered water pitcher from the fridge, then stepped over to grab three cups from one of the cloudy milk-glass-lined cabinets.

Looking at the two sisters together he could see the family resemblance. Sun-kissed olive skin tones, high cheekbones with straight noses, dark brows framing light brown, in Lilí's case hazel-green, eyes.

"Water's fine, thanks," Diego replied when Yaz raised the pitcher toward him.

"So how exactly do you two know each other?" Lilí asked. She leaned a hip on the counter edge, turning to include her sister in the question.

"From the center," Diego offered. Might as well throw her a bone.

She thought about it for a few seconds, before her face lit up as her memory flipped to what he figured she'd already known but simply hadn't recalled. "The dance program Yaz kicked off. How were you involved with that?"

She angled her head to aim the skeptical question at him.

"That's a story for later," Yaz answered, placing their water glasses on the breakfast bar between them. "More importantly, is the center where you two connected with each other?"

Diego started to answer, but Lilí quickly jumped in. "He filled in with my class last night when the regular assistant had a sick child."

Interesting telling of the tale. Not really a lie. More like a skirting of the original question. Or skipping important details she wanted to avoid. Smooth evasion tactic on Lilí's part.

He leaned his elbows on the cool marble bar top and waited to see if Yaz pressed for more info. Arms crossed, she stood to Lilí's left, in the corner created by the counter's L shape.

"And tonight? This 'incident' Rosa mentioned?" Yaz stressed the word, her suspicion clear. "The one that led you to the police station. You wound up there together how, exactly?"

Lilí took a sip from her glass, eyeing him over the rim. Her expression practically begged him to keep quiet.

Okay. This was her show. Her sister doing the grilling. He'd follow her lead. Step in if he felt the evasion veered into untruth territory. Hitching a shoulder the tiniest bit, he gave her the go-ahead sign.

Her lids fluttered closed. Relief cleared the frown between her brows as she carefully lowered her water to the counter.

"Diego and his partner are working a case involving one of my clients. No big deal."

He noticed that she didn't face Yaz. Keeping her body angled away from her sister, avoiding eye contact, Lilí ran a finger through the circle of moisture her glass had left on the counter.

Oh, the tangled web we weave . . .

Or something like that. It was one of the few lines he remembered from a college class when he was getting his bachelor's degree online. Only because the quote had reminded him of experiences on the job. How perps inevitably tripped themselves up once they started spinning outlandish tales.

"And?" Yaz pressed.

"Aaaand, something happened earlier today, so I

called Diego. Turns out the cops on duty have it under control. I simply had to go ID someone tonight. It's all good."

Lilí twisted to face Yaz, a fake, see-nothing-to-worry-about grin he was not buying plastered on her face. Turns out, neither was Yaz.

She stepped toward Lilí. Reaching to cup her sister's right elbow, Yaz examined the dark bruises Tito's fingers had left when he'd grabbed Lilí's arm.

Concern blanketed Yaz's features. "What's going on, Lilí. *Dime la verdad.*"

"I *am* telling you the truth."

The two sisters stared at each other, a poignant contradiction with one visibly worried and the other desperate to remain the strong, independent woman she yearned to be in the eyes of her *familia*. The one he saw when he looked at her.

The stare-down continued, a tense silence building.

Diego squirmed uncomfortably on his stool. He felt like somewhat of a voyeur, peeking in on a private conversation. Yet he couldn't look away. Couldn't cut the tie that bound him tighter to Lilí the more time he spent with her. As crazy at that might be.

Instead, he sat there, holding his breath. Waiting to see which sister would win this round.

In the end, Lilí caved first.

"It's the truth, just not all of it," she admitted, her words heavy with dismay.

Rather than rail at her for the partial lie, what typically happened when he and Lourdes actually tried having a conversation, Yaz grasped her little sister's arms and pulled her in for a hug.

"*Chica,* you cannot hold out on me. That's not how we work."

"I know," Lilí mumbled.

"And you definitely can't keep stuff from Rosa. You know she's wired with some kind of antennae and can always sense when something's wrong with any of us."

"I'm sorry." Lilí's arms wrapped around her sister's slender frame. She grasped Yaz's long ponytail where it hung down the center of her back, squeezing it like a lifeline.

The gesture poked at a yearning Diego rarely admitted to himself. Much less to anyone else.

The love between the two of them was evident in the way Yaz leaned back to gently brush Lilí's bangs out of her eyes. How Lilí clung to her big sister's waist. He saw it in the affectionate expressions on their faces.

This is what he missed with his sister.

There'd been a time when he and Lourdes had been close. Eons ago, when he was a kid. If Mami worked a late shift at the cleaners, Lourdes had been the one to cook his dinner, review his homework, and read him a bedtime story. She tucked him in and said prayers with him.

Then things had changed. She started hanging with the wrong friends. Crushed on the wrong guy. Took a wrong turn. Along the way he'd lost his sister.

With his mom gone now and the majority of their relatives back in Puerto Rico or scattered around the New York boroughs, Lourdes was his only local connection to family. A messed up, frayed connection he couldn't figure out how to mend.

"Come on, let's move to the living room so you can fill me in." Yaz linked elbows with Lilí, making it impossible for her to disagree. "I've gotta have something to tell Rosa when she calls me. And you know she will."

"Better you than me," Lilí grumbled, earning a grin from Yaz.

That was his cue to leave. Enough family talk for him. "I should get going," he said, sliding off the metal stool.

"Okay!" Lilí answered quickly.

"*Oye, nena*, why are you being so rude? Mami taught you better than that." Yaz swatted Lilí's forearm. "Besides, I'd like to hear Diego's version of the story. I'm sure he won't mind filling in any details you *conveniently* forget. Right, Diego?"

Yazmine's heavy-handed invite for him to stick around paired with her superior manner reminded him of how she'd managed to corral the rambunctious kids who'd shown up for her dance classes at the center. Without raising her voice, she had a knack for getting them all to fall in line, quit acting up, and listen. All while remaining enamored with her.

But he'd already intruded on their together-time enough, and he wasn't really the family type. Exhibit A: his own dysfunctional *familia*.

Ready to say thanks but no thanks, Diego caught Lilí's almost imperceptible shake of her head. Once again her expressive eyes spoke to him. This time they screamed, *Don't do it. Don't do it.*

He got the message. She didn't want him ratting her out and letting her sisters know what had really gone down with Tito. He could respect her bid for independence.

At the same time, she'd put herself in danger over the past week by stepping beyond the line of professional duty. Bringing Melba González home with her, then convincing her to go to the shelter, were moves that had set Tito off. If Velma hadn't been leaving the building tonight when Tito confronted Lilí, who knows what might have happened to her.

Sure, she'd been subdued while they were at the station. Answering Shapiro's and Jordan's questions with a sort of shell-shocked lack of emotion. Taking extra time with the photo array. When she and Melba met in the office on their way out they'd been all hugs, Lilí wiping away tears on the sly.

Had she learned from the scary experience? Would she think twice before putting herself in the same situation with another client?

For his own peace of mind, he had to be sure the answer to both questions was yes.

For her peace of mind, he should probably give her some space.

In the end, whatever would make her feel better won out over everything else. Granted, her eyes pleading with him might have swayed his decision. A little.

Diego turned his wrist, pretending to check the time. "You know, I didn't realize how late it was getting and I've got an early AM appointment."

"Are you sure you can't stay?" Yaz asked.

"Yeah, I should go."

Triumph flashed across Lilí's face. That look made him nervous. Had him wondering what she'd wind up revealing to her sister. More importantly, what she'd leave out.

"Lilí, I'm sure you want to walk me to the door. Being the good hostess that you are," Diego said, purposely not phrasing his words as a question.

Lilí gave him a blank look, clearly not following.

Yaz got his drift. She slid her arm out of the crook of her sister's elbow. Her arched brow telegraphed that she knew he was angling for a moment alone with

Lilí. Whether she thought it was personal or police business, he couldn't be sure.

He was fine leaving her to wonder. Frankly, he wasn't sure himself.

Taking advantage of having caught Lilí off guard, Diego grabbed her hand to tug her behind him down the short hall to the foyer.

"Oh, okay. Sure," she murmured, linking her fingers with his as she followed him. Her tiny hand intertwined with his, reminding him of her petite frame and the damage Tito, or any other deranged spouse, could inflict on her.

"I'll see you at the center," Yaz called out.

Diego glanced back to find her already settled on the black leather sofa in the living area. "Let me know if you need anything."

"I'll be in touch, and please say hi to Gloria for me."

"Will do," he said.

At the end of the foyer, Diego unlocked the dead bolt, then opened the door to usher Lilí outside. Surprisingly, she, who seemed to have a contradictory opinion when it came to most of his ideas, didn't object to being led out into the hallway.

"So who's Gloria?" Lilí asked as soon as the door had shut behind them. "Is she your ex or something?"

Was that a hint of jealousy he detected? Wishful thinking. Her question was probably more like nosiness.

She let go of his hand to prop a fist on her hip. Her orange blouse slid down her shoulder, tempting him.

He wanted to trade the missing warmth of her palm pressed to his with the warmth he knew he'd feel if he cupped her shoulder. Or bent down to sample her skin. Sucked in a breath to fill his lungs with her tropical scent.

Instead he shoved his hands in his back jeans pockets. He shook his head, trying to get his thoughts off the crazy, lust-filled track they continuously jumped on around her.

"Gloria?" she repeated.

"Kid from the neighborhood," he explained. "She's one of the founding students in the center's dance program. Adores your sister."

Lilí's dubious expression relaxed, replaced by a smile brimming with admiration. "Yeah, most of Yazmine's students do. She's great at her job."

"So are you," he said.

She ducked her head. Her bare shoulder lifted and fell in a shrug.

It was interesting, this change in her attitude now that her big sister was here.

The confident, determined, kiss-my-ass advocate who'd manhandled him in her bid to get inside Melba's place that first night had melted away like the Wicked Witch hit with a bucket of water.

"Hey, as much of a pain in the butt as you can be, you look out for your clients. At a time when most of them need someone in their corner."

"Yeah, well, sometimes, actually a lot of times if you ask my sisters"—one edge of her full mouth hitched up in self-derision—"I get in over my head."

Gently he brushed the back of his fingers over the ugly bruises on her arm.

She winced and he pulled back.

"Case in point," she mumbled.

"Look, it's not my place to get in the middle of your conversation with your sister." He jutted his chin at the door behind Lilí. "Nor to tell you how to do your job."

She frowned. "I sense a *but* coming next."

He nearly laughed at her put-upon grumble. "But

what happened tonight with Tito, could have been a lot worse. *Tienes que tener cuidado.*"

"I *am* careful. Despite what my sisters think. To them I'll always be that rambunctious kid with too much energy, racing around the playground while taking care of the little ones in our church nursery."

She leaned back against the door, her beautiful face a mix of wounded pride with a hint of resignation. A flash of white against the rosy pink of her lips snagged his attention as she worried her bottom lip.

The urge to cover that lip with his own, soothe the bite marks with the stroke of his tongue, made his gut clench. Unable to resist his desire to touch her, Diego placed his right hand on the side of her neck. His thumb caressed the soft skin behind her ear.

Lilí gazed up at him, her lashes fluttering over a hazel-green stormy sea he wanted to dive into.

"You need to level with Yazmine," he said. "If not, her imagination will conjure a worse scenario and the worry will grow. The hen-pecking will get worse out of fear. Happens all the time with spouses and family members of cops."

"I know," Lilí muttered.

He let his thumb trace her jawline, coming oh so close to the curve of her lip.

"But whatever goes down during your conversation with your sister, don't forget the good you've done with Melba. With Omara and the rest of the girls in your self-defense class."

Lilí's eyes narrowed speculatively. "Why are you being so nice to me all of a sudden?"

He grinned. It was a better alternative to kissing her till her toes curled. That might earn him a punch in the belly.

"Seeing as how you've yet to listen to any advice I've given you, I'm asking myself that same question."

A shadow of her cheeky smile curved her lips at his words.

"And maybe, like I keep telling you, I'm one of the good guys."

Her hands fluttered in the space between them, then she pressed her palms to his chest. Desire shot through him and he swore his pec muscles twitched at her soft touch.

"*Gracias*," she whispered.

Damn if he didn't want to seal her thanks with a kiss.

But her sister was waiting inside. And all the evidence pointed to his unsuitability when it came to Lilí Fernandez.

So instead, he forced himself to take a step back. His hand slowly caressed her slender neck before dropping to his side, cutting their connection.

"Anytime," he answered. "It's late, and you've had a long day. You should get some rest."

She nodded and reached for the doorknob. Once inside, she pulled the door close, leaving her trim figure to fill the opening. "Will I see you at the center tomorrow? The girls and I have our second class."

"Yeah, I'll be there."

"Good. I'll see you then." She flashed a quick smile, then shut the door.

He waited to hear the bolt click before turning to head down the carpeted hallway.

Of course, there was no specific reason for him to be at the center. Guitar class was only on Tuesdays.

Then again, some of the guys liked to run his butt up and down the basketball court. Talking smack. Occasionally even talking through a problem.

At the elevator bank Diego pushed the call button. He stared at his reflection in the metal door and shook his head.

Who was he kidding?

He wasn't heading to the center to shoot hoops.

He'd go down there tomorrow night because Lilí would be in the building.

Fool that he was, no way would he pass up an opportunity to see her.

"Okay, so when are you going to tell me what's going on with you and Diego Reyes?"

Lilí winced at her sister's question.

They sat together on the sofa, Yaz wedged in one corner, legs spread along the length of the cushions, arms wrapped around Lilí, whose back was to her, mimicking her position.

Lounging like this had been a lot easier when Lilí was five or six and she'd sat on her older sister's lap watching TV or jabbering about something that had happened on the playground. After Mami died, then Papi, they sometimes cuddled like this in the quiet. Memories of their parents' laughter and love swirling around them.

Once in a while Rosa joined, the three of them snuggling together on the sofa, reminiscing.

Tonight, though, Lilí had already sidestepped several questions from Yaz about Diego. Her emotions were too raw to discuss him. Out in the hallway, during the onslaught of his nice guy pep talk, with the tingle-inducing feel of his hand along her neck, his thumb tracing lazy circles on her sensitive skin, lust for him threatened to boil over.

¡Diantre! Had Yaz not been waiting inside the condo,

Lilí would have dragged him back to her room and had her way with him.

Then probably regretted it in the morning.

So, she'd closed the door, reminding herself that she and cops rarely mixed well in social situations. She'd had enough debates and bad dates to prove that.

Instead she'd trudged back into the living room to find Yaz sitting on the couch, Lilí's favorite snuggling throw draped over her long dancer's legs.

"What? No more third degree about my job or Melba González?" Lilí responded, thinking she'd rather hear a lecture about either of those than delve into the topic of Diego Reyes.

The man confused her. Annoyed her. Totally turned her on.

"Come on. Spill it." Yaz shimmed her shoulders, jostling Lilí.

"There's nothing to spill. The guy helped me out a few times. No big deal."

"That was nice of him."

"That's his job," Lilí stressed.

"He didn't have to come when you called him. Or fill in with your class when you needed someone. I'd say he's going out of his way for you. Don't you think?"

Uh-oh. Lilí knew that matchmaking tone when she heard it.

"I think, he's a cop," she reminded her sister.

"Who's pretty easy on the eyes."

Lilí smacked Yazmine's thigh playfully. "What would Tomás say about that?"

"He'd say I have good taste."

"Ha!" Lilí scoffed. "*Estás loca.*"

"If I'm crazy, then you're bananas."

The old line they'd thrown at each other when Lilí

was little brought a warm sense of contentment and comfort.

Yaz squeezed her arms around Lilí in a hug. "So no interest in Diego? No tingling of attraction?"

"Any tingling I get lately is satisfied by a good vibrator."

Yaz howled with laughter.

Lilí leaned to the side and glanced at her sister over her shoulder, enjoying her role as the mischievous one.

When Yaz's outburst had died down, Lilí settled back against her sister and asked, "What makes you so sure Diego's a good guy?"

"*Ay*, give me a minute. That was too funny." Yaz wiped a tear from the corner of her eye. "I can't stop picturing Rosa's face if you'd made that vibrator comment to her."

Lilí grinned. She'd actually already had a conversation about the topic with Rosa.

That girl had some mad research skills. She could find anything on the internet. Case in point, their foray into "erogenous zones," thanks to a new toy Rosa had brazenly decided to try. Mind you, their search had taken place on Lilí's laptop. Rosa hadn't wanted that kind of site showing up in her internet history, especially if Maria borrowed the family computer while visiting. That was their sister secret, the type they'd started sharing only in the last few years since Rosa had started coming out of her shell after her marriage to Jeremy.

Lilí pulled the edge of her comfy throw higher up her chest, burrowing closer to Yaz.

"So, how do I know Diego's a decent guy?" her sister asked. "Because when you watch someone interacting with kids, or when you see kids react to an adult in a trusting way, you can tell he's doing something right."

"You mean at the center," Lilí said.

"*Sí.* I've watched older boys gravitate to him, looking for a decent role model. Even if they can't or won't admit it." Yaz ran her fingers through the fuzzy throw material draped over Lilí's arm.

"And this Gloria you mentioned? He said she's a kid in his neighborhood."

"Yeah, she's a sweetie. I'd say she's probably eight now, since she was five when we started the program. Diego was a lifesaver at that first recital."

Lifesaver, huh?

Lilí could see that. Sure, sometimes his Superman complex wandered into the area of controlling, but she sensed a deeply personal reason for him being that way. *Sensed* being the operative word since the big lug wasn't much into sharing personal details. His "none of your business" jab still rankled.

"Gloria volunteered to do a dance solo. The kid was all in. Then, two days before the show, stage fright hit her like a bolt of lightning. Fried all her gumption. She really wanted to do it. I could see it in her eyes. But she was scared."

Drawn by the story, intrigued by Diego's role in it, Lilí sat up, turning to face Yaz. "What happened?"

"Diego."

Her sister's smug grin had Lilí rolling her eyes.

"Seriously," Yaz said. "He shows up at rehearsal with his guitar. Tells Gloria he'll play the song for her, on stage, so she won't have to be up there alone. And they're both a hit in the recital."

Lilí's heart melted a little more. Seriously. The man could not be any sweeter.

Or salty, given the way he'd dismissed her attempt to offer some advice with his sister earlier.

Ay, the push-pull from him had her feeling like a yo-yo. Something she did not need when her job demands could be so emotionally draining.

Propping her right elbow on the couch, Yaz leaned her head against her open palm. "See what I mean? Good-guy material."

Lilí huffed, twisting back around to lie back against Yazmine.

"Do you remember what Papi said in his letter to you?" Yaz's softly whispered question trapped Lilí's breath in her chest.

She thought about the letter Papi had written to her before he died, like he'd done for all of the girls. Lilí's was safe in her nightstand, along with the photograph of her, Papi, and Mami at her fifth birthday. They'd celebrated with friends at the park. The picture had been taken right before she blew out her candles. Her smile was snaggle-toothed, Mami's and Papi's brimmed with joy as they stood behind her, each with a hand on her shoulder. Always protecting. Loving. Guiding.

The words in Papi's letter were emblazoned on Lilí's brain. And in her heart.

Yo conozco tu buen corazón. Tu compasión por los demás. Ahora tú estás forjando tu camino. Con tu propio músico allí afuera esperándote.

The words echoed in her mind, translating back and forth between Spanish and English.

I know your good heart. Your compassion for others. You are forging your own path now. With your own Music Man out there waiting for you.

The nickname she had often called Papi pricked at the scab of pain that losing him so early had formed on her heart. No matter how much time went by, it would never heal.

Her sisters knew that, felt it themselves.

"You can*not* bring Papi into a conversation about a guy I've known for a week," Lilí demanded. "It's not fair."

"He plays the guitar."

"I know."

"He feels his music the way Papi did."

"I *know*."

Dios mío she'd seen it. Been blown away by it. So much that she'd craved his fingers on her body, playing her as skillfully as he played his guitar.

The intensity of that attraction scared her.

She could not be with someone who didn't understand what she did, why it was so important, or who couldn't see the intrinsic value of feeling your way through those gray areas of life. She'd witnessed how the system, intentional or not, could betray its victims. How it ignored different facets, emotional consequences, and the psychology behind victim advocacy. She'd lived through that with Karen in college. She experienced it every day with her clients.

No matter how mouthwateringly sexy he might be, or how his music made her heart sing, Diego Reyes was not the *músico* Papi referred to in his letter. He couldn't possibly be.

As much as that might disappoint her, she'd do well to remind herself of that when she ran into him again.

Chapter Ten

"Here you go."

Lilí looked up from where she hunkered down next to an equipment duffel bag to find Omara holding out one of the red padded protective gloves they'd used during the self-defense class. "Thanks."

She did a quick scan of their corner of the gym, noting that while the other students had bugged out, Omara's group waited for her near the edge of the bleachers about thirty feet away.

Kent Smith had already left with two duffels of equipment. She'd told him she could handle the last two on her own. They'd hang on to the items to use during the final class next Tuesday.

"I appreciate you noticing this was left out," Lilí told Omara.

"Sure." The girl quirked her neck in a typical teen "whatever" head tilt. She jammed the toe of her pink-and-blue striped sneaker into the court. Evidently she had something else she wanted to say.

Lilí waited. Omara would either speak her mind or leave it for later. Best she not feel pressured or she'd clam up. That would only detract from the progress they'd made tonight. And thankfully for all the girls, because they were the ones that mattered here, progress *had* been achieved.

For starters, they'd all come dressed appropriately. Omara's clique still sported full makeup and cute hairstyles—Lilí hadn't really expected otherwise. After all, there were teen boys in the building to impress. But their exercise gear allowed them to practice the self-defense moves much easier and they'd all given 100 percent. That wasn't always the case with some classes, despite Lilí's best efforts.

Finished picking up the last of the protective gear, Lilí tugged the zipper closed on the duffel.

"You did a great job tonight. I hope you feel proud of yourself," she told Omara.

Arms crossed, nearly covering the words "All That" scrawled in black script across the front of her tight gray T-shirt, Omara gave a tough-girl chin jut to indicate her friends. "Yeah, sure. Look, the girls and I thought we oughtta say thanks for doing this and, you know, for acting like you care. Or, whatever."

The unwitting glimpse of Omara's softer side made Lilí want to hug the girl. Of course, she refrained. That wouldn't be a cool move.

Instead, Lilí rose from her haunches and met Omara's gaze. Tentative acceptance lingered in the girl's dark eyes. Doubt twisted her lips.

"There are a lot of people here rooting for you. Willing to help you develop the tools so you can be successful and healthy. I'm one of those people." Lilí pressed a palm to her chest.

Several beats passed.

She could tell by the way Omara's eyes narrowed

the tiniest bit that the girl was weighing her options. Trust or not trust. It had to be earned in this neighborhood.

"You were pretty bad-ass going up against Officer Smith tonight," Omara finally said.

"Well, we were both wearing protective gear, and it was simulations. But I can hold my own."

"Like with that jerk who came at you last night?"

Surprise had Lilí drawing back a step. "How did you . . . um, what did you hear?"

Omara tossed her head, sending her black ponytail swinging behind her. "Melba González lived down the street from us. My mom knows her. If you ask me, it's 'bout time she cut loose her *sinvergüenza* of a husband."

Lilí barked out a short laugh at Omara's apt description—no doubt about it, Tito had no shame. Definitely no conscience. That's part of what made him so dangerous.

The memory of yesterday's confrontation silenced Lilí's laughter.

"To be honest, I was scared." Palms splayed in front of her, she looked Omara straight in the eye. It was vitally important for the teen to recognize the severity of the situation. "But I did my best to use that fear and adrenaline to drive my actions. I looked right at him and didn't flinch. I used strong, forceful, *loud* words so that I got his attention and to make sure anyone in the vicinity could hear me. I stomped the inside of his foot like we practiced tonight and I kneed him in the groin. Twice."

"Sweet." Omara's expression was a mix of pugilistic rapture and pissed off. Not quite the attitude Lilí was hoping for.

"The thing is though, had my coworker not come

out of the clinic, I'm not sure I could have gotten Tito off of me."

Omara sobered. Her tan complexion blanched a shade and she cast a nervous glance at her friends.

Lilí stepped closer to bring the girl's attention back to her. "You want to remember, our classes and these moves aren't about kicking someone's butt. They're about trying to get you *out* of a situation. Either before it happens or before it escalates. But the moment you have an opportunity to get away, you take it."

"I know." Omara's head bobbed in rapid nods.

"Good. That's real good." Tension she hadn't even been aware of eased from Lilí's shoulders. She forced a smile to lighten the mood. "Next class will be all simulations. I've already warned Officer Smith that you girls won't go easy on him."

Omara grinned. She arched a carefully plucked and shaded brow, her queen bee cover firmly back in place. "You got that right. We'll be ready."

"I'm counting on it."

With a loose-fingered wave, Omara backed away. "See you around. And . . . thanks again."

"Anytime."

Their exchange of friendly smiles warmed Lilí's heart. Diego was right. Omara was a good kid. She joined her friends, and a couple of the other girls waved to Lilí as they rose from the bleachers and headed toward the gym doors.

Lilí turned to give the area another once-over, making sure none of the equipment had been left behind. Satisfied that all was taken care of, she swung her messenger bag over her head and across her body, then snagged the hard plastic handles on the two rolling duffels.

Tonight they'd brought pads for all the students, as

well as Kent. Next week, during the final class, Kent's partner would gear up for simulations with more than one aggressor. It was the last opportunity for the girls to get comfortable with the moves. After that, Lilí prayed they never needed to use them.

She reached the gym's double doors and one of the basketball players trotted over to hold one open for her while she pulled the bags behind her.

Halfway down the hall leading to the bustling lobby, she spotted Diego standing in front of the waist-high counter. The center's assistant manager, David, stood on the other side.

Based on the cajoling look on David's thin face, Lilí figured he was trying to talk Diego into something. Tall and gangly with a friendly personality, what the barely thirty-year-old lacked in experience he made up for with his commitment to the center. David was also a born sweet-talker with a knack for convincing you to volunteer for something before you even realized it.

That's how Lilí had wound up agreeing to chaperone the middle school kids' day trip on Saturday. Of course, it didn't hurt that the event involved attending a Cubs game. Now that her cousin Julia was dating an ex-player and local sports figure, Lilí might luck into tickets more often, but still she rarely passed up a chance to catch her Cubbies in action. Something David knew, and had taken advantage of in his wily way.

The assistant manager caught sight of her, waved, then flipped his palm and bent his fingers in a "come here" gesture.

Diego turned around the second after her eyes had landed on his firm butt, which looked pretty fine in his faded jeans. He smirked. Probably because he'd caught her checking him out.

She slowed her steps as she approached. No need to seem in a rush to meet up with him.

Because she wasn't.

Not really anyway.

"Hi, David, what's up? Diego." She gave the too-hot-for-her-own-good cop a nod in greeting, determined to focus on keeping things platonic.

It didn't matter that she'd had a vivid sex dream about him last night. So vivid she'd woken up reaching for him beside her only to find cool sheets and an empty pillow.

He didn't have to know about that.

Besides, this morning over coffee and Greek yogurt with berries, she'd vowed to squelch any attraction. It was unhealthy and pointless. His inability to have a simple discussion about his sister had proven that.

"*Hola*, Lilí, how was class?" Diego asked.

"Great." She couldn't hold back her grin. "The girls were fantastic. A few actually said they're excited for our last class next week."

"Nice." Diego clasped his hands on top of his guitar case propped up in front of him. The motion accentuated his muscular arms and drew her attention to the bottom of the crown-of-thorns tattoo wrapped around his right biceps. The same tattoo she'd kissed in her dream.

She squelched that thought before it dragged her back to other, more enticing images from dreamland. Although she had to admit, Diego Reyes in the flesh was equally enticing.

Tonight he wore another Chicago Bears tee, the football team's logo in deep orange and white standing out against the shirt's navy cotton material. He hadn't shaved, so his five o'clock shadow gave him a scruffy bad-boy vibe that made certain parts of her body take notice.

Cálmate, she cautioned her racing pulse. As if demanding it to calm down would actually work. Then she remembered something he'd mentioned when they were at his apartment, talking about his music.

"Wait, didn't you say that you taught your guitar classes here on Tuesdays?" she asked.

"Yeah, usually." He reached up to scratch his jaw, shooting a quick glance at David. "Sometimes I'll throw in a free class if any of the kids want extra practice."

A look she couldn't decipher passed between the two men.

Suddenly, David got busy shuffling papers around, but she could have sworn a corner of his mouth quirked before he ducked his head.

"Thanks again, Diego!" A cute middle school–aged kid with shaggy brown hair and an adoring grin for Diego ran up to them. The boy switched an old battered guitar case from his right to his left hand, his excitement palpable in the way he bounced on the balls of his feet. "I think I got the fingering down now for that song."

"Anytime, buddy," Diego answered. He shared a quick fist bump with the kid. "You know I'm always up for practicing if I'm not working."

Omara strolled up behind the boy and Lilí realized he must be the younger brother Diego had mentioned.

"*Hola,* I'm Héctor. You're the lady who's been teaching Omara self-defense, right?" The kid stuck out a skinny arm to shake hands with Lilí.

"That's me. Lilí Fernandez. Pleased to meet you, Héctor."

He grinned, his demeanor friendly and open.

An older boy in long basketball shorts and a saggy tank shirt approached them, his deep voice rumbling Omara's name as he drew near. Lilí noticed the protective hand Omara placed on her younger brother's shoulder as she tipped her head in response when the teen strolled by.

Point made. Big sis had her brother's back. In their neighborhood, oftentimes that was vital for survival.

Lilí's heart softened even more for the loyal queen bee as Omara exchanged polite hellos with the adults.

"I heard class went well," Diego said.

"You shoulda seen Lilí tonight. Girl kicked Officer Smith's a—uh—booty." Omara swapped the word after dropping her gaze to her little brother.

"No way!" Héctor said, bringing a fist to his mouth to cover his laugh. He gave Lilí an appreciative head bob. "She's got game, huh?"

Normally not one to embarrass easily, that was Rosa's thing, Lilí was surprised by the warm blush she felt climbing up her neck and into her cheeks. Mostly thanks to the heat in Diego's eyes as they traveled from her head to her toes and back again.

"Yeah, she does," he said, his husky voice a raspy caress to her already haywire senses.

"You two coming or what?" A boy in saggy khaki shorts and a white tee with a small towel slung over his shoulder called to Omara and Héctor from the youth center's front door.

"We better get going. It's safer to walk with the group once it's dark." Omara patted her brother's shoulder for emphasis.

"'Kay. I'll see you on Saturday for the game, right, David?" Héctor asked. He took a couple steps backwards, but paused when the assistant manager shook his head.

"Actually, I can't make it now. I'm working on finding a replacement." The expression on David's thin face spoke of his disappointment, then it quickly brightened when he pointed to her. "But Lilí's the other chaperone, so it'll be fun."

"You are?" Héctor perked up.

"Are you kidding me?" One hand on her hip, she gave him a raised-brow head waggle with some of the attitude his sister carried in spades. "A July afternoon at Wrigley? I'm not missing that."

"Sweet!" Héctor balled a fist and pumped it in front of his chest. "*Nos vemos el Sábado.*"

"Sure thing, see you Saturday," she repeated, waving as the two siblings headed out.

"You don't know how relieved I am to hear you're still in," David said. "I was just telling Diego about my sister planning some surprise for my mom. Didn't bother letting the rest of us know, but, there you go."

He swiped a hand through the air, obviously annoyed with whatever was going down in his family. "Anyway, I can't make the game and need to find someone to take my place. Eight kids is too many for one person to keep track of in a crowded ball park. I just hate canceling since Ben got us the tickets through his Cubs connections. And they're bleachers seats. The kids are gonna love that!"

"Me too! Julia and I connected via phone last week since she and Ben are on the road, and she mentioned that he was working on it. I'm glad he was able to come through. Shouldn't be too hard to find someone to replace you, right?" Lilí asked. "I mean, who doesn't want to catch a free Cubs game?"

"This guy, apparently." David gave Diego a bug-eyed, what's-up-with-that? look.

Diego held up his hands in surrender. "Hey now, I didn't say no. I said I needed to see about rearranging some plans."

Lilí's belly flip-flopped. The idea of Diego tag-teaming with her to take the group of middle school kids to Wrigley Field made her both giddy and nervously excited. Or maybe it was excitedly nervous.

Either way, it didn't bode well for her. Feeling nervous was a warning—stay away from fire or you'll get burned. Excitement, while it could lead to fun, oftentimes got her into trouble.

Rosa's "look before you leap" cautionary motto wove through Lilí's brain.

"I'm sure I can find another volunteer with security clearance," she told David. Sidling up to the counter, she leaned against the edge. The corner dug into her hip through her black leggings. "There's gotta be someone else interested in spending a sunny day at the ball park."

"Wait a minute. I didn't say I couldn't go," Diego protested.

He slid his guitar case to his left and matched her stance, leaning his right hip on the counter and facing her.

At the other end of the long check-in desk, one of the shift employees called out to David.

"You two hash it out," he told them before stepping away. "All I can say is, you'd be doing me a solid if you would both say yes."

Lilí waited for Diego to respond, but the pesky cop

evidently continued to perfect his man-of-few-words routine.

"Look," she finally said. "You've got plans, don't sweat it. I'll find someone else."

She crossed her arms and blinked up at him like it was no big deal.

All the while her interest caught on the short whiskers darkening his jawline. The faint scar above his left brow. His earthy cologne invaded her senses. The same way it had when she'd roused from sleep, convinced he lay beside her.

"Why do I get the feeling you don't really want me to go?" he asked, giving her a narrow-eyed, speculative look.

"Oh, I'm fine either way. Go. Don't go."

Please go.

She shushed the traitorous voice in her head.

"I haven't been to a Cubs game yet this season," Diego said. "Hanging out with kids from the center is usually a fun time. Hanging out with you has been—"

"You better say something nice or I'm gonna have to practice one of the class moves on you," she warned.

He chuckled, the sound rich and throaty. And inviting. The laugh lines marking the corners of his eyes deepened.

Lilí couldn't resist grinning back at him. *Diantre*, resisting his charms was about as easy as saying no to Rosa's flan. That had yet to happen in Lilí's lifetime.

"I was about to say 'interesting,'" Diego replied. He dug his left hand into his back pocket, the motion stretching his tee across his muscular chest. "Amongst several other adjectives, but that one might be the safest."

"Wise choice."

"That's me, a wise guy." He punctuated his words with a flirty wink. "So, what time are we meeting here on Saturday?"

His question made her heart stutter step. Uh-oh, that meant trouble.

"You're really going to chaperone?" she asked.

"Sure, why not? It'll ease some of David's stress."

Sí, while adding to hers.

Now she'd spend the entire afternoon distracted, trying not to admire the easy way he connected with the kids, like when he'd filled in for Kent in her class. The same way he'd apparently done with little Gloria during Yaz's dance recital. As well as with young Héctor. The man had been here an extra night this week offering the boy another free lesson.

How could she not be attracted to a guy who put these kids, many of whom needed positive role models like him, first?

Despite how wrong he might be for her.

Because, *Dios mío*, no matter how many times Rosa had told her not to play with fire when they were growing up, Lilí had always been the type that had to get burned before learning for herself. With Diego, if nothing else, everything leading up to the burn would feel really, *really* good.

"The kids were told to meet here at nine forty-five in the morning," she said. "That gives us a little time for stragglers, then we'll take the bus to Clark and Division and hop on the Red Line to West Addison. We wanna be at Wrigley when the gates open at eleven twenty."

"Sounds like a plan."

"David's, not mine really."

"And now ours." A spark flared in Diego's dark eyes, warming her. "Guess I'll see you Saturday morning."

"Yeah, baby! That's what I'm talking about!" Lilí yelled.

Diego watched her high-five Héctor, then reach across the kid to slap palms with one of the girls in their group.

He'd known she was a Cubs fan and had found out about her six degrees of separation connection to the team thanks to her cousin's boyfriend. Apparently she also had cousins in Puerto Rico who played ball. But when she'd shown up at the center decked out in a Cubs ball cap and jersey, miniature Cubs baseball-cap earrings dangling from her lobes, Cubs sneakers on her feet, a leather Cubs watch strapped on one wrist, and a Cubs wallet dangling from the other . . . he realized that when it came to her baseball team, Lilí put the "fan" in fanatic.

Get the girl inside the ballpark and her eyes lit up with excitement like a rookie cop's after making their first collar.

Arriving at Wrigley Field just as the gates opened had meant the kids could take advantage of reduced food prices for the first hour. Lilí took a group who wanted to eat right away while Diego and the rest of them headed to find their seats.

Twenty minutes later she'd shown up with a hot dog and fries in one hand, a soda in a collector's cup in the other. A bag of roasted peanuts wedged between her left elbow and side, her broad smile had rivaled the kids' as she plopped down in the seat next to him.

Her shoulder had bumped his and he'd grabbed her hot dog as the foil-wrapped food threatened to roll off the paper boat of fries. Then, he'd nearly swallowed his tongue when she stretched out her shapely, toned legs and tugged on the hem of her too-short-for-his-own-good jeans shorts.

Now, the game was in the bottom of the fifth inning with the home team ahead by two, thanks to the home run that had precipitated Lilí's high-five fiesta.

Food had been devoured and peanut shells littered the cement floor at their feet. Giver that she was, Lilí had shared her bag with him. He and a couple kids had just returned to their seats with soft-serve ice cream, his with an extra spoon for Lilí.

The beer man walked down the aisle, hawking his wares. He paused at the end of their row.

Diego shook his head when the guy made eye contact. Lilí had already waved the beer man off earlier. No alcohol when they were on chaperone duty.

"Yes!" Lilí cried, balling her fist and punching the air as she capped off her run-scoring cheer and fell back in her seat.

He held up the miniature plastic batting helmet full of chocolate and vanilla swirl ice cream.

"For me?" she asked, her eyebrows rising with her obvious glee.

She reached for the extra spoon when he nodded.

"Wow, you sweet talker, you." She grinned, a little giggle escaping from her mouth.

He laughed, amused by her playful personality. Another side of her he found himself drawn to, along with the sexy, the determined, the dedicated, and even the hardheaded ones.

"What?" she asked around a spoonful. She slid the

utensil slowly from her mouth, then stuck out her tongue to lick some cream off the back side. The provocative gesture sent blood surging south in his body and Diego nearly groaned.

She furrowed her brow in question. "You okay? Did you get a brain freeze or something?"

Or something, all right.

He shook his head, relieved when George, to his left, elbowed him to get his attention.

Lilí stuck her spoon back into the ice cream, her free hand sliding to cup his underneath the container to steady it. Her touch sent heat waves rolling through him, stronger than those beating down from the hot July sun.

"We get to stay for the whole game, right, Diego?" George asked.

"Yep, till the last out is called," he answered. "And hopefully we'll get to sing 'Go Cubs Go' at the end if the Cubs win."

"*When* the Cubs win." Lilí leaned over him, her upper arm grazing his chest as she held their dessert steady and shook her spoon to emphasize her point. "No *if* about it. When the Cubs win, we'll sing at the top of our lungs. Got it?"

"Got it!" George fist-bumped Lilí, who sat back in her seat with a satisfied grin.

"We better eat this before it turns back into milk," she told Diego, snagging another bite with gusto.

Diego stared at her in awe, continuously amazed by her many facets.

The positive energy she exuded with the kids, the sexy tomboy vibe she had going on thanks to her team gear, and the sparkle of mischief in her hazel-green eyes were a one, two, three punch combination pummeling his recent conclusion that he and Lilí's relationship could remain both friendly and professional.

Volunteering to chaperone today had been his way of testing the friendship waters. Instead, he'd wound up leaving those slow-moving, placid depths and veering into the raging rapids of full-blown lust.

Life on the wild side was dangerous, but with Lilí he had a strong notion it would be worth it.

She tapped her plastic spoon on the edge of the mini Cubs helmet. He obliged, taking a bite of the melting dessert. The cold concoction tasted sweet on his tongue, but what he really wanted was to taste it on her lips. Lick the drop of chocolate caught on the corner of her mouth.

Whether she sensed his focus on her mouth or not, Lilí reached up to swipe the chocolate off with the back of her hand.

"Here." Diego dug in a front pocket of his khaki shorts for one of the napkins he'd grabbed.

"Thanks," she mumbled around another spoonful. "It's getting messy, huh? You should finish it." She pushed the container in his direction, then wiped her face with the paper napkin.

The Cubs players took the field and Lilí joined in with the cheering crowd.

Diego sat back to enjoy the atmosphere, especially the kids' enthusiasm at being inside the ballpark. For many it was their first game and he was happy to be a part of their first Wrigley Field experience.

Lilí was a font of information when it came to her team's history. Since most of the kids were budding baseball or softball players, they listened to her every word, off and on throwing questions at her. Despite her keen interest in following the game, she gave each child her undivided attention, ensuring they understood that whatever they had to say was important. That they mattered to her.

For a couple of the kids, this type of unconditional love wasn't something they saw much of at home. The fact that she either knew this or was naturally an attentive, giving person made him respect her even more.

At the top of the eighth inning, Diego's phone vibrated in his pocket. He dug it out to find a text from David, sent to him and Lilí.

> Family party got over early. I'm down the street from Wrigley in the center's van. Will meet you on the corner of Sheffield & Addison after the game.

Lilí was so engrossed in the Cubs manager's pitching change decision, she didn't seem to notice her phone had received the message.

Diego held his cell out to her. "Hey, David says he can pick us up so we don't have to bother with crowds on the "L" and the bus."

"Oh, okay." She barely glanced at his phone, instead stretching up in her seat to yell at the umpire, "Come on, ump! Give me a break! That was a strike!"

Her fervor encouraged Héctor and a couple others to join in the cries. Diego made a mental note: In a tight game, don't count on Lilí to contribute to important discussions.

While Lilí, the kids, and thousands of other Cubs fans in the park cheered as the pitcher struck out the next batter, Diego typed a message to David.

> Sounds good. Will text when we're outside.

David replied with the thumbs-up emoji.

A short while later the opponents were down to their last out. All the fans stood on their feet cheering, ready to sing the Cubs' winning anthem and wave their white flags with the dark blue W signifying the team win.

The batter swung and missed and the crowd went wild. Including Lilí, who raised her arms high with a triumphant cry of "¡Wepa!"

Before he knew it she threw her arms around him for a celebratory hug. She smelled like sun and sweat with a hint of her coconutty-lime lotion. Absolutely delicious.

The hug was over much too fast for his liking. Then she was on to slapping high fives and singing along with the forty thousand plus others in the park. Including Héctor and the rest of their gang, who jumped up and down with huge grins on their faces.

Standing there, in the midst of all the chaos and cheers, it hit Diego. For the first time in a long while, everything seemed right in his world.

He had planned to spend today working on small renovations in his home. Trying to upgrade things that his *mami* had always talked about updating, but never gotten around to. Or more likely, hadn't had the money for. Every completed project assuaged his guilt over not being able to provide enough before she had died.

Most days that guilt weighed heavily on his mind. But today, thanks to Lilí, he hadn't thought about it at all.

Suddenly, as happy as everyone else was that the Cubs had won, Diego wasn't ready for the afternoon to end. Not yet anyway.

Once the song had finished and fans started

streaming out of the ballpark, while the kids were gathering their commemorative cups and anything else they'd brought with them, Diego grasped Lilí's elbow gently.

She glanced at him, a question lingering in her eyes.

"What do you say to us letting David take the kids back, and we stick around to grab a drink at the Cubby Bear to celebrate? You up for it?" he asked her.

Lilí's infectious grin spread across her kissable lips. "Heck yeah!"

And with that, his afternoon got even brighter.

Chapter Eleven

"Thanks again!" David called from the driver's seat in the van.

"Anytime." Lilí bent down to peer at him through the open front passenger window, still riding the high of her team's win.

A round of thank-yous and catch-you-laters were shouted by the middle schoolers in the moments before Diego closed the vehicle's side door, giving it a pat to alert David that he was good to go.

She and Diego stood on the curb, waving as the white fifteen-passenger van with the youth center's multicolored helping-hands logo on the side pulled away. Around them Cubs fans of all ages crowded the sidewalk, laughing and joking, recalling, even reenacting, an amazing play from the game. Overhead the "L" rumbled to a stop on the raised train's platform crossing Addison Street.

"You sure you're up for a drink at the Cubby Bear or Sluggers?" Diego asked.

The smart thing to do was beg off and take the stairs up to the platform. Or hail a taxi and head home.

Lilí considered herself a smart person. However,

with the joy of sharing the Wrigley experience with the kids sparking her enthusiasm and after spending the past few hours hyperaware of Diego's every move beside her, she wasn't ready to walk away from him. Not yet anyway.

Besides, they'd be in a crowded bar, what could she possibly do that she'd regret?

"Sure, let's go," she answered.

Diego grinned, then gestured for her to precede him. Like he had the other night when he'd driven her home after the photo ID, he looped an arm around her lower back, angling his body to shield her from the jostling fans at his side. The protective gesture was endearing, if old-fashioned, but since it put him a little closer to her, she didn't mind.

"Great game, huh?" he asked.

"Any game that ends with us winning, is a great one," she answered.

The bill on his cap created a shadow over the top half of his face, leaving his eyes shaded, but his white teeth flashed with his smile. She returned it with one of her own, a lightness in her step she recognized stemmed from the anticipation of spending more time with him.

One block later they reached the bar, showed their IDs to the bouncer, and waded into the revelry. Diego's hand slid from her lower back to reach for hers. She linked her fingers with his, telling herself the gesture was simply to avoid them getting separated in the crowd.

It took them a good fifteen minutes before they were able to belly-up to the bar and order their beers. The place was a madhouse, packed with post-game partyers.

While they waited for their drinks, she and Diego

chatted about the game, the kids . . . It was hard for Lilí to follow at times, seeing as how they stood facing each other, her thighs and hips occasionally brushing his in the crush.

Someone bumped into her from behind and Lilí stumbled into Diego. His arms looped around her to steady her and she grabbed on to his waist.

"Sorry," she mumbled.

"You okay?" He peered down at her, his hands resting low on her back, his long fingers skimming the top part of her butt.

She nodded. All the while savoring the tingles of awareness his touch sent shimmering through her.

"I wasn't thinking about how packed it would be," Diego said, bending closer so she could hear him over the din.

"Yeah, it's always like this after a game. But the positive energy is invigorating."

Or maybe it was *him* invigorating her.

He craned his neck to take in the crowd, before tipping his head toward her. "We're packed in here like sardines, yet you manage to find the silver lining. It's one of your best qualities."

"Among many, right?" she teased.

A light flared in the depths of his eyes. His fingers flexed on her back and she pressed closer to him.

Diantre, he smelled delicious. Sweat and sunscreen and the earthy scent she would always associate with him. She wanted to bury her nose in his neck. Breathe him in.

Instead, she curled her fingers in his belt loops underneath his Cubs tee, trying to hold on to her sanity at the same time she held on to him.

"Here you go!" the bartender called.

Diego released her to pass the guy some cash in

exchange for their pints. Holding them aloft, he called to her over his shoulder. "Let's see if we get lucky and find an open table somewhere in the back."

She nodded, then grabbed a handful of his shirt so they could stick together.

As luck would have it, an older couple stepped down from their stools at a high-top table at the same time the crowd spit out Lilí and Diego nearby. The gentleman waved them over to take their places.

"Thanks!" Diego told the couple.

"Sure, go Cubs!" the older man answered with a grin.

Lilí offered her thanks as well, before clambering onto the black bar stool and making herself comfortable at the small round table.

"Cheers!" Raising his pint glass, Diego clinked it with hers. "To a successful day all around."

"Definitely! The kids had a great time. I'm thrilled the Cubbies were able to give them a win today."

Diego nodded as he took a healthy swig of his beer. "So how'd you get to be such an avid Cubs fan? I'm thinking the genesis had to have been long before Ben Thomas and your cousin hooked up. It's her brothers who play, right?"

Leaning her forearms on the faux wood tabletop, Lilí nodded, wondering how he knew so much about her family. More than likely David, who thought very highly of Ben, had blathered. Ben was actually a major donor to the center's sports program and, along with her cousin Julia, actively involved with the entire Chicago youth center system's fundraising efforts.

"I mean, you're like a walking Google search on the team's history," Diego added.

She chuckled at his exaggeration, but his question made her think back on her first game at the park. "You know baseball's big on the Island, especially winter ball. So naturally, my Papi was a huge fan. I grew up watching or listening to Cubs games on WGN with him. He and I came to my first live game when I was about six."

"Without your sisters?" Diego asked. He mimicked her position, leaning on the table, head angled toward hers.

"Mami and Papi always made a point of spending one-on-one time with each of us girls. Time when we had their undivided attention. Papi's and my trips to Wrigley were part of our father-daughter outings together."

"That's a pretty cool idea. In my family it was a little different."

"How so?"

"*Bueno.*" He drew out the word, as if thinking back on his childhood. "My *mami* was a single mom, so even when she wanted some peace and quiet, she was the only one we could turn to. Looking back, I rarely recall her doing something just for herself. She was always working, volunteering at the church, and looking out for my sister and me."

"What about your dad?" Lilí held up a hand before he could answer. "I'm sorry. That might not be something you want to share."

"Nothing earth-shattering to tell." Diego took another drink, then plunked his pint glass on top of the table. The corners of his mouth curved down with what she thought might be indifference. "Raúl was never around much. Then, when I was about five, he took off for Puerto Rico and never came back."

It was a story of abandonment she commonly heard from the women and children who came into the clinic. Still, its commonality didn't make it any less painful for those who experienced it. Empathy welled inside her and Lilí placed a comforting hand on Diego's forearm.

His gaze cut from the scratched tabletop to meet hers. She expected anger and resentment. The apathy in his eyes was probably worse.

"Do you ever hear from him? Or see him?" she asked.

"No. I reached out to him twice. Once when I was Héctor's age. Again before I left for the army. Both times asking for the funds needed to cover a decent rehab program for my sister."

He paused. Ran a finger down the condensation on the outside of his glass.

She waited, hoping he would elaborate, but it wasn't her place to push if Diego didn't feel like talking about it. Even though she honestly believed doing so might be a good thing.

"He responded with some lame song and dance. Excuses to avoid his responsibility." Derision sharpened Diego's features, curled one corner of his mouth. "I deleted his contact from my phone after the last time."

Lilí winced at the harsh move.

Then again, maybe the young Diego had learned what it took many others much longer to grasp: You can't control how others behave or think. You can only control yourself. Do what's right for you and your loved ones. It was a recurring topic at the clinic.

Cutting off contact with a man who'd shown no interest in being a loving, contributing member of his own family might have been the healthiest way for Diego to cope. That didn't make it any less difficult.

"I'm sorry you had to go through that," she said softly.

"It's not the first time you've heard something like

this. If you stay working where you are now, it won't be the last."

"Doesn't mean it hurts any less."

Diego's chin dropped to his chest and he shook his head slowly from side to side. "Damn, how do you do that?"

"Do what?"

The music switched to a popular party anthem and Lilí ducked closer so she could hear him.

He angled his head, piercing her with a look so full of longing it stole her breath. "How do you manage to say the right thing? Validate someone's crappy feelings, even when they're pretending to ignore them, so they . . . they feel less crappy?"

"Oh, I don't know that I really do—"

"Stop." Diego sandwiched her hand with his on his forearm. "Don't discount yourself. What you do is amazing."

She stared up into his dark eyes, moved by the sincerity in their depths. "Thank you for saying that."

"It's the truth."

His fingers lightly caressed the back of her hand. A slow, tantalizing motion that made her yearn for his touch in other places. She watched his gaze slip from her eyes to her mouth. Instinctively, Lilí licked her lips, remembering his taste.

Diego's head moved a fraction closer. Paused.

Lilí held her breath, wanting more than anything to feel his lips on hers again. To experience that connection she'd only ever felt with him, that evening in his living room. Instinctively she leaned toward him.

"Go Cubs goooo! Go Cubs gooooo!"

The cry sounded right behind Lilí, making her start and jerk back in surprise.

Diego grabbed her shoulder to keep her from

falling off the bar stool as a group of college guys burst through the crowd chanting the tune. Fists pumping the air, beers sloshing, they were in full celebration mode.

A shaky, nervous laugh bubbled up from her chest as she mimed a fist pump back at one of them. Disappointed as she was by the interruption, Lilí had been in their shoes many times in the past. In this same bar. No way could she be annoyed by their poor timing.

Settling back on her stool, she sat up tall. Farther away from Diego's delicious temptation.

He lifted his ball cap and adjusted it back on his head. The sheepish grin he shot her was reminiscent of Héctor's when the boy had tried sneaking one of her fries during the game. Just as she'd willingly offered more to the kid then, she most certainly wanted to offer more to Diego now.

That might be dangerous.

Or not.

She couldn't decide, especially when she was with him and the fire simmering between them sparked into an inferno.

"Anyway," Diego said, sitting up on his stool as well. "Raúl was, still is I guess, nothing like your dad. Reynaldo, right?"

Lilí nodded, pleased he'd remembered Papi from the Puerto Rican Festival performances.

"Based on the way you talk about him, seems like Reynaldo was a great father."

"*Ay*, we were lucky. My *papi* was the best. Mami used to say they broke the mold after they made him." The memory of the love on Mami's face whenever she spouted that line made Lilí smile. "My sisters and I pretty much agree. About both our parents, really."

She took a swig of her beer, the hoppy tang rolling

over her tongue as happy childhood memories flashed in her mind.

"My mom, Alma, was the same." Diego picked up his glass and saluted toward the ceiling. *"Que descanse en paz."*

Lilí had murmured that same prayer for a loved one to rest in peace countless times when thinking about her own parents. She gave a respectful sign of the cross and Diego acknowledged it with a "thank you" tilt of his head.

"Mamí worked long hours to provide for my sister and me," he continued. "But she always made sure it was clear that we were what was most important to her. She had a fun side, could play dominoes for hours, and oh how that woman loved to dance."

The faraway, almost blissful expression on Diego's face as he spoke about his *mami* was like a lasso looped around Lilí, drawing her to him. It spoke of a kindred yearning for those who had shaped their lives, and continued to do so, even though they were no longer with them.

"I remember one year at the Fiestas Puertorriqueñas, Reynaldo and Los Paisanos were playing, which of course meant my mom *had* to be there."

Despite his beleaguered tone and twist of his lips, Lilí couldn't resist holding up a hand to cut in. "Can I just tell you, Papi would have been thrilled to hear you say that. He really enjoyed playing for people who loved the music as much as he did."

"Yeah, I know what he meant," Diego answered. "I've never played for a big crowd like Los Paisanos have, but I understand the feeling of knowing your audience truly appreciates your art."

Witnessing the pleasure Papi had found in his music mirrored in Diego pushed Lilí closer to the edge, leaving her on the verge of thumbing her nose at caution and taking that leap she kept telling herself to avoid. *Dios mío*, the other night she had definitely appreciated his talent. Among other things.

Yazmine's reminder of Papi's letter when they'd been sitting on Lilí's couch together whispered through her head.

Lilí silenced it. Diego was not her *músico*. He couldn't be.

"*Pues*, my mom was definitely a Los Paisanos fan," Diego continued. "I've got her CDs to prove it."

Lilí laughed, contentment washing over her at his wry chuckle.

"She sounds like a wonderful woman," Lilí said. Alma Reyes had to be if she'd raised a good man like him all on her own.

"She was." The love, pride, and ache of absence he felt for his mom colored Diego's words. They were evident in the way he rubbed at his chest, directly over his heart.

Captivated by his deep emotion, by his ability to share those feelings with her when many men would hide them, Lilí's insistence on their incompatibility dissolved a little more. Maybe she had judged him too harshly.

Diego cupped his hands on either side of his empty pint glass, gliding it back and forth through the condensation pooled on the table. "My mom was strong, determined. She had a quick sense of humor and cared deeply for others. Like you."

He grasped the glass with one hand, stopping its motion. The same way his words ensnared her heart.

The revelry and music surrounding them faded to a dull roar in Lilí's ears.

"*Gracias*," she whispered, too moved to say much else.

One of his broad shoulders rose and fell in a half shrug. An earnest, almost tender look crossed his features when he glanced at her out of the corner of his eye. "Like I said before, it's the truth."

Ay. Dios. Mío.

Scared she might be falling for him, too hard and much too fast, Lilí pushed herself into the familiar role she had assumed with her family after Mamí had died. When Lilí had learned to hide her pain and uncertainty behind laughter or a joke to ease the discomfort of others.

"*Pues*, in my world, unlike yours, there are shades of truth." She wiggled her hand playfully in a so-so gesture. "What you view as determined, Rosa usually calls stubborn or hardheaded. You say humor. Yazmine says I need to take things seriously. But I do know how to lighten the mood when needed. And that's a key skill."

She winked, pretending his words hadn't affected her as much as they had. Wishing she hadn't finished her beer so she could wash down the truth trying to force its way out. The truth that somehow he managed to see the real her those closest to her didn't.

"I'm sure they're aware of your skills," Diego countered. "Maybe I don't know your sisters that well, but you can tell the three of you have a strong bond. That's something my *mamá* would call a blessing." He paused, his thick brows creasing with a frown before he continued. "I used to have that with—"

His cell phone vibrated on the tabletop. Diego glanced at the screen, then pushed the side button to ignore the call.

"With whom?" Lilí asked when he didn't go on.

He'd been talking about her sisters and she wondered if he'd started to share something about his. The one who, according to him, had chosen incorrectly when it came to right and wrong. The one she'd bet he deeply missed. If not, why the anger and latent disappointment?

His phone vibrated again. The same local area code and phone number flashed across the front.

"I should probably get this. Make sure it's not something for work." He picked up the phone, but instead of answering, he asked, "Do you mind?"

"*¡Ay, no! Por favor.* I'd do the same if it was my work." She waved off his question, then swiveled on her stool to give him some privacy.

"Reyes here," he answered, his voice that same gruff, I-mean-business tone he'd used the first night they'd met.

Lilí watched a young couple nearby dancing to the music's heavy beat. Well, more like grinding, but who was she to judge. She'd done her fair share of dirty dancing. Still did with the right partner. Like say . . .

"Lourdes? Is that you?"

The anxious tone in Diego's voice drew Lilí's attention and she spun back around to face him.

"What's going on? Where are you?" He fired off the questions. With the phone at one ear, Diego stuck a finger in the other to block out the noise. He slid off his stool. His body tense. His face a hard mask of stony resolve.

"*Cálmate.* Lourdes, *calm down.*" He repeated the order firmly, shaking his head at whatever his sister was saying on the other end. "I can't . . . you're not making any sense."

His mouth thinned as he listened to whatever his

sister was saying. His expression grew even more intense in the moments before he ordered, "Look, tell me where you are and I'll be right there."

He gave a brisk nod as if his sister could see. "Don't leave. I'm on my way."

Diego stabbed at the icon to end the call. When he glanced at Lilí anger and concern stared back at her. "I'm sorry. I have to go. My sister—"

"Hey, no need for you to apologize." Lilí stepped down from her seat and slipped her wristlet wallet onto her arm. "*Familia primero.* That's what my parents always taught us. Go take care of your sister. Family first. Always."

"Thanks." His frown deepened as Diego started to move away. All of a sudden he doubled back, bending down to brush her cheek with a kiss.

"I hate leaving like this. You deserve better," he said softly.

His knuckle grazed her jawline in a gentle caress. Then he disappeared into the crowd, leaving her wondering what he meant.

And wanting so much more.

Diego pulled up in front of the dilapidated corner store in the seedy part of Burnside, tires squealing.

The entire drive he'd racked his brain, working to piece together how the hell Lourdes might have wound up all the way down here on the South Side of Chicago. And who the hell she'd gotten herself mixed up with this time.

He spotted her leaning against the side of the store building, right by the Plexiglas® front door. Smart move. In her current position she could easily see and be seen by the clerk inside. Having a witness might offer some semblance of protection from whatever loser she was trying to get away from.

Her curly brown hair was longer than the last time he'd seen her. What, six months ago? Now it hung past her shoulders in a bedraggled, knotted mess. The skintight, cropped red tank and minuscule black skirt she wore left little of her curvy body to the imagination. More than likely she figured her outfit, capped off by a pair of high-top Converse wedge heels, made her look stylish. Guaranteed to catch a man's eye.

Yeah, the wrong type of man.

Had their *mami* been here, she would have told Lourdes to go change into something less revealing. Preferably something in Lourdes's size rather than clothes meant for the likes of the plastic dolls she used to play with.

Her gaze jerked to his Charger when he screeched to a halt. Fear flashed across her face. The fresh bruise on her left cheek had anger rising in his chest.

Diego jammed the button to roll down the passenger window.

"Get in!" he called out.

Lourdes leaned forward to peer at him, but stayed where she was, uncertainty stamping her features.

"If you want my help, you're gonna get your ass in my car. I'm not hanging around here." He kept his gaze trained on the group of men gathered in a close huddle near the entrance to the back alley. All sported loose T-shirts and saggy pants belted below their butts, their necks weighed down by thick gold chains.

One held a big wad of bills. Another dug deep in his front pocket for something. The others were obviously relegated to lookout based on the way they kept busy scanning the vicinity.

Diego had no intention of finding out what might

be going down between them. His focus was on getting his sister out of harm's way. For that to happen, she had to stop being difficult.

He ground his teeth in exasperation, waiting to see what his hardheaded sister would do.

She approached his car in a moody shuffle, but didn't reach for the handle.

"*Tú me llamastes a mi, Lourdes,*" he reminded her.

"Yes, I know I called you," she grumbled, finally opening the door. She tossed a worn, oversized backpack onto the floor and plopped down in the passenger seat.

He didn't even bother waiting for her to get settled before he pulled away from the curb.

"Buckle up," he ordered.

"I am. Give me a minute. You're hauling outta here like El Cuco is on our heels."

Her reference to the Spanish bogeyman that had terrified him as a kid might have made him laugh if the situation had been different. The memory of him being four or five and her sitting on the end of his bed until he fell asleep flashed at him in a blast from the past. He pushed it away.

That had been before things went downhill. Before their *mami* had died.

The thought of his mom and the stress Lourdes had caused her soured any sweet trip down memory lane for him.

"Where we headed? I ain't going to no shelter or rehab joint. Don't need it." Arms crossed, Lourdes shot him a glare.

He took a right turn, driving toward South Greenwood Avenue. "Going to Burnside Park. I figure it's a safe place to talk. You can tell me what you've got going on."

Hopefully being in an open spot would calm her. Keep her from getting too anxious and blowing him off like she had the last time they'd spoken.

She'd called him in a state of panic. Same as today.

They'd met at a fast food place in Englewood. Some run-down joint where the employees stayed behind protective glass and the tables could barely support a plate of the greasy food they doled out. It had been obvious that Lourdes was in between scores, in need of a fix. She'd been nervous. Antsy. Easily agitated.

He'd been pissed. Worried. Disappointed in both of them.

No amount of trying to convince her to go to rehab had worked. She'd felt pressured and had ultimately stormed off in a profanity-laced snit.

Flash forward six months and here they were. Same story, different day.

They reached the park and Diego pulled into a shaded spot facing the playground. The late afternoon sun hung lower in the sky, casting long shadows from the trees and park equipment.

"You wanna get out? Maybe sit at an empty bench?" he asked.

"Sure. Whatever."

His frustration over her sullen attitude threatened to boil over. "Look, I'm trying here. But you don't make it easy."

"You think I wanna hafta call you like this?" She shoved a hand through her curls, the motion drawing attention to the various shades of purple marring her cheek.

The thought of someone putting their hands on his sister kicked his protective, man-of-the-house machismo into overdrive. "Who did that to you?"

Lourdes ducked her head so that her wild curls covered her face. "It's nothing."

"A bruise the size of my fist isn't 'nothing.'" His fingers clenched on the steering wheel. "Tell me who it is and I'll have a conversation with him about the consequences of punching my sister."

"You don't know him," she sidestepped.

"Looks like you shouldn't either."

She huffed out a breath. "Always preaching, *hermanito*, aren't you?"

Unbuckling his seat belt, Diego twisted to face her. "That's because your *little brother*"—he stressed the nickname she'd used—"wants what's best for you."

"And you know what that is, huh? You have all the answers and I know nothing. ¿*Verdad*? Right!" She answered her own question, then tugged on the door handle and pushed out of the car, grumbling the whole time.

For a second he was afraid she was already blowing him off. Set to disappear again like she had the last time. Then he noticed her backpack on the passenger floorboard.

Relieved she wasn't bugging out, but not taking any chances, Diego slid out of his car and clicked the lock button. If she took off again, she'd have to get in touch with him for her bag.

He followed Lourdes to a dark green, thermoplastic-covered table shaded by a large oak tree about twenty feet away. Off to the right, a group of kids ran around the playground in a rousing game of tag. Their cries screeched through the air. A young mom pushed her toddler on the baby swings, the little boy's legs kicking his glee in the yellow booster seat.

Lourdes jerked her chin at him as he approached.

"When'd you turn into a Cubs fan? Thought football was more your thing."

"I took some kids from the youth center to the game today with a gir—with another chaperone." He tried to amend the explanation, hoping to avoid any questions, but it was too late.

Lourdes's face brightened with interest. "Oh, so you gotta girlfriend now?"

"No. Just a friend. Someone I know from work. Kind of, anyway."

He rubbed at the tight muscles in his neck, avoiding eye contact with Lourdes as he stepped over the bench seat across from her. His relationship with Lilí wasn't a topic he cared to discuss with his sister. Not when he couldn't figure it out himself.

"I see how it is." Waving her pointer finger through the air at him, Lourdes bobbed her head side to side with attitude. "You can ask me twenty questions, expecting answers. But you're gonna hold out and zip your lips when I ask one."

"It's not like that," he said on a heavy sigh.

Coño, he knew better. A harsher word than "damn" burned the tip of his tongue at his foolishness. Interview Techniques 101 taught him that if he wanted Lourdes to trust him, he had to build a rapport. "I responded to a DV call recently. The other chaperone works at the Victim's Abuse Clinic in the Humboldt Park area, so she knew the victim. Turns out she volunteers at the youth center, too."

"Hmm, so you been spending time with her, huh? Any sparks?"

More like fireworks.

Lourdes waggled her eyebrows like she'd read his mind.

"It wouldn't work." He brushed aside her teasing.

"She sees the good in everything. In everyone. She's out to save the world, and I'm . . ."

"You're a hard-ass." Hands clasped on the table, Lourdes gave him the frank look he remembered from his childhood.

At one point in their lives, she'd been the hard-ass. If their mom was working late and he tried talking his way out of doing a chore or going to bed on time, Lourdes had called him on it. Rarely cutting him any slack.

But then things changed. For a long time now their situations had been reversed.

"Only when I have to be. And for good reason," he said.

His gaze roamed over his sister, seeking signs of drug withdrawal. Her pupils weren't dilated. No tremor or shakes indicating restlessness. Sure, her hands were clasped, but the last time he'd been with her, her knee was bouncing so fast he thought she might come out of her skin.

"You got your fill?" She arched a brow at him. "I'm clean. Haven't had anything in nearly four weeks. Plan to stay that way."

He squelched a spurt of joy at her claim. Four weeks wasn't all that long, and he'd heard this same promise before. Had fallen for it countless times. So had their mom, one time too many.

"I'm serious. *Me tienes que creer*," she insisted, spreading her hands palms-up across the table toward him.

His heart pounded in his chest. *Dios*, how he longed for that to be true, but their history had jaded him. "I don't *have* to believe anything. I want to, but you've made that pretty difficult."

"Fine, be a prick then."

She pulled back from him, mouth twisted in a

derisive scowl, as if she didn't care either way. But in the seconds before she turned to stare out at the playground, he caught the flash of pain in her dark eyes.

A breeze kicked up and she speared a hand through her curls, pushing them out of her eyes. "Did you answer my call so you could just be a jerk to me then?"

Nuh-uh. He wasn't going to RSVP for her pity party either. It wouldn't do her any good, and that's all that mattered to him, ensuring she got the help she needed. From him or someone else.

Maybe someone like . . .

He stopped that line of thinking before he got any further. No way was he getting Lilí involved with his sister. He refused to play any role in stripping Lilí of her optimism. If that happened, he'd never forgive himself.

"I answered because we're *familia*," he told Lourdes. "But you're not leveling with me. You call in a frenzy, and now won't tell me what's going on. What is it, you need a place to stay?"

"Believe it or not, I'm working on a plan." She picked at the chipped red polish on her short nails. "Like you'd let me stay with you if I needed to anyway."

"I would."

That got her attention. Hope sparked on her face. The same way it used to spark on Mami's when Lourdes would show up out of the blue. He, on the other hand, had learned to be leery.

Sure enough, Mami would welcome her back, under certain conditions, only to have Lourdes wind up making another bad decision and taking off again.

"You always have a place with me, as long as you abide by the rules."

She sucked her teeth dismissively. "Yeah, *your* rules."

"Same ones Mami had. Stay clean. Get a legal job.

Stay away from the people who aren't your real friends."
He counted off each one on a finger.

Lourdes pressed her lips together in a sullen pout.

He refused to back down. Despite Lilí's caution
that not everything was black and white, he knew that
with his sister, he couldn't waver. For her own good,
as well as his.

A sound trilled and Lourdes reached deep into her
cleavage to pull out a burner phone.

How the phone had managed to stay wedged in
there when her chest looked like it was ready to pop
out of the small crop top, he had no idea. Then again,
he'd seen some uncanny ways undercover cops stashed
their weapons. Lourdes might be able to teach a few
of those guys a thing or two.

He waited while Lourdes read the text message.
Her shoulders relaxed a fraction, then her thumbs
started tapping away at the keyboard in response.

"Patricia says I can stay with her," Lourdes finally
said.

"Wait, Patricia, your friend from high school?"
Pushing his palms into the table's curved edge, Diego
leaned back in surprise. "The one who's been in and
out of rehab, damn, I lost track how many times now?"

Lourdes shoved the phone back into her cleavage.
"Don't judge."

"Yeah, right." He shook his head, bewildered by the
idea that this might be his sister's plan. "Let me get
this straight. You don't wanna stay with me because I
have too many rules. But it's okay to stay with the
person who introduced you to your first dealer?"

Lourdes blanched, her tan skin turning a pasty
color.

Exasperated by the fact that she'd choose to stay
with Patricia instead of accepting his fair offer and

coming home, Diego pushed to his feet and stepped over the bench. He stalked a few paces away before spinning back around to face her. Arms extended out at his sides, he gaped at her, completely confused by her lack of reason. "In what world is that a good idea, Lourdes?"

Anger tightened her jaw. The purple bruise on her cheek gave her a tough, brutish look that matched her narrow-eyed glare.

"In my world." She stood up, hands fisted on her hips. "Look, I know I've screwed up. A lot. Some mistakes, you may not ever forgive me for." Her voice broke on the last few words. Her chin trembled and he could see her struggling to fight off tears.

Was this the way it would always be between them? Arguments, hurt feelings, unspoken accusations.

At a loss for how to fix the situation, Diego scrubbed a hand over his face. Desperation tightened his chest, despair choking the words in his throat. Had Lilí been here, this entire conversation probably would have been handled differently. Then again, it was always easier to deal with things when you had no skin in the game.

"I called you because I was scared."

His gut clenched at Lourdes's softly spoken admission.

"But you can't 'fix' me, Diego. I gotta do that myself. On my terms."

He wanted to rage that she was wrong. Yet deep inside, he knew she wasn't.

The water under the bridge separating them was murky. Far too many times it had risen to make the bridge impassable. If he was honest, there were times it had been his fault as much as hers.

Like after Mami died. Back then, the blame game between him and his sister had been brutal.

It didn't matter how badly he wanted Lourdes to be safe and healthy, and in his life. Or how much he felt he owed it to his mom to see her wish for her daughter to have a good life come true. Lourdes needed to want all that for herself.

If she was clean now—big IF—she might be on the right track. Though he seriously believed that relying on Patricia was a big mistake.

"Fine," he said, on a heart-heavy, guilt-laden sigh. "You want me to back off. I'll back off and we'll do things your way."

"You being real with me?" Lourdes eyed him with skepticism. The lack of trust in her narrowed gaze was like a shank to his midsection.

"Yeah, I am. Come on, I'll drop you off."

He'd drive his sister over to Englewood, then he'd start keeping an eye on the comings and goings at Patricia's house. He wasn't leaving anything to chance.

Chapter Twelve

"Hi, David, how's it going tonight?" Lilí strolled up to the front desk at the youth center late Tuesday evening after the last self-defense course.

"Hey, nice to see you! I heard some of the girls chatting before they headed out. Sounds like the class was a success."

He held up a hand for her to high-five, a huge grin splitting his thin face.

"Yep," she answered. "They kicked butt. Kent and his partner were impressed."

Lilí couldn't have been more proud of the girls. They'd all arrived ready for business. Omara and her posse even claimed to have practiced the moves in their living rooms.

"Thanks again for chaperoning over the weekend. Amazing game, huh?" David stepped to his left as a teen approached the counter and held out a paper. David's fingers tapped away at the computer keyboard a few moments before he nodded. "Okay, Joey, you're all set."

Lilí smiled at the teen as he headed back toward the gym.

"Yes, awesome Wrigley experience for the kids," she told David. "Seemed like they all had a good time. I snapped a couple pics and sent them to Julia to pass along to Ben as a thank-you for getting us the tickets."

"Good thinking!" David's grin broadened.

"Sure. Hey, did Diego mention anything about the game when he came in tonight?" She gave herself a mental pat on the back for her smooth move trying to get some intel on Diego without making it obvious.

David's chin-length sandy blond hair brushed his jaw when he shook his head. "Dude was in and out of here like a flash. Said he had something going on at his place."

Interesting.

Bueno, more like, disappointing.

She hadn't spoken to Diego since the Cubby Bear. For a crazy moment, in the midst of the celebratory atmosphere, between the talk about her parents and him opening up about his mom, she'd thought they might have maneuvered over a speed bump.

Knowing he missed his *mami* as much as she missed hers. Finding out how Papi's music had tied them together, without them even knowing each other. Silly, maybe, but she'd found herself drawn to Diego in a way she'd never been drawn to anyone before.

Then he'd gotten that call from his sister and his whole demeanor changed. The stoic mask had descended on his face and he'd hurried off. Well, after making that cryptic comment about Lilí deserving better. Whatever that meant.

The guy was the epitome of "strong and silent" when he wanted to be. Talk about frustrating.

Diego hadn't answered her call Saturday evening. Nor had he bothered responding to her "just wanted to see how you were doing" message. She'd waited until Sunday afternoon, then called once more. This time she hung up when she got his voice mail.

Yesterday she'd sent a text. A simple: **Hope everything's okay with your sister.**

His response had been a curt: **Working on it.**

She hadn't been able to get him, and everything he'd shared, off her mind. It was driving her bonkers.

The advocate in her felt the need to offer professional assistance.

The friend wanted to offer an ear to listen or a shoulder for him to lean on.

The wannabe lover . . . ha, she had all kinds of ideas involving Diego, but that *chica* needed to rein it in.

All three voices merged into one loud cry for her to swing by his place on her way home. At this point, she just might be crazy enough to do it.

"Well, I should get going," she told David, then remembered something she'd meant to ask. "Oh, are we still on for the middle school healthy relationships, cyberbullying, and harassment class next month?"

"Yep. Kids are already signing up for it. But that doesn't mean you can't make yourself useful around here before then." He shot her a playful wink.

She grinned back. "Oh, you won't get rid of me that easily. Yaz is already trying to recruit me for her summer dance extravaganza."

"I knew I liked your sister!" David said on a laugh. "She's supposed to stop by later this week. I'll let her know she can count you as a yes."

"You two make it hard to say no." Lilí waved

good-naturedly and headed toward the main door. His belly laugh widened her grin as she stepped out into the humid night air.

To knock or not to knock, that was the question of the hour.

Lilí sat in her Corolla across the street from Diego's town house on West Haddon Avenue, debating which to do. Rosa would be proud to know her habit of pro-con list-making had rubbed off on Lilí. Sort of.

The flickering light behind the curtains in Diego's living room led her to believe the television was on. Seeing as how it was barely nine forty-five, he was probably awake.

Was it rude to drop by uninvited at this late hour?

Would he find that too presumptuous of her?

¡Ay Dios mío! She thunked herself on the forehead with the palm of her hand. What was the matter with her? She'd never been accused of overthinking things before. Why the hell start now?

Removing her keys from the ignition, Lilí stepped out of her car. She squared her shoulders, tugged the bottom of her "Girl Power" tank a little lower over her black exercise leggings, then started across the street.

Moments later, her fist hovered over Diego's front door, motionless. *Ay, knock already*, she chided herself.

Several Mississippi-length seconds later, she heard the bolt slide on the other side.

Diego opened the door, holding on to it with his right hand while leaning his left forearm on the door frame. Not exactly a "come on in" stance, seeing as how his muscular body, looking all casually sexy in a

Chicago PD T-shirt and navy basketball shorts, blocked her entry.

"Uh, hi, what's up?" he asked. Subtext of his frowny-faced expression: Surprised to see you here.

"Not much." She toed his welcome mat with her sneaker. "What about you? How're you doing?"

"I'm good." He bobbed his head as if to emphasize his point, but the death grip he held on the door, and the tension evident in his hunched shoulders, told her differently.

"Your text yesterday was a little cryptic."

Lilí gave herself a mental thunk on the forehead as soon as the words left her mouth. *Dios mío,* she sounded like a whiny girlfriend. Neither of which described her. She did not do whiny, and allowing a guy to get to second base didn't make her his girlfriend either.

"There's been a lot going on, you know?" Diego said.

"No, not really."

An uncomfortable expression crossed his face and he tossed a quick glance over his left shoulder. Like he couldn't wait to be done with their conversation so he could get back to whatever he'd been watching on the television.

Annoyed by the strange awkwardness between them, hating that she felt foolish for dropping by in the first place, Lilí made herself meet his gaze. "Look, you don't owe me an explanation. I guess I thought we were . . . I don't know, friends, maybe? And that you might need someone to tal—"

"Who is it, Diego?"

The female voice coming from inside his town

house stalled Lilí's next words. Seemed like he already had someone to talk to.

An embarrassed flush crept up Lilí's neck, burning as it climbed into her cheeks. Mortified, she backed away. "I'm sorry. I'm interrupting."

"No, it's not what you think."

Footsteps padded across the hardwood floor in his house, signaling someone else's approach. Diego glanced over his shoulder again, then dropped his forehead to rest on the arm propped against the door frame.

Lilí held her breath, part of her wanting to see the kind of woman Diego would give her the brush-off for. Part of her screaming at her to get the hell out of there and save face.

Before she could decide, Diego swung his arm back to make room for a curvy, buxom woman wearing a skintight, low-cut blouse and cut-off shorts. The woman's brown hair was a mass of tousled curls, leaving Lilí to believe she'd interrupted something more than TV watching.

The stranger glanced from Diego to Lilí, then back again, her gaze assessing.

"So, is this the chaperone?" she asked Diego.

Lilí frowned, not following.

Diego stared at Lilí, the gold flecks in his eyes intensifying with something that looked a lot like regret. He nodded at the strange question.

"¡Ay, que buena suerte!" The woman's strange squeal over whatever good luck she claimed to have startled Lilí.

Diego actually winced.

Elbowing past him, the woman stuck out her hand

toward Lilí. "*Hola*, I'm Lourdes, Diego's sister. And you are?"

Lilí blinked. Manners, ingrained from years of Catholic school, had her instinctively accepting the handshake.

"I'm . . . the chaperone, apparently?" She drew out the words, shock over finding Lourdes here robbing her of the ability to form an intelligent response.

A cackle of laughter pulled Lourdes's mouth in a wide grin.

"I like her." Lourdes elbowed Diego in the ribs again.

Now that his sister had moved into the entryway light, Lilí caught the resemblance to the younger girl in the family picture on Diego's living room wall. The years between hadn't been easy on her. The toll of her hard life was evident in the lines of fatigue creasing her face and the dark shadows looming under her eyes. The purplish bruise her makeup didn't quite hide on her left cheek worried Lilí. On multiple levels.

Diego hadn't been kidding. He did have a lot going on if his prodigal sister was in his home.

"Did you come over for pizza?" Lourdes asked.

"Uh, no, Lilí just stopped by for a minute. Right?" Diego's wide-eyed, *please go with me on this* expression was almost Three Stooges comical. Funny how the tables had turned. Last week she'd been desperate to get him away from her sister. Now he couldn't do the same fast enough.

"Are you sure?" Lourdes asked.

Once again, Diego jumped in before Lilí could respond. "Yeah, we're sure."

Lourdes's smirk told Lilí the woman knew what her brother was up to. Namely, keeping the two of them apart. "Pity. It was about to get interesting. Maybe next time . . . Lilí, was it?"

"Yeah." Lilí returned Lourdes's friendly smile with a tentative one of her own.

Maybe Diego's sister seemed a little rough around the edges, but her eyes were steady and clear. Her coloring, despite the ugly bruise, was healthy. She appeared worn and tired, but not bitter. Her laughter was quick, yet not hysterically so. Those were all positive signs.

For Diego's sake, Lilí was relieved by what she saw.

For Lourdes's sake, Lilí hoped the woman might finally be on a healthy track.

"It was nice meeting you," Lilí called out as Lourdes turned to head back toward the living room. "Hope to see you again."

"Oh, I'm sure you will," Lourdes answered, shooting her younger brother a saucy wink.

Ignoring his sister, Diego stepped out into the hallway and pulled the door shut behind him. "Look, I'd invite you in, but things with Lourdes are kind of touch and go. She's staying with a friend over in Englewood and this is the first time she's been over in ages."

"Hey, like I said, you don't owe me any explanation." Lilí held her hands up, palms facing Diego. More a reminder for herself of the wall she should be keeping between them. "My mistake for coming over unannounced. Won't happen again."

She edged away, embarrassed that she'd barged into a family dinner he obviously didn't want her to be a part of. And why would he?

"Wait! Please."

If not for the soft entreaty she would have kept

on going. But the sincerity in his voice, the earnest expression on his face rooted her to the spot.

"I just . . ." Diego edged closer, invading her personal space.

Lilí told herself to step away, but what she really wanted was to close the distance between them.

"Thanks for checking up on me," he said. "No one's done that in a long time."

Feeling painfully self-conscious, while at the same time battling the crazy desire to wrap her arms around him in a comforting hug, Lilí went with what she did best in uncomfortable situations. She made a joke.

"Yeah, well, David said you had something going on at your house. I figured he meant a party and my invite must have gotten lost in the mail so . . ."

A corner of Diego's delicious mouth curved. Tired lines fought with laugh lines at the edge of his eyes. "No party here. Just working on figuring some things out."

"I might be of some assistance, you know."

He shook his head, the refusal to acknowledge her capabilities an unwitting jab at her professional skills. "I don't want you getting involved with this."

"How many times do I have to say, it's my job to get involved in situations exactly like this." Arms crossed, Lilí dared him to refute her.

There went that head shake again. This time his lips pressed in a thin line of disapproval before he said, "Maybe somebody else's. Not mine."

His words were a punch to the solar plexus. And she, like a newbie on the first day of self-defense class, hadn't had the presence of mind to shield herself from the blow. No, *idiota* that she was, she'd come over here asking for it.

Disappointment flooded her system. Her eyes burned with the prick of tears.

"*Ay por favor*, don't take it like that." Diego reached out to her, but Lilí stumbled back. Her shoulder slammed into the wall behind her and she sucked in a sharp breath.

His rejection hurt. Way more than it should.

It was crazy. Silly, really. They hadn't known each other all that long. But the conversations they'd shared about their families, the things he'd said about her making a difference at work, the idea that he saw something in her that even her closest relatives couldn't . . . She must have read more into all of it.

Once again, she'd leapt without thinking. And if he touched her now, the tears threatening would fall. She refused to let that happen in front of him.

As if he sensed her withdrawal, Diego dropped his hand to his side. A pained, uncomfortable expression pinched his handsome face, stretching the scar above his left brow. "I have to handle things my way."

"Of course, I get it." She did. Finally. As much as he claimed otherwise, he didn't believe in her. Or respect her professionally.

She took another step to the side, suddenly desperate to get away from him.

"Lilí—"

"No, it's all good." She nodded up and down like one of those silly bobblehead dolls. Trying to convince herself as much as him. "I really hope things work out for Lourdes, and you. I'll see you around."

Her heart heavy, Lilí turned toward the building's front door.

Diego didn't say another word. He simply let her leave.

It wasn't easy, but Lilí held her head high as she

walked back to her car. They'd run into each other again, that was inevitable. When that happened, she'd be cool and professional.

No matter how hard she had to bite her tongue to keep the wannabe lover inside of her, the part that yearned for him to open up to her, from saying something completely inappropriate.

Priceless.

That's the best description Diego could come up with for the stunned look on Lilí's face when she walked into her family's living room Friday evening to find him sitting on the couch, shooting the breeze with her brothers-in-law.

Her expressive eyes widened. Her jaw dropped open. Head tilted in question, her long braid hung at her side as she jammed her hands in the back pockets of her ripped jeans.

"What the hell are you doing here?" she groused, hip cocked at a peeved angle.

"*Oye*, language." Yazmine's husband, Tomás, pointed at Susana Marta and Rey, ages four and three if Diego remembered correctly. The two kids were busy playing with a pile of large-sized Lego blocks on the floral area rug.

Rey was Yaz and Tomás's youngest. Back in the kitchen, their eleven-year-old daughter Maria had been recruited for duty earlier. Susana Marta belonged to Rosa and Jeremy, along with baby Nico, who napped in a cradle nearby.

Lilí eyed the kids with a grumbled *humph*.

"Fine then," she drawled, belligerence dripping from her words. "How is it, dear Diego, that you happened to be in our humble abode, all the way out here in Oakton, nearly an hour away from yours?"

"Smart aleck," Jeremy murmured, though Rosa's husband wisely kept his eyes on the Cubs baseball game on the TV rather than engage a moody Lilí.

Her less than gracious greeting clued Diego in to the fact that he was a surprise guest. Which was actually a surprise to him, too. He'd figured Yazmine had run the idea by Lilí before inviting him earlier today.

"Hey! Lilí's home!" Yaz breezed into the living room carrying beer bottles for him and the other two guys.

"Um, yes, I am." Lilí frowned at Diego before turning the same frown on her sister. "And so is . . ."

"Diego. Here you go." Yaz handed out the drinks, then tossed her curtain of black hair over her shoulder once her hands were empty. "We had a meeting about the dance extravaganza at the center this afternoon. Diego was at loose ends, so I asked him to join us."

"And, Diego, you felt inclined to accept because . . ."

"Because he's a nice guy," Yaz interjected before he could answer. "What gives?"

Lilí stared at him, her gaze so intent he figured she was trying to send him some telepathic message. More than likely it wasn't a very nice one, based on the churlish slant to her lips.

"I could use a little assistance in here," Rosa called from the kitchen. "These *tostones* aren't going to fry themselves!"

"Come on." Yaz waved for Lilí to follow her toward the connected dining room that led to the kitchen. "Rosa's hostess-with-the-mostest routine is in high gear tonight."

"Let it be known that you said that, not me." Jeremy raised his bottle at Yaz for emphasis.

Diego grinned, recognizing a man who knew when to not get on his significant other's bad side.

"Wise guy." Yaz batted at the back of Jeremy's head as she passed behind the dark brown sofa where he and Diego sat. "Anyway, when I told Rosa that Diego was joining us, she broke out her stash of *alcapurrias* from the deep freezer. Let's go help."

Diego licked his lips in anticipation of the meat-filled *yautía* and green plantain fritters his *mamá* used to make.

Lilí didn't budge. Instead, she continued her faulty telepathic messaging at him. Hands fisted on her slender hips, gold strappy sandal tapping her annoyance on the hardwood floor, she dared him to say something.

The way they'd left things on Tuesday, he knew he owed her an explanation for being here. At some point he'd have to justify why he'd accepted Yaz's invite. Without revealing that he hadn't been able to get Lilí out of his head and had jumped at the offer.

When Yaz realized her sister hadn't moved, she pivoted, coming back to hook an arm through Lilí's. "Stop already. Whatever's eating at you from work, let it go for now."

Ha! Diego knew it wasn't work bugging Lilí.

"Fiiiine," she groaned as she was dragged away. "But this?" Lilí waggled a finger back and forth between the two of them. "This discussion isn't over. *¿Me oyes?*"

Yeah, he heard her all right. So did everyone else in the living room.

Four pairs of eyes stared at him. The kids' with

youthful *uh-oh* expressions that said someone was in trouble. The two men with commiseration.

Once the sisters had cleared out, Diego leaned back against the sofa with a relieved sigh. He glanced between Tomás, a tan, dark-haired Latino who was a VP at a well-known advertising firm, and Jeremy, a blond and blue-eyed computer whiz from the prominent Taylor family in Chicago. Despite their different backgrounds and social circles, in the half hour or so Diego had been in their company, he felt a growing kinship with both.

"Man, I don't know what you did to *piss her off*"— Tomás lowered his voice on the last three words, in deference to the kids—"but good luck with that." He scrunched his face in sympathy and settled deeper into the ottoman angled to the right of the sofa.

Jeremy laughed, leaning over to clink his drink with Tomás in solidarity.

"Lilí's good-hearted, but feisty," Jeremy warned.

"Tell me about it," Diego said. "I've seen both sides and more."

And he was crazy about them all. Sipping his beer, he considered how—*carajo*, probably more like if—he'd be able to smooth things over with her. It wouldn't be easy.

Lowering his bottle he caught the big-brother stares the other two men aimed his way with laser-sharp precision.

Uh-oh.

"Here's the thing." Jeremy splayed his left hand on Diego's knee. More a warning than a friendly gesture. "Lilí might not want anyone to know it, but underneath that determined, don't-mess-with-me-or-anyone-in-my-care façade, lies a soft heart. She's a great kid."

"Who's not really a kid," Diego qualified.

One thing *he* knew for certain was that Lilí wanted her family to take her more seriously. By grouping her in with their children, her sisters and their husbands were doing her a disservice.

"She's a vibrant woman who makes an incredibly positive difference in the lives of a lot of people in my neighborhood. They're lucky to have her in their corner."

Tomás's dark eyes assessed Diego for several seconds before he tilted his head in acknowledgment. "I have to agree."

Jeremy released his grip on Diego's knee, but gave him a measured look that said he wasn't off the hook yet.

Diego got that in the stratospheric social circle Jeremy had grown up in, rubbing elbows with everyone who was anyone in Chicago and beyond, he probably dealt with many who weren't what they appeared to be on the surface. The same could be said for Diego's line of work.

Jeremy might be a tougher nut to crack than Tomás, if Diego felt like cracking any. But he was more interested in what Lilí thought. How she felt. And whether or not there was a way for them to have . . . something.

"Papi, can I habs some *florecitas, por favor*? I is hungy." Rey climbed up onto his father's lap, a tower of red Lego blocks in his hands.

"I know you're hungry, *papito*, but no cookies right now." Tomás ruffled his little boy's black hair. "I'm sure Mami and your *tías* have dinner almost ready."

Rey's question brought Susana Marta over to clamber onto the couch between Jeremy and Diego. She was a welcome distraction from Jeremy's appraising stare as he hunched over to ooh and aah at the sculpture she'd made from the pile of blocks.

The warm father-child ties, dropped into the setting of the living room where Lilí had grown up, provided Diego with another welcome peek into the life of the woman who'd stormed into his.

He could easily picture a younger Lilí running through the house with her usual exuberance, probably banging on the bongo drums positioned on opposite sides of the cherry-stained entertainment center, stomping up the stairs leading to the second floor when she was in a grumpy mood, announcing dinner was ready in a booming—

"Dinner's ready!" Maria called from the archway connecting the dining and living rooms.

"¡Sí!" Susana Marta and Rey clapped with excitement.

Tomás shushed them softly, pointing to baby Nico sleeping in his cradle, tucked in a corner near the large table.

The three Fernandez sisters trooped out of the kitchen, arms laden with various dishes. Diego's mouth watered at the delicious smells of *pernil, alcapurrias, tostones,* and *arroz con gandules.* He hadn't enjoyed a home-cooked meal like this in ages. Sure, he'd eaten the roast pork, fritters, fried plantains, and pigeon pea rice at area restaurants, but it wasn't the same as a home-cooked meal.

A wave of nostalgia for his *mamá*'s cooking washed over him as he followed the group to the table.

The little ones were lifted up into booster chairs and Tomás and Jeremy flanked both ends. Not wanting to intrude if the others had regular spots as well, Diego waited for the sisters and Maria to take their seats.

Maria gave him a shy smile, motioning for him to sit between her and Lilí.

Lilí grabbed her niece's elbow and dragged the girl to stand beside her. That left Diego to take the empty spot on the other side of the young girl, at Jeremy's right.

Okay, obviously Lilí continued to hold a grudge. He'd let her stew while he enjoyed the treat her family's meal and company provided.

"Diego, thank you for joining us." Rosa offered him a soft smile, her round face friendly.

"I appreciate the invite."

"Humph," Lilí grumbled.

Rosa shot her younger sister a warning look.

Funny, Diego had seen that similar I-mean-business expression on Lilí's face when she'd been trying to get past him to reach Melba that first night.

The resemblance between the three sisters was obvious—same wide mouth, straight nose, shape of the eyes and coloring. But he found the differences interesting. Rosa quiet and studious. Yazminé tall and slender. Lilí, the shortest of the three, yet the one that snagged his attention with her sassy attitude, high ponytails and braids, athletic build and quick smile. Or her quick snarl, depending on her mood.

He'd take either from her at the moment. They sure as hell beat her silence over the last few days.

Leaning forward slightly, Diego peered around Maria. He caught Lilí's gaze and winked.

She narrowed her eyes, but bad poker player that she must be, she couldn't hide the upward tilt at the corner of her mouth.

The hint of her smile lightened the weight of guilt he'd been carrying around since he'd rushed her out

of his place like a bouncer at closing time. It'd been
for her own good. He didn't want her getting involved
with the problems Lourdes often created. Still, he'd
known Lilí was upset by his bum's rush routine.

"Maria, would you like to say grace for us?" Yazmine
asked.

Diego joined hands with Maria and Jeremy. Head
bowed, with Maria's youthful voice reciting the prayer
Diego's *mamá* had taught him at a young age, he
closed his eyes and savored the moment.

Family time.

Togetherness.

Tradition.

This is what he missed. This is what he wanted for
him and Lourdes. What he feared they might never
have again.

This is what he'd felt for the first time in a long
while when he and Lilí had talked about their families
after the game the other day. Before Lourdes had
called and he'd started keeping watch on the comings and goings at Patricia's house when he wasn't
working.

"Amen," Maria finished.

A chorus of amens answered.

Soon plates were filled. Chatter turned to pre-
school and middle school starting in the fall. Jeremy
mentioned the Cubs' current win-loss record, which
brought up the subject of the sisters' cousin Julia.
Apparently she was traveling with her boyfriend,
Ben, the former professional ballplayer who was
coaching at a youth baseball clinic out of state. Rosa
asked Diego about their field trip to the game last
Saturday, but Lilí jumped in with a noncommittal

reply and quickly tossed the conversational ball to Maria by asking about the young girl's summer camp.

He got the hint. Obviously Lilí wasn't keen on discussing anything involving her and Diego.

The family chatter continued throughout the meal. Jokes were shared. A little gentle teasing ensued when Tomás mentioned Yaz had tried convincing him to be her demo partner for the center's parent-daughter dance. Diego learned that's how the couple had first met, when Maria enrolled in Yaz's dance class.

At one point, Diego caught Lilí making silly faces to distract little Rey from getting antsy when he grew tired of sitting in his booster seat.

Diego laughed at the little boy's attempt to copy his *tía*. She'd grinned at Diego, then seemed to catch herself and turned her attention back to her nephew. She didn't look Diego's way again until everyone had finished eating and Rosa mentioned serving her flan for dessert.

"No, don't get up," Lilí told her sister, holding a hand out to stall Rosa from pushing her seat back. "Diego and I can get it. Right, Diego?"

The stiff smile she flashed told him she wanted more than an extra pair of hands in the kitchen.

Time for him to face the music.

"Good luck," Jeremy murmured for Diego's ears alone.

He took that as a good sign, seeing as how Jeremy had seemed to reserve his judgment earlier. That the guy cared enough about Lilí to watch over her made Jeremy okay in Diego's eyes.

Two steps into the kitchen, she rounded on him, fists balled at her sides. Her dark pink tank left her toned arms bare, but he had little time to admire her figure as she jumped into her interrogation with full steam.

"What are you doing here?" she snapped.

Loaded question.

He went with the obvious. "Eating dinner with your family?"

"Because it's okay for you to break bread with mine, but not for me to join you and your sister, huh?"

Direct hit.

It was the reason why he'd felt that stab of guilt earlier when he'd realized she had no idea Yaz had invited him. At the youth center he had wondered if he should say no, maintain the distance they'd kept the past few days. But his desire to see Lilí again had been too strong to resist.

"Your family's not the same as mine. There's no potential danger here," he tried to explain.

"Please." Lilí spun around on the muttered word, moving farther into the kitchen. "Don't feed me that line."

Diego followed, his cop instincts noting a small square table and four wooden chairs off to the right, along with an opening to the downstairs hallway leading to the front door.

"It's not a line," he insisted. "You have enough to contend with at work. Why would you want to get involved with whatever mess my sister might cook up?"

Lilí strode past the sink and oven on the left side of the room, stopping in front of the fridge. She reached for the handle, turning to give him one of her classic "duh!" glares over her shoulder.

"Maybe because I deal with situations like this every day and sometimes on weekends."

"Which is why you don't need to deal with my crap on top of that." Not to mention, someone he cared about had already gotten caught in the crosshairs of Lourdes's bad decisions. He didn't want that to happen again.

He stepped closer. Fighting this desperate need to take her in his arms, bury his face in the warmth of her neck, and breathe in her sweet citrusy scent. Instead, he reminded himself to be satisfied he was even here.

"Look, I don't want to fight," he said softly.

"Well, I might want to fight with you," she grumbled.

The grumpy tone in her voice softened the edges of her earlier annoyance. He could hear the smile she fought and he sought to coax it out of her.

"How about if we arm wrestle?" he countered playfully. "If I win, you cut me some slack. Let us enjoy tonight."

"And if I win? What do I get?"

He nearly laughed at her foolhardy question. Nearly, because he caught the flash of competitive spirit in her beautiful eyes. But he outweighed and outmuscled her by a considerable amount; no way she'd beat him. Certainly she didn't think he was serious . . .

"What? You think I can't take you?" Lilí released the fridge handle, spinning to lean back against the door. She gazed up at him, chin tilted at a confident angle. "I tell all my self-defense students, if the right opening presents itself, determination and focus can beat brute force."

All playfulness inside him vanished at her words.

Diego took another step toward her, until less than a foot separated them.

"I'd never use brute force with you. With any woman. You know that, right?"

She placed her palm on his chest, preventing him from moving closer. Her touch burned through his polo shirt, scorching him with the need for more of her.

"Yes, I do. But that doesn't mean you can't hurt me in other ways."

Her honesty gutted him.

"The absolute last thing I ever want to do is hurt you. The other night I did, and for that I'm sorry. It wasn't my intent." He covered her hand with his, willing her to believe him. To believe *in* him. "I missed you this week," he admitted. "And I thought, I guess I'm hoping, maybe we could—"

"Um, Tía Lilí?"

Maria's voice had Diego jumping back to put a respectable distance between himself and the child's appealing aunt.

"My mom said to hold up on dessert. We're gonna show Papi and everyone else the dance I'm co-teaching for the extravaganza. We're, um, kinda hoping Diego wouldn't mind, maybe, playing for us on Abuelo's guitar."

Diego did a double take. He hadn't planned on being asked to play for Lilí's family. The last time he'd given her a private concert . . . *pues*, the results had not been exactly family friendly.

His blood heated at the memory of their heavy make-out session in his living room. Uh, yeah, definitely not kid friendly.

He met Lilí's gaze. The green in her eyes darkened, exactly as it had in the seconds before she'd yanked off her shirt, then tossed it through the air. She had to be remembering that evening. If he was lucky, she wanted to relive it as much as he did.

Footsteps sounded in the hallway as her sisters and the others headed to the basement.

"Okay, we'll be right down," Lilí answered, her voice huskier than usual.

"Cool!" Maria raced from the room.

"I guess it's showtime for you, huh?" Lilí said once they were alone again. "It's not very often we let someone play my *papi*'s guitar."

A new weight of responsibility suddenly pressed down on Diego.

Picking up Reynaldo's guitar to serenade his family would be an honor. Based on what Lilí had shared, he figured listening to someone bring their father's music to life again, especially in their home, would be an emotional, hopefully uplifting experience for the sisters. He wanted to give them that.

Hell, there were countless things he wanted when it came to Lilí. He simply wasn't sure if he deserved them.

Chapter Thirteen

"He's really good," Rosa murmured.

Lilí nodded at her sister's assessment of Diego's mad guitar skills. Though "really good" didn't even begin to describe his mastery.

Once again she was entranced by the way he became one with the guitar, the emotion flowing from his soul through his fingers to the strings. Eyes closed as he gave himself up to the music.

Ay, ay, ay. She could watch this man play all day. And night.

Which was why she'd distanced herself from where he sat on the piano stool across the basement.

She and Rosa stood near the bottom of the stairs while the rest of the family was scattered throughout the finished room. Tomás and Yaz danced in the middle of the pale gray laminate floor, their bodies swaying to the Spanish ballad Diego strummed. Little Rey held on to Maria's hands, shaking his hips as he and his sister danced alongside their parents. Jeremy sat in the recliner in Rosa's reading section in the back corner. Susana Marta snuggled on his lap, holding her favorite baby doll.

Rosa had actually missed the start of Diego's "show" because she'd been upstairs breastfeeding Nico. The little bugger now gurgled contentedly in her arms, his pudgy cheeks even fatter with his grin.

What had begun as Diego simply accompanying Maria and Yazmine while they performed their number had morphed into him being asked to play one song, then another, and another.

"We haven't had someone play live for us since—" Rosa broke off, the pain of losing Papi crossing her features.

"I know. It's hard. I miss him *and* his music."

Needing a distraction from the sorrow, Lilí poked a finger at Nico's chin. She was rewarded for her googley-eyed expression with a giggle from her precious nephew.

"*Bueno*, with someone like Diego around, you wouldn't have to miss the music."

"*Por favor*, not you, too." Lilí rolled her eyes at her sister.

She had a hard enough time on her own remembering why it wasn't a good idea to get mixed up with Diego. If her sisters started egging her on to "go for it," she might wind up getting hurt.

"I'm just saying . . ." Rosa gave her the same raised brow look she had since they were kids. The one that said: *You should listen to me; I know what I'm talking about.*

"He's a cop. Who doesn't understand what I do," Lilí stressed. Though there'd been times his words and actions indicated otherwise.

"Yet, he's helped with your class and the incident that resulted in your visit to the police station. Sounds to me like you're both committed to helping protect people," Rosa countered. "That says a lot, if you ask me."

"We're too different. It wouldn't work out."

"That's what I used to tell myself about Jeremy. And look where we are now." Rosa playfully tugged on the end of Lilí's braid. "Despite you deciding to grow out your hair once you started working, I keep thinking of you as the girl with that sassy pixie haircut who used to drive me crazy, but also made me laugh. I know that's not always fair to you, and for that I'm sorry. *Pero*, you'll always be my baby sister. I want you to be happy and loved, like you deserve."

"I am loved, by this precious guy." Lilí held out her arms for her nephew, who dove toward her with gusto. She laughed, squeezing him to her in a big bear hug.

When she opened her eyes, she caught Diego watching her. His gaze intent, unreadable. Hypnotic. Drawn by him, by his music, Lilí shuffled her feet to the rhythm, moving to join Yaz and her family on the basement's makeshift dance floor. Baby Nico nuzzled into the curve of her neck and shoulder, his baby scent teasing her with the thought of what-ifs.

Ay, they'd held countless "dances" down here over the years. Sometimes Papi played on his own. Sometimes Los Paisanos practiced while their families ate, drank, and mingled. But other than during Papi's wake and the few times they'd put on a Los Paisanos CD to commemorate his passing, the basement had been silent of his music.

Until now. Until Diego.

As Lilí swayed with her nephew, Diego's song wrapped around her, weaving its way into her heart. She thought about his words earlier.

I don't want to hurt you. I missed you.

Her gaze connected with his again. Held.

Tonight Diego had easily fit right in. Finding common ground with her brothers-in-law. Attentively listening to Maria's tales of the goings-on at school and dance class. Not seeming to mind the noise and mess that came with having rambunctious little ones at the dinner table. Impressing her sisters when they asked about his volunteer work at the center.

And now, gifting them all with something they'd been missing without Papi here.

Lilí wanted to be mad at Diego for pushing her away the other day. But her anger had dissipated in the face of his heartfelt apology.

Standing here in the basement, surrounded by her family's love, with Diego's music filling her soul, she finally admitted a truth she'd been avoiding all evening.

When she left here tonight, there was no way she planned on going home alone.

"Are you sure?" Diego asked for the third time since she'd propositioned him in her family's driveway after saying good-bye to everyone else inside.

Exasperated, Lilí leaned her forearm on his open driver's-side window.

Diego sat in his idling car, hands gripping the steering wheel, across the street from her building. Thankfully they'd lucked into two open spots near each other.

"Yes, I'm sure," she answered. "Unless you're getting cold feet. It's only a drink, but, whatever."

She started to step away, but Diego grasped her forearm to stop her. Lilí bent down again to peer at him.

"With you and me, a drink might not be enough," he said, his voice a deep rasp.

In the dappled streetlight streaming through the branches and leaves of a nearby tree, Lilí saw the glimmer in Diego's dark eyes. The promise of what lay ahead if he went upstairs with her.

It was a promise she intended him to keep.

"I know," she answered, looking squarely at him, so there was no doubt in her meaning. "That's kinda what I'm hoping for."

She backed away, leaving him to make his decision.

Diego rolled up his window and exited the car. Staring intently back at her, he pocketed his keys, then held out his hand.

Their fingers linked, palms pressed together. Diego slowly raised their joined hands to press a soft kiss along the back of hers. Need shot through Lilí like a starter pistol, galvanizing her steps as she pulled him toward her front door.

Inside the building she waved hello to Stan, working the security desk. She politely asked about his wife and kids, but didn't stop to chitchat like normal. Tonight she had other things on her mind.

At the elevator bank she and Diego stood in silence, her right leg jittering with anticipation as they waited. Once inside the elevator, she pressed the button for her floor, then stayed by the panel, their linked hands stretching their arms to span the distance she'd left between them.

"*¿Estás bien?*" Diego asked, his dark brows angling down at his question.

"Yeah, I'm fine. Just staying over here to avoid giving the extra pair of eyes a show." She pointed to the dark orb-like security camera in a corner of the ceiling. If she got too close to him, she might jump his sexy body right here. Regardless of who could be watching.

He answered by brushing his thumb along the

center of her palm. Tingles of awareness shimmied up her arm.

Back and forth. Back and forth. The motion teased her, had her body craving more of his touch.

She forced herself to focus on the elevator lights blinking their ascension. All the while cursing the contraption for not moving faster. Blessedly they finally reached her floor and the doors opened with a muted *swish*.

They hurried down the carpeted hall, Lilí releasing her grip to dig her keys out of her messenger bag. Hands shaky with pent-up anticipation, she missed the dead bolt keyhole on the first try. Fumbling to get both locks undone.

She pushed the door open and stepped inside, only to hear Diego behind her asking again, "Are you positive?"

"*Ay por favor,*" she said on a groan.

When she spun around to face him, he stood on the edge of the threshold, as if hesitant to enter.

"Why do you keep asking me that?" Lilí dropped her keys into her bag, the jangling mimicking her rattled nerves.

Diego shoved his hands in his back jeans pockets. An uncomfortable, embarrassed look marched across the hard planes of his handsome face. "Because you're a good person. With good intentions. Usually for a lot of other people instead of for yourself. And I don't, uh, I don't want to hurt you. I—" He stopped, cleared his throat. "I care about you. Is that so bad?"

Warmth spread through her chest at the same time other parts of her throbbed with excitement. *Dios mío,* she needed to get this man inside her apartment. Right. Now.

Because he seemed to be a man of action rather than words, Lilí grabbed a handful of Diego's navy polo shirt and tugged him into her condo.

She was in his arms, his lips on hers before he could even kick the door closed. It clicked shut behind them and Diego broke their kiss long enough to flip the dead bolt and slide the security chain in place. He turned back to her, a sexy grin pulling at his lips. Crinkling the edges of his dark eyes.

His shirt was still clenched in her fist and she released it, spreading her open palm on his chest. His heart beat strong, steady. Fast.

Diego palmed her hips, pulling her closer as he stared down at her. The gold flecks in his eyes burned bright, fueling the desire threatening to boil over inside her.

"I'm guessing that's a no. Caring about you's not so bad?" he said.

"Good guess."

She meant to give his chest a playful pat, but it turned into more of a caress, which became an exploration of his muscular pecs.

His pupils flared with desire. "So, what I really want to ask is, where's the bedroom? But I know . . ."

He bent closer, his warm lips pressing a toe-curling kiss to the bare skin on her shoulder near the edge of her tank top. She held her breath as he placed another on the curve of her neck. Another on the sensitive spot just behind her ear.

Her head lolled to the side, giving him better access. She felt the moist heat of his tongue along her skin, sending spirals of heat swirling to places that cried out for his attention.

"Or the gentleman in me knows"—soft kiss along

her jawline—"I should at least make a show of"—kiss on the corner of her mouth—"politely sharing a drink. But first I need—"

His lips covered hers, silencing her moan of pleasure.

She opened her mouth for him, her tongue brushing and twisting with his, savoring the pulse-pounding sensations he evoked within her. He tasted like the café con leche and flan they'd had for dessert. Sweet and oh so sinful.

His hands slid from her hips to her backside, kneading her glutes with his strong fingers. She pressed herself against him, the evidence of his reaction to her, the proof of what his body wanted from hers, heightening her arousal.

She wound her arms around his neck, her fingers brushing the cropped hair at his nape. All the while his deft hands continued their massage along her backside. Stoking her desire. Threatening to push her over the edge. He sucked her lower lip, then gently caressed it with his tongue before devouring her mouth with his once again.

Needing to touch him, feel him, she yanked his polo and undershirt out of his jeans waistband. She trailed her hands along his abs, over his smooth pecs, around the curve of his rib cage in a wanton study of his body. The muscles along his back rippled under her touch and she rolled her hips languidly against his.

Diego groaned. His hands cradling her butt, he held her against him, their hips moving to a rhythm they created together.

Más.

The word pounded in her head, just like when they'd been together at his place.

More. She needed more.

Desperate for a closer connection, Lilí grabbed the hem of his shirt with both hands and jerked it up.

Diego seemed to take her hint because he arched back so he could pull his polo and undershirt up and over his head, dropping them to the hardwood floor at their feet. Then he stood before her, the curves and dips of his muscular chest bare, hers to delight in.

Lilí sucked in a sharp breath, awed by the sight of him.

The timer on the living room lamp had clicked it on while she was out. Now the lamp's soft glow shone into the foyer, painting Diego's tanned skin in muted tones and shadows.

Lilí let her gaze wander over his six-pack abs, following the light trail of hair arrowing down to his waist. Despite the temptation to follow that trail farther, she found herself inexorably drawn by his tattoo. It was an artfully designed rosary in deep red and black that lay haphazardly strewn over his heart, its tail dangling down the center of his rib cage. The loop of beads encircled a name in script, Alma. A date from several years ago inked the space under his *mamá*'s name.

Lilí gently traced the loop of beads with her index finger, captivated by the proof of how much his mother had meant to him. His need to carry her close to his heart. The same way the memory of her parents remained in hers.

She glanced up at Diego to find him staring down at her.

Sorrow dimmed the desire that had flashed in his brown eyes moments before. She pressed her palm lightly over the loop of beads, as if doing so would soothe his pain. He brushed her bangs out of her eyes with the softest of touches.

"I got the tat the day after we buried her," he shared, his voice raw with emotion.

"It's beautiful."

"She would have told me not to mark myself. But she'd left an indelible mark on my life already. I had to honor her in some way. Had to atone for not being here when things got so bad with my sister."

Guilt.

Ay, she understood that emotion when it came to family responsibilities and loss.

After Mamí's death, Lili's guilt manifested as others worried about her when they had their own pain to deal with. She had coped by playing the role of silly prankster, quickly learning that the laughter her antics created eased her sisters' and Papi's sorrow. Lightened their burden. Her playful personality had made her a staple in the church nursery and kept her on neighborhood parents' speed-dial for babysitting services.

That had been the genesis of her idea to go into a field where she could use her people skills along with her desire to help others. Karen Fowler's assault in college years later solidified Lili's decision.

Although, despite having moved into adulthood and begun her professional career, her family still viewed her as the fun-loving girl always good for a laugh. The one who needed to take things more seriously.

But Diego saw her another way.

That realization both excited and rattled her. Had her falling back on humor to settle the nerves flapping faster than a hummingbird's wings in her chest.

"She'd have to give you props for maintaining the

same theme throughout all of your tattoos, right?" she asked, purposely keeping her tone light.

Diego's head tilted in question.

With her finger, Lilí outlined the crown-of-thorns tattoo circling his right biceps. Something she'd yearned to do from the moment she'd noticed the ink peeking out from under his shirtsleeve.

"Jesus's crown of thorns, Mary's rosary beads. It's hard to find fault with religious symbols, don't you think?" She glanced at him from under her lashes before ducking down to press a soft kiss to the crown of thorns.

He sucked in a quick breath. The ragged sound sparked her pulse, fueling her exploration.

Sí, now it was her turn to play.

Moving her attention from his arm to his chest, she pressed a tiny kiss on one bead. Then the next. And the next. She followed the loop with feather-soft kisses, eventually reaching the rosary's tail. Bending her knees, she slowly lowered herself to continue her fun.

"Lilí." He uttered her name on a groan.

"Mmmm."

One kiss. A second kiss. A final kiss on the last of the three beads leading to the crucifix at the end of the chain.

Her hands dropped to his waistband. Her thumbs hovered over the button on his jeans as she knelt before him.

"Lilí, if we go any further, I may not be able to stop. Are you sure?"

The tension in his voice alerted her to how difficult it would be for him if they halted. But she knew he would if she said the word.

Diego claimed she was a good person. *Pues*, she'd say the same about him. Despite their varying perspectives when it came to dealing with his sister, everything else she knew about him confirmed it. In her heart, she trusted him.

Slowly rising from her crouch, she slid her body along his until the evidence of his arousal pressed against her lower belly, heightening her desire. Her soft curves molded to his powerful frame in delicious perfection. His warm, earthy scent filled her lungs as she sucked in a deep breath, then dove headfirst into the deep end.

"There are few things in my life I've ever been more certain of than what I want to do right here. Right now. With you." Grasping his shoulders, she lifted on her tiptoes and covered his mouth with hers.

Diego groaned with satisfaction as he deepened the kiss. He grabbed her hips, lifting her up so she could wrap her legs around his waist. His hands on her butt, he held her tightly, all the while making love to her with his mouth. His lips. His tongue. Then he was teasing her ear, licking its shell and blowing a hot breath that made her shoulders shiver with lust.

Desire, hot and heavy, pulsed through her, shooting straight to her core.

"Which way?" he grumbled as he took a few steps forward.

"Mmmm," she murmured, tilting her head so he could lick along her neck. His teeth grazed her sensitive skin and she moaned her pleasure.

"Which way to your bedroom, Lilí, or we're gonna end up on the couch."

The strain in his voice had her eyes fluttering open. She blinked, trying to clear her desire-addled brain.

Need sharpened Diego's features. The five o'clock shadow darkening his jaw added to his tough, bad-boy vibe that had her insides quaking with excitement. The muscles in his arms flexed as he tugged her tightly against him, leaving no doubt about his body's reaction to hers. Or his intent once they made it to her bed.

She cupped his cheek. Smoothed her thumb over his lower lip. *Dios mío*, he was absolutely beautiful. And right now, he was all hers.

"My room's on the left," she answered.

The gold flecks in his eyes flared, an answering desire flooding her system as he strode purposefully down the hall.

Diego stepped into his jeans and pulled them up just as he heard the water shut off in Lilí's adjoining master bathroom.

He pictured her stepping out onto the yellow mat she kept on the white tile floor in front of the walk-in shower. The same shower he and Lilí had figured out was big enough for two people if they got close enough. Much to his, and her, satisfaction.

His pulse picked up speed.

Man, if he'd thought a night in Lilí's bed might cool his desire for her . . . he'd been dead wrong.

Leaving her to finish washing up in the shower while he got dressed had been an effort in self-control. Their delectable bath-time fun made him itch to tug her back under the sheets. Tease another seductive smile or gut-clenching moan of pleasure from her.

The bathroom door opened and a wave of humid air seeped into the bedroom. Lilí emerged, her trim figure wrapped in a fluffy pink towel that hit her mid-thigh. Her tanned shoulders were dewy with moisture. Her long hair tousled and wet.

Diego nearly swallowed his tongue at the sight of her. His blood instantly flowed south and his fingers stalled in the act of buttoning his jeans.

She smiled at him, the corners of her eyes crinkling. The urge to sample her sweet lips once more hit him hard and fast. But then he caught a hint of uncertainty, something his feisty do-gooder rarely displayed, in the hazel-green depths seconds before she dropped her gaze.

That uncertainty kept his feet rooted to their spot. Had him reaching for his shirt where he'd dropped it near the black-stained wood nightstand after their late-night snack run to the kitchen.

It wasn't easy—c*arajo*, nothing involving how he felt about Lilí was easy—but he willed his libido to calm the hell down.

Twenty-four hours ago she'd been pissed at him for giving her the brush-off at his place earlier in the week. Despite their mind-blowing night together, or how badly he craved a repeat, he couldn't say he still wouldn't do his best to keep Lilí away from his sister.

Yeah, that was probably messed up, especially since he'd been invited over for the Fernandez family dinner. Had relished being included in the generational mix, even swapping stories about the sisters' father. The mini jam-session in their basement, watching Lilí cuddling with her baby nephew on the makeshift dance floor . . . everything about last night had shone a bright searchlight on a secret longing he wasn't quite ready to admit.

A longing for a connection. With her.

For that to happen, he needed to let her in. But his

family life was different from Lilí's. Until he knew for sure Lourdes had turned a corner, he'd be leery of Lilí getting caught up in his sister's drama.

"*¿Tienes hambre?*" she asked. "I can whip up some pancakes and eggs pretty fast."

Yeah, he was hungry all right. For more than the food she offered.

Lilí held the knot of her towel with one hand, just above the birthmark he'd discovered on the curve of her left breast. The same slightly darker spot he'd kissed in the shower moments ago.

The memory heated his blood.

"What time are you supposed to meet your neighbor?" she asked, pulling him out of his mind's delicious meanderings.

Another reason why he shouldn't be thinking about rumpling the sheets with her again.

They both had their own plans for the day. She, meeting with a group of ladies at the shelter. He, helping a buddy do some work on his car, followed by lunch with Lourdes. Then he and Stevens had the third watch at four PM.

"I've got a little over an hour," he said, noting the time on his cell before slipping it into his back jeans pocket. "Breakfast sounds good."

Any one-on-one time with her sounded good. It was only outside these walls, or with his messed-up family anyway, that he needed to figure things out.

Her smile widened. "Okay then. I'll be ready in a few."

She reached for a pump container of lotion on top of her dresser, part of the black-stained wood set that matched the nightstand and headboard. The dark color was a contrast to the bright spring accents in the area rug and the floral pattern of her comforter.

Altogether, the room was a perfect study in Lilí.

Chunky dark furniture that was strong and sturdy, like her resolve to make a difference for the women and children who depended on her. The bright colors in the throw pillows and the modern art piece above her bed, along with the picture frames holding family photographs scattered around the room, were flashes of her personality—the epitome of her quick smile and wit, positive outlook, and devotion to her loved ones.

The yin and yang that swirled together to create the amazing woman he hadn't been able to get off his mind.

Diego watched as she propped her left foot on the corner of her bed. The pink towel parted to give him a peek at the length of her toned thigh. His gut tightened at the tantalizing view.

When she started lathering her coconutty-lemon lotion on her tanned skin, leaning over her bent knee to skim her hands over her shapely calf, his self-control threatened to dissolve.

"Um, I'll go get the coffee started," he mumbled. Spinning on his barefoot heel, he made like a speed-demon and hightailed it out of her room.

"You only have to turn on the Keurig!" he heard her call.

But he wasn't stopping. Not with temptation crooking its wicked finger at him.

Halfway down the hall his phone vibrated in his back pocket. He pulled it out to catch a text message from Lourdes illuminated on the screen. His footsteps slowed as he read it.

Call me. We need to talk.

In the past, a cryptic message like this typically meant bad news. A problem. He didn't want that invading this private space with Lilí. Not yet anyway.

He hesitated, torn between responding or leaving well enough alone for now.

"Fried or scrambled?"

Lilí's question startled him. He spun to look back over his shoulder at her, quickly sliding his cell in his pocket. He'd get back to Lourdes when he left here.

"Um, either's fine," he answered. Guilt over ignoring his sister's message warred with this new desire to lose himself in Lilí and the good she represented.

"Scrambled it is then."

She shimmied past him in the hallway, looking all perky in a cream sundress with skinny straps, orange and yellow circles dotting the material. A thin tan belt cinched her waist, matching the tan sandals on her feet. Even her pink-tipped toenails gave off a positive vibe.

The satisfied grin on her full lips that dared him not to smile back and the wispy bangs framing the impish twinkle in her eyes were like the icing on top of the Lilí Fernandez cupcake he craved.

Needing a taste of her, he linked his fingers with hers, tugging her gently back toward him. She arched a brow in question, but willingly stepped into his arms.

"Is there something you wanted?" she said, a playful note in her voice.

Her smile broadened. For him. Because of him.

Releasing her fingers, he draped his arms around her lower back. Lilí leaned into him, her hands gently resting on his shoulders near the curve of his neck.

"I had a great time last night," he told her.

"Me too."

"Not only here, with you." Instinctively his arms

tightened, drawing her hips closer to his. He liked how comfortably she fit in his arms. How right it felt. "Though that was pretty amazing."

She grinned. "Yeah, I was pretty amazing, wasn't I?"

He chuckled. Man, he loved her cheekiness.

Love? His choice of word surprised him. Had he said it out loud, he would have laughed it off as an expression. Privately, he couldn't ignore the depth of emotion tightening his chest. An emotion that both scared and emboldened him.

"Pretty sure of yourself, aren't you?" he teased, backing her up against the wall. Desire flared in her eyes.

"Oh, I didn't hear you complaining, wise guy."

No, and she wouldn't.

Burying his face in the crook of her neck, he took a deep breath, her intoxicating scent filling his lungs. Her deft hands caressed his shoulders, sliding around to knead the muscles along his upper back. His blood heated, and that quickly there was no doubt as to where his body wanted this bit of foreplay to lead.

And yet, while he craved physical intimacy with her, there was so much more that drew him to Lilí than her body. As luscious as it was.

He pressed a wet kiss on the area below her ear, his arousal growing at the tiny shiver he felt her give. It'd be so easy to scoop her up and take her back to bed. She'd willingly go. He'd willingly join her.

Instead, Diego eased back. He pressed his forehead against hers, a little puff of her minty breath caressing his lips.

"You're right, no complaints from me," he admitted.

Her grin widened.

"But I also meant, dinner with your family. I really

enjoyed meeting everyone, sharing your father's music with them."

"Hearing Papi's music again." Her lids fluttered closed. Her chest rose and fell on a soft sigh before she met his gaze again, warmth brimming in her expression. "That was an unbelievable gift. You gave my family something we haven't had in a long time."

An embarrassed flush crept up his cheeks at her sincerity. "I, *bueno*, I felt the need to say thanks for letting me join you."

Lilí pushed his chest playfully. "That was Yazmine's doing, not mine."

"But I would have left if you had asked me to."

The playfulness drained from Lilí's face, replaced by a tenderness he hadn't seen before. She cupped his cheek, her palm soft, gentle. "I know. That respect, that soft side you have, is part of why we're here right now."

"Soft side?" He balked.

Her playful grin materialized again. "Oh, you might think you hide it, but I know it's in there."

She patted his chest, then rose up on her toes to brush her lips against his. "Come on, I'm getting hungry. One thing you should know, and my sisters have taken great joy in relaying this to my boyfr—to everyone: If I'm not fed regularly, I can get a mean, hangry attitude."

With a playful wink, she trounced down the hall, leaving him wondering about her slip of the tongue. Had she nearly said her "boyfriend"?

Actually, he liked the sound of that. A lot.

In the kitchen, Lilí tugged open the fridge, then pulled out a carton of eggs. Just as he opened his mouth to ask what she'd like him to do, the vibrating in his pocket picked up again. This time it continued, indicating an incoming call.

For a couple seconds he ignored it and allowed himself to enjoy watching Lilí going about her business. Carefree, humming some tune as she put together the ingredients for their breakfast. The first of what he'd like to be many, if he could get his personal life squared away.

The vibrating stopped. Then started up again.

A sliver of unease weaseled its way into what, until now, had been the perfect morning-after. He dug out his phone to see Lourdes's name flashing at him. Disappointment had him squeezing his cell in his a fist. A call this early from her rarely meant good news.

History told him this was not a conversation, more than likely an argument, he wanted to have while standing in Lilí's living room, the brightness of her chipper attitude rivaling the sunlight streaming in from the wall of windows along the right side of her condo.

"I've gotta . . . I should take this," he mumbled.

"Hmm?" She glanced up, her hand poised to crack an egg on a blue ceramic bowl. "Oh, sure, feel free. I've got this covered."

Sliding his thumb across the screen to connect the call, Diego strode toward the balcony's sliding glass doors. "*Hola, Lourdes, qué pasa?*"

"Hi, little brother. I'm good. Or . . . I will be."

The pause in her voice made the back of his neck prickle with unease. He recognized that conciliatory tone. Something was up.

Disappointment blew through him like a dog-days-of-summer heated breeze.

Sensing Lili's gaze on him, he reached for the

metal door handle, tilting his head toward the balcony to indicate his intent. She waved him on.

Outside, the cool morning air and far-off sound of traffic rumbling through the city streets greeted him. He slid the door closed behind him, leaving Lilí, and any thoughts of how he could make it work between them, inside her condo.

"*Me oíste?*" Lourdes asked.

"No, I didn't hear you. You were cutting out," he answered, when he realized his sister had kept talking.

"I said I have to take a rain check on lunch today."

His disappointment morphed into anger, pushing his tone to the edge of civil. "What's wrong?"

"Nothin'."

"You better be straight with me."

"I got some stuff to take care of," she whined, "that's all. *Cálmate.*"

Calm down? Right. When it came to her, remaining calm was impossible.

"What stuff?" he pressed.

"I'm not doin' anything wrong."

"I didn't say you were."

"*Pero lo estás pensando.* I know it," she accused him. "You're always thinking the worst."

Diego clamped his lips together, forcing himself to simmer down. This was not an argument he intended to have with Lourdes while Lilí was nearby, milling about her kitchen.

"Don't do this," he begged his sister. "Not now. Is something going on at Patricia's?"

"I got it under control."

"What's the problem? Are you using again?"

The accusation slipped out before he could stop

it. The question was guaranteed to make his sister blow—

"Enough with the twenty questions already!" she demanded. "Back off!"

Diego smacked his hand on the metal balcony railing in exasperation, the force reverberating up his arm.

Part of him wanted to say to hell with it. Wish his sister good luck and wipe his hands of the mess she inevitably created. But that's not how *familia* worked. His *mamá*'s voice rang in his head, reminding him that *familia* had your back. Stuck together through whatever crap life threw your way.

As a young soldier, he'd promised her he'd return home, college money practically in hand, ready to earn a degree and get a decent job to provide for their *familia*. He owed it to his mom to do that.

"Lourdes, no games here, okay? Are you in trouble?"

"No."

Despite her moody gruffness, relief loosened the tension seizing his chest.

"Not yet."

That quickly, anxiety snatched him back in its clutches.

"But I'm handling it," Lourdes assured him. Too bad he wasn't convinced. "I just gotta cancel lunch and take care of something. I'll be in touch."

"Wait!" Worry that she might go off the grid and he'd lose contact with her again had him crying out in fear.

A beat passed and he pulled the cell away so he could glance at the screen, make sure she hadn't already disconnected.

"What?" Her voice already sounded far away. He was losing her.

"*Déjame ayudarte*," he pleaded. When she didn't answer, he repeated his entreaty. "Please, let me help you."

"The fact that you want to, despite everything that's gone down before . . ." She spoke softly, making him strain to hear her words. "It means a lot to me, *hermanito.*"

"I'm not your little brother anymore, unable to get you the right resources. You know that."

"*Sí*, I do. Only, it's time I figured out things for myself. Like I said, I'll be in touch."

The call disconnected before he could respond.

Tightening his fist around his phone, he fought the ridiculous urge to fling the device over the balcony railing. Why did this keep happening with her?

Anger, frustration, and guilt for his ineptitude melded into a conglomeration of hostility so intense, it threatened to consume him. Clutching the railing like a lifeline, he hung his head, at a loss for what to do.

No telling how long he stayed there, his thoughts in turmoil, before the *swish* of the sliding glass door opening clued him in to Lilí's arrival. Head still bowed, he watched her tan sandals and pink-painted toes on the tile floor as she approached.

She placed a gentle hand on the middle of his back. A warm, comforting gesture he wanted to lean into, but the conflict between letting her in or keeping the ugliness away from her paralyzed him.

"You okay?" she asked softly.

He swallowed around the knot of emotion clogging his throat. "Just the normal up and down with my sister."

"Is she—"

"About to bug out." He shrugged, as if that happening was no big deal. As if the agony of failing with her once again wasn't a burning ache in his chest. "Looks like it, anyway."

"If there's anything I can do for you or her. For both of you . . . I can try," Lilí offered.

And risk her getting hurt as well? Put her in a position where she'd wind up being disappointed and frustrated, the same way he inevitably did when Lourdes was involved?

This wasn't Lilí's problem to deal with. It'd been his to shoulder alone for a while now.

No way was he going to sully her hands or put her in danger because of his family bullshit.

Her brothers-in-law would make him regret it.

Her sisters would skin him alive.

Worse, he'd never forgive himself.

Anxiety rising, Diego pushed off the railing. He spun away from her, pacing the length of the balcony. On the streets below cars honked, engines revved. Saturday morning city traffic picking up its pace. The hum and buzz of activity matched the disquiet buzzing in his head.

At the far end of the balcony he skirted the two wicker barrel chairs with their black and white cushions, the matching hourglass-shaped table nestled between them. A comfy spot to relax at the end of the day. Or the perfect place to start one.

He could easily picture Lilí sitting there, a mug of coffee cradled in her hands. Feet tucked underneath her as the sun peeked around the buildings to say hello. Hair tousled, mouth curved in her inviting grin, her eyes alight with mischief. The same way she'd greeted him when he woke up beside her this morning.

"Whatever nonsense you're trying to decide how to spit out, do it already." Lilí's bald statement brought his pacing to a halt.

He turned around to find her standing with her feet in a wide stance, arms crossed, her chin at her typical determined jut. The same don't-mess-with-me attitude she'd thrown at him that first night at Melba's.

"I offer to help, you back away. Or brush me off. It's like a scene from a bad movie on instant replay."

"It's not like that," he hedged.

"Then tell me how it is." She arched a brow, a small challenge that felt more like a line drawn in the sand between them.

He wanted to wipe that damn line away with a swipe of his foot. Take her back to bed and forget everything else, except how right it felt to be with her.

But he couldn't risk it. Couldn't risk her.

"Look, this is me. It's how I operate." He opened his arms wide, baring himself to her. "Being a cop, I've made a point of handling the crap Lourdes gets involved in by the book. Keeping my emotions out of it. I do the best I can. On my own. That's how it has to be."

Lilí stared back at him, not giving an inch.

"Maybe I should go," he said. There was nothing else he could say that would make her understand.

She huffed out a breath, giving him her signature eye roll. "I figured that was coming next."

"Come on." He stepped toward her, reaching out, hating the way their morning had devolved. Kidding himself that maybe they could find some common ground to stand on. "Don't be like that."

"Like what? Realistic? Truthful?"

When she kept her arms crossed, rejecting his outstretched hand, he shoved it deep in his front pocket. "Look, I don't want to fight with you."

"Then don't shut me out."

"It's for your own good," he countered.

Her lips twisted with derision, and dejection wrapped its heavy weight around his shoulders.

Several tense beats passed.

"Fine. Be mad at me, but what I'm doing is for the best." For her. Definitely not for him. But she's the one who mattered most here. "Thanks for a—"

"No." She shook her head forcefully, her long, satiny hair swaying against her back. "Save me the 'thanks for a memorable night' speech. *Por favor.* I want you to respect who I am. What I'm capable of doing. If you'd only let me in."

Each statement from her landed with an archer's accuracy, piercing his heart, wounding his soul. Yet they didn't change his mind. He couldn't let them.

"I'm only trying to protect you, Lilí, the best way I know how."

Jaw muscles clenched in obvious anger, she stared at him. But whereas her eyes had always been a window into her emotions, now their expression remained flat, unreadable.

"Well then," she finally said, her voice clipped. Detached. "You know your way out. Don't let me stop you."

She moved to the railing, grasping it with both hands as she stared out at the buildings and the sun rippling off the waters of Lake Michigan in the distance. Effectively dismissing him.

Disappointed, Diego trudged toward the balcony door, pausing at her side. He racked his brain for something, anything, that might change her mind. Unfortunately, he came up empty.

Man, how he wanted to rewind the clock an hour. Go back to when the morning had held so much promise. But there was nothing left to say, and nothing that would ameliorate their current standoff.

Regret strangling him, he walked away without another word.

Chapter Fourteen

Lilí left the women's shelter after the group meeting and headed toward the clinic several blocks over. There was nothing pending at work, but the thought of going home, where she'd no doubt relive the argument with Diego this morning, depressed her.

Which pissed her off.

Which then made her need to find some way to be productive.

There was always plenty of work to be done at the clinic, so why not make herself useful.

The end-of-July sun beat down on her, warming her shoulders. By the time she rounded the corner onto North Kedzie Avenue, beads of perspiration dotted her upper lip. Despite the brutal heat, a cold shiver ran between her shoulder blades when she drew near the vacant building next to the clinic, the memory of Tito body-slamming her against the car vivid in her mind.

She forced herself to look away from the line of cars parked on the side of the road. If not, she would have missed the figure sitting on the vacant building's steps. Shoulders hunched, with her curly dark brown shoulder-length hair partially covering the woman's face, Lilí couldn't be sure, but it looked like . . .

Lourdes Reyes scrambled to her feet when she caught sight of Lilí approaching. Somehow Diego's sister didn't seem as surprised to run into Lilí on the sidewalk as she was.

Tugging the hem of her jeans shorts, Lourdes scrambled down the three steps. Admirable considering her three-inch-high red Converse wedges.

Lilí slowed her steps, trying to gauge the other woman's current state. Given what Diego had shared earlier today, she was worried Lourdes might be back on her latest drug of choice.

"Hi, I'm not sure you remember me," Lourdes said. She pushed her hair out of her face with a hand Lilí noted appeared steady. "I'm Diego's sister."

"Yeah, I do. Good to see you, Lourdes. Everything okay?"

The momentary relief that brightened Lourdes's eyes when Lilí said her name, faded at the question.

Biting her lower lip, Diego's sister shook her head. Her gaze traveled up and down the street, as if anticipating someone else's arrival, before focusing back on Lilí. She fiddled nervously with the tassels on the front of her olive hobo bag. Her motions weren't quite fidgety enough to be labeled agitated, but definitely enough to relay the message that she had something she was trying to figure out how to say.

Ironically, Diego had beaten around the bush on the balcony this morning, until Lilí had told him to man up about it. Which of course had led to an argument. Not necessarily the best tactic for getting someone to talk reasonably.

With Lourdes, especially without knowing for sure

if the woman had started using again, Lilí waited to follow her cues.

"I'm in a bad place right now," Lourdes admitted in a halting voice. "And I, *bueno*, I heard around the neighborhood that this might be a safe place. That you've helped others, too."

Lilí nodded, keeping her expression open, inviting. "That's true, on both accounts."

"Good." Lourdes's entire body relaxed on a rush of breath. She rubbed her nose, a gesture that could mean something. Or nothing. Still, Lilí noted it, and kept watch for any signs of relapse.

"Look, I know you're friends with my brother."

Kind of. Maybe. Last night Lilí would have said they were more. Had hoped for more. Today, who knew?

"He's been through a lot 'cause of me," Lourdes continued. "I owe it to him to straighten things out."

The projection tactic wouldn't wash with Lilí. Not when it came to getting an addict to take ownership of their problems.

"What about for yourself? What do you want?" she asked.

Lourdes's face crumbled. She sank down onto the bottom step in a heap, her legs bent akimbo.

Lilí joined the other woman on the warm cement.

"I want out," Lourdes rasped. "I need to get out of Patricia's place and the temptation to slide back into old habits."

"Is that what's happening?"

Lourdes nodded, her expression pained. She swiped at her left eye with a knuckle, then rubbed her nose again. "Her old boyfriend keeps hanging out. Bringing stuff that—that only leads to trouble."

"Have you taken anything he's offered?"

The fact that Lourdes didn't answer right away was answer enough.

Lili's heart sank. Diego would be so disappointed. It might manifest as anger, but she'd stake her training on the fact that it only masked his pain.

Right now though, her focus had to stay on his sister.

"And you came here because?" she asked.

"I came here hoping to see you. Or ask whoever's inside to call you so we could talk."

That answer caught Lilí by surprise. She'd only had one brief conversation with Diego's sister before this. Why seek her out specifically?

"Look." Lourdes shoved her hobo purse onto her lap as she turned to face Lilí. "My brother trusts you. And I don't think he does that a lot with others. That tells me something."

Shocked by Lourdes's claim, Lilí drew back. "I'm not sure I'd say that."

"It's true. So if I'm gonna do this, you're the one I trust to make sure it's all good."

"Do what?"

Lourdes sucked in a breath, her dark eyes wide with conviction. "I wanna check myself into rehab. Without my brother feeling like it's his responsibility."

No matter what happened with Lourdes, Lilí was sure Diego would feel responsible. That's what happened with family. What affected one, affected them all. At least, it did with Lilí's.

She'd heard the guilt in Diego's voice when he talked about his mom and his sister. No doubt about it, he'd take this on his shoulders, too.

But Lourdes was right. She needed to do this on her terms. For herself.

"Are you sure?" Lilí asked.

"Mm-hmm," Lourdes answered. The nervous bite of her lip, the shaky hand tucking her curls behind her ear, they could be due to anxiety over her decision. Or residuals of whatever she had alluded to taking from Patricia's boyfriend.

"Okay then." Lilí stood up, holding out her hand to Lourdes. "If you're serious, then we should head inside and see when and where we can get you into a program."

Lourdes pushed herself to a stand before she took Lilí's hand. "I need the *when* to be today. Like, let me go grab my backpack and get the hell outta there. *La situación está muy mala.*"

The wide spectrum of what entailed a "really bad situation" like Lourdes claimed to be in, plus the bruise Lilí recalled seeing on the other woman's cheek when they'd originally met, worried her.

"If you can get me into a place today, maybe we can swing by Patricia's and grab my stuff. Before they get back from their, um, errands."

The cagey way Lourdes stumbled over the word *errands* clued Lilí in to the fact that Patricia and her scumbag boyfriend had probably gone out to score. If so, Lourdes didn't need to be there when they got back.

Enough said.

"Okay then, let's get inside. I'll make some calls, while you fill out some paperwork, and we'll go from there."

For the second time in as many weeks, Lilí found herself at a client's home, picking up their belongings.

This time she'd not only submitted the proper paperwork and alerted others in her office of her whereabouts, she was intent on maintaining the right boundaries. Something she'd wavered on . . . Who was she kidding, she had totally obliterated a boundary by taking Melba to her condo.

Trouble was, she couldn't honestly say she'd do anything differently given the same situation.

Keeping a professional perspective wasn't always easy. Especially right now, when she remembered how upset Diego had been this morning.

While Lourdes dug for her keys in her hobo bag, Lilí thought back to her argument with Diego on her condo's balcony. *Dios mío*, things had gone downhill so fast.

One minute she'd been humming a Prince Royce song in her head while scrambling eggs. The next, she looked up to see Diego's tense figure hunched over the railing, dejection curving his broad back.

She'd gingerly approached him. Hoping, praying, he'd accept her willingness to shoulder whatever Lourdes's call had brought.

When he'd looked up at her, his handsome face etched with misery, her heart swelled with the need to comfort him. To ease the disillusion haunting his features. Far too quickly though, resignation tightened his jaw as he pushed her away. Again.

Despite his propensity to disregard her professional guidance, Lilí felt compelled to alert him about the current situation. Reassure him that Lourdes was actually making a smart decision.

Worrying about a family member, when there was little you could do about their health or safety, drained a person. Kept you in a constant state of apprehension as you waited for the other shoe to drop. Throughout Papi's battle with cancer, she'd flinched every time a call had come from home. Afraid it meant bad news.

Knowing Diego would be relieved about Lourdes's decision to go to rehab, yet not sharing the information with him, caused a pang of remorse that seared Lilí's chest. But client confidentiality warranted that she keep the information to herself. If Lourdes wanted her brother to know what was going on, it was up to her to tell him.

Still, as they entered the tiny, run-down apartment near the 3300 block of West Walnut Street, an area known for its particularly high crime rate, Lilí tried, but failed, to squash a niggling sense of guilt.

Clear proof as to why becoming personally involved with a client inevitably created an ethical dilemma.

"I just need to grab my stuff from the spare room. You can grab a seat out here." Lourdes waved an arm to encompass the small living area with the kitchen off to the right.

Lilí glanced around, taking in the worn carpet, dilapidated pressed-wood furniture, and sagging couch, its cushions faded and stained. A bookshelf in one corner leaned to the right, one of the shelves hanging off-kilter and dipping down to rest on the shelf below it. Beer bottles, open chip bags, dirty napkins, and several empty pizza boxes littered the area.

Her perusal skid to a halt when she spied two crack pipes, haphazardly strewn on the coffee table, along with a lighter, a piece of tubing, and a wire kitchen scrubber. Mundane household items easily used to assemble a makeshift crack pipe.

All that was needed for an addict's party was the rock cocaine.

"*Ay, ching*—" Lourdes bit off the muttered curse when she noticed what had caught Lili's attention. "I ran out as soon as they were gone, but didn't realize they left their crap out."

"Is this the norm around here?" Lilí asked, wondering if, or how often, Lourdes had joined the party.

Lourdes shook her head, her brown curls swaying across her shoulders. "It wasn't when I moved in last weekend. But I came home from work at the laundromat on Wednesday and Patricia's ex was sprawled on the couch like he owns the place. The guy's a loser. Dragging her down with him. Patricia promised me Octavio wouldn't bring anything into the house."

Lilí figured her expression must have relayed her "yeah right" thoughts because Lourdes pursed her lips and nodded.

"I thought I could resist what he's been pushing. But things were crappy at work yesterday and . . . and I got weak." A mix of shame and anger flashed across her round face before she turned her head away from the drug paraphernalia.

"Today, when Octavio and his buddy showed up, I headed back to my room," Lourdes continued. "When they started talking about a plan to score, I waited for them to leave, then hopped the bus to your clinic."

"You did the right thing," Lilí assured her, placing a hand on Lourdes's forearm.

"*No me puedo quedar aquí.*"

Diego's sister was right, she couldn't stay here. Not if she wanted to get clean, rebuild her relationship with her brother, or lead a decent life.

Lilí didn't say any of that though. Lourdes obviously knew all of it already or she wouldn't have sought help. She simply had to believe it. And believe in herself.

"Maybe it's better if you come with me instead of waiting out here," Lourdes suggested. "They won't be back anytime soon, but you'll probably be more comfortable away from . . . from all that."

Lilí followed her to the open hallway that ran parallel to the living space. The two bedrooms bookended this half of the apartment, with the shared bath in the middle.

Lourdes motioned to the room on the left. "That one's mine. Let me just grab my toiletries. Everything else is already packed."

Pushing open the door, Lilí found the room decorated in an I-don't-give-a-damn motif that matched the rest of the place. A twin mattress with no boxspring lay in the center of the floor, an upside-down plastic crate serving as a nightstand beside it. A short, white dresser, several knobs missing from the drawers, sat off to the right. Along the far wall, one of the closet's accordion-style doors hung haphazardly off the track.

A battered, oversized gray backpack sat on top of the dresser, unzipped. A pair of jeans stuck out of the top of the bag, one leg hanging over the edge as if it couldn't decide whether it wanted to stay or go. More clothes lay in a heap beside it.

"I'll be right back," Lourdes said. "Then we can get outta here."

Lilí edged into the room, moving to the foot of the bed. A nervous shudder skittered across her shoulders. Crouched halfway down to sit on the edge of the mattress, she noticed the stained sheets and changed her mind. Instead, she crossed to the dresser and made herself useful by folding the clothes.

The fact that all of Diego's sister's belongings fit into this one bag tugged at her heart. Lourdes had a brother waiting, desperately wanting to be there for her as she built a new life. Unfortunately, Lilí's experience had demonstrated that another person's desires weren't enough to help an addict.

That Lourdes had recognized the danger of slipping back into addiction if she stayed here with Patricia and had sought out the clinic was a smart step toward recovery.

"Okay, I think I got everything," Lourdes said, entering the room. She gripped the hem of her shirt with one hand, holding it up in front of her to create a makeshift carrier for her toothbrush, a tube of toothpaste, a bottle of lotion, some hair mousse, and several other items.

She'd taken about three steps in when they heard the front door open.

"*¿Oye, Lourdes, estás aquí?*" a woman called out.

Lourdes's eyes bugged out, her gaze shooting to snag Lilí's.

"Where else she gonna be? Lourdes, get your ass out here!" a man yelled. The front door slammed shut, punctuating his rude command. "Yo, Stevie, you remember to grab the bag of food from the back seat?"

Patricia and Octavio, Lourdes mouthed before holding a finger up to her lips, indicating Lilí should remain quiet. Reaching back, she carefully pushed the door, leaving it open a crack but hiding them from view.

"Hey, Lourdes, are ya here?" Patricia repeated.

"Yeah! Give me a minute," Lourdes answered, before lowering her voice to a whisper. "Can you take this stuff?"

She jiggled her shirt, the toiletries rattling against each other.

Her heart pounding, Lilí grabbed as many things as she could, dropping them onto the folded clothes.

"I thought you said they'd be gone for a while," she said in a hushed tone.

"They were supposed to be. Octavio said his dealer was hanging out in Englewood and then he had to meet with some guy about a job," Lourdes whispered. "Maybe they won't stay long. It's better if they don't know you're here. Octavio has a pissy temper when he's high."

"Patricia, make yourself useful and bring me a beer!" the jerk ordered, as if on cue.

"Make that two," another man yelled. "Hey, you want the Doritos or the potato chips?"

"Potato. And pass me one of them pipes. I wanna try this shit."

With Lourdes's room on the same side of the apartment as the living area, the men's heavy footsteps were clearly heard through the thin walls. No doubt they were getting settled on the grungy couch. Spreading their stash on the scratched coffee table along with the other paraphernalia.

"This place is a dump," Octavio complained, his voice sounding so close, the hair on Lilí's arms stood on end. "How come you ain't picked up this trash yet, woman?"

"*Sinvergüenza*," Lourdes muttered, her lip curling with disgust.

Lilí had to agree with her assessment. But having no shame was probably the nicest thing you could say about Octavio.

The heavy bass of a popular reggaeton song kicked on, the *thump-thump* beat of the Spanish rap tune reverberating through the room. Lilí's stomach sank. So much for Lourdes's idea that the group might not stay. Seemed like these people were gearing up for a party.

Not good. If this Octavio guy started lighting up whatever drugs they'd managed to score, no way Lilí wanted to be here. And no way should Lourdes be around that kind of temptation.

"Are you sure we can't just walk out and head straight for the door?" Lilí suggested. "They can't stop us."

"Uh-uh. When he's been smokin', Octavio gets hyper paranoid." Concern and fear laced Lourdes's hushed voice. "He'll block our way. Or order his flunky Stevie to do it while he starts asking questions, demanding answers. If he gets wind that you're from the clinic, who knows what that crazy bastard'll do."

Elbows bent, Lourdes balled her fists in front of her chest, her face scrunched in obvious frustration. "*¡Ay, que estupida soy!* I shoulda come back on my own and met you later."

Lilí wouldn't have gone along with that idea. Not willingly, nor without being afraid Lourdes might not show up in the end.

Sure, Lourdes could still change her mind about checking herself into the rehab facility. That was her prerogative. But if she did, Lilí planned to talk her through other alternatives. Definitely provide her with better living situation options along with information on outpatient counseling and Narcotics Anonymous meetings.

Someone banged on the wall separating Lourdes's room from the front of the apartment, startling her and Lilí.

"You in there snoozing? Get your ass out here and try this shit! My treat!" Octavio crowed.

"I said give me a minute!" Lourdes yelled back.

Octavio answered with a few more insistent thumps on the wall. Gruff, almost wild laughter sounded on the other side.

Lilí's stomach clenched. Panic-laced fear ratcheted up inside her as memories of Tito's attack flashed in her mind. His smelly breath filling her lungs. His grungy body pressed against hers. The pain shooting across her shoulder blades when he slammed her against the car.

Blood rushed in her ears and she forced herself to take a deep breath. Count to ten. Slowly release it, willing the fear to leave her body along with the air.

"You gonna be okay in here if I go show my face to shut him up? I'll tell 'em I'm not feeling well."

"I don't think that's a good idea. I don't want you to get hurt," Lilí insisted. She grabbed on to Lourdes's forearm, desperate to keep Diego's sister safe. "Let's just go. Together. Who knows how long they'll be out there."

"Let me give this a shot. It's our best bet," Lourdes said.

They stared at each other for what felt like an eternity and the blink of an eye at the same time. Ocatvio banged again.

"I can do this," Lourdes assured her.

"Be careful!" Lilí begged.

Lourdes nodded and turned away.

Lilí watched her reach down the front of her peach tank top and surprisingly pull out her cell. Lourdes tapped the screen, then put the device to her ear as she reached the door. After mumbling something Lilí couldn't make out, Lourdes tucked the cell into her cleavage again.

"Whatever happens, don't come out there," she

warned, before opening the door enough for her to slip out.

Lilí's stomach bottomed out at the dire order.

"*Oye*, she's alive," Octavio crowed a few seconds later.

The reggaeton music drowned out whatever Lourdes or anyone else responded.

Anxious, Lilí stepped around the end of the dresser so she could press her ear against the wall, hoping to make out something. Anything.

All she could hear was the mix of male and female voices. More footsteps approached. These were softer, so maybe Patricia had joined them from the kitchen.

Lilí made out the occasional *no*, and what she thought might have been an "*esto está bueno*," which could only mean someone had lit up one of the pipes and the drugs they'd bought were "good."

There was some kind of deep shuffling, scraping noise, like maybe one of them had scooted the coffee table over or moved some piece of furniture. Lilí couldn't be sure so she pressed her ear harder against the wall.

All of a sudden the voices got louder. More heated. Frantic. The rumble of their exchange rose in intensity.

"I said no!" The anger-laced desperation in Lourdes's words had Lilí clenching her fists. Considering ignoring the other woman's advice and going out there to offer backup.

A cackle of derisive male laughter rang out, followed by a loud crash.

A woman screamed.

Something slammed into the wall on the other side of Lilí and she yelped in surprise. Stumbling backward, she tripped over the end of the mattress. The weight of her messenger bag threw off her balance and she went down, smacking her elbow on the milk crate and upending the pseudo nightstand.

The yelling outside intensified, a cacophony of Octavio's and Stevie's deep voices melded with Lourdes's and Patricia's.

"Get the hell off me!" Lourdes cried.

Fear galvanized Lilí and she scrambled to her feet. Adjusting her messenger bag on her shoulder, she scanned the room, desperate for some sort of weapon.

Her gaze landed on the end of a baseball bat sticking out of the closet at the same time the argument moved into the short alcove between the bedrooms and bathroom.

"Leave her alone," Patricia whined.

"Shut up!" Octavio screamed back. A woman cried out in pain. "I'm offering you something. You say *gracias* and take it!"

The wild, unhinged words had Lilí clambering over the mattress to grab the bat.

"I said I ain't interested. Get outta my face!" Lourdes yelled.

"Don't disrespect me in my house!" Octavio screamed. "*¡Vete pa'l carajo!*"

A male grunt followed Lourdes's "go to hell." Then she flew into the room, shoved the door closed behind her and turned the lock.

"We need to get outta here. Now!" Her chest heaved with ragged breaths as she rushed over to snatch her backpack off the dresser.

"Open up, damn it!" Octavio banged on the door. The thin wood shook, threatening to give way.

Lourdes shoved her curly hair out of her face and Lilí noticed the other woman's bloodied lip. Anger detonated inside her.

Tightening her grip around the bat handle, Lilí crouched into her fighting stance. She wobbled on the old mattress, but swung the weapon up onto her shoulder. Ready to wield it.

"Come on!" Lourdes raced to the window.

The cheap metal blinds rattled in complaint as Lourdes jerked on the string to raise them. She unlocked the window, grunting as she struggled to push it up, then gestured for Lilí to crawl through it onto the fire escape.

The doorknob jiggled at the same time Ocatvio banged again.

Lilí scrambled awkwardly off the bed, her pulse racing.

"Good thinking. But let me have it." Lourdes held her hand out for the bat. "If that asshole breaks down the door, I'll take care of him. You get away."

"We're both getting away. Together. You hear me?" Lilí said. "I'm proud of you." She squeezed Lourdes's arm in a show of support. Lourdes offered her a wobbly smile.

"Bitch! You can't hide in there all night."

On that threat from Octavio, Lilí hiked up her sundress, stuck one leg through the window, and hopped out onto the metal walkway. She grabbed the rusty handrail to steady herself when her sandal caught on the windowsill.

Lourdes quickly joined her, the bat in one hand and her backpack slung over a shoulder. They scrambled down the metal fire escape to the third floor, shooting occasional looks above, Lilí petrified they'd find Octavio following.

By the time they reached the second floor and were struggling to slide the ladder down the track to the street level, a police siren sounded in the distance.

"Amen!" Lourdes muttered.

With the high-pitched scrape of rusted metal, the ladder finally lowered.

"Go!" Lourdes ordered.

Lilí didn't waste any time scurrying down the rungs.

Once on the sidewalk, she waited for Lourdes to join her before they raced up the alley. They reached the street at the same time a cop car screeched to a halt in front of the apartment building, lights flashing.

Diego jumped out of the driver's side of the squad car and rounded the hood.

Relief washed over Lilí like a surfer's wave drenching the shores of Tres Palmas in Rincón, nearly knocking her to her knees.

"Over here!" Lourdes called out when Diego ran toward the building's entrance.

He spun in their direction, his handsome features a mask of fury and intensity. His gaze met Lilí's and he faltered a step. Shock skittered across his face for an instant before fury descended once again.

Lilí slowed her pace, allowing Lourdes to reach her brother first.

"Lourdes, what the hell? How did you two . . . who hit you?" Diego's litany of questions drew to an abrupt halt on the last one. He grasped his sister's shoulders, peering at her in the early evening shadow cast by the building and the setting sun.

Lourdes swiped at her lip with the back of her hand. "It doesn't matter. I'm okay."

Stevens stepped around the siblings to meet up with Lilí. "Are you hurt?"

A hand pressed to her chest as if that would slow her racing heart, Lilí nodded her head. She peered over her shoulder, afraid she'd find Octavio hot on their heels.

Thankfully, the alley remained empty.

Her insides trembled. A shakiness with an epicenter deep in her core vibrated out to her extremities. Despite her resolve to stay strong, Lilí's knees weakened and she sank down on her haunches.

"Whoa! Let me—"

"I'm good," she said when Stevens hunkered down beside her. "Just catching my breath."

He put a hand on her back. Foolishly, she found herself wishing it was Diego's.

The police radio attached to Stevens's shoulder squawked, the dispatcher putting out a call about a disturbance in the area. Diego and his partner ignored it.

"What happened here, Lourdes?" Diego asked.

Lilí tilted her head to peer up at him through her lashes.

His motions sure, adept, he briskly checked his sister for injuries—running his hands down her arms, tilting her chin to get a better look at her fat lip. The pain drawing his brows together heightened Lilí's unease.

"And you?" Disbelief filled his dark eyes as he pierced her with a sharp gaze. "How the hell did you get involved with this? You should know to be more careful."

Adrenaline still thrumming in her system, Lilí straightened. No way would she let his he-man cop routine intimidate her. Even if his argument held a grain of truth.

"Don't be a jerk to her," Lourdes jumped in before Lilí could respond. She pulled her chin from her brother's grasp, shifting to her right as if to shield Lilí from him. "I'm the one who got her into this mess."

"No, we got in this together," Lilí answered. "But Octavio's the one who did wrong here. Not you."

The sincerity in the look of thanks Lourdes gave her eased the knot of anxiety tangling Lilí's insides. Then she peered over Lourdes's shoulder and met Diego's furious expression.

Chapter Fifteen

Never in the four years he'd been on the force, had Diego been more bone-chillingly afraid than when he'd received Lourdes's call.

Or rather, when she'd called him so he could listen in on her conversation with Patricia and her dirtbag boyfriend, Octavio.

Less than five minutes in, he'd known the situation was heading downhill. Fast.

Smartest move he'd made recently was getting Lourdes a new phone under the condition that she activate the location-sharing feature. A quick check confirmed that the two women were at Patricia's place.

Moments before her call, he and Stevens had radioed dispatch to put their car down for a quick dinner break. Stevens had already been headed toward a sandwich shop on the corner. As soon as Diego heard his sister mumble "We need help," he'd hollered at Stevens to forget the food and get the hell back in the car.

Lights flashing, sirens blaring, Diego had floored the gas pedal, white-knuckling the steering wheel the whole way. Hell-bent on getting to the women before things got bad.

Of course, the "we" he'd assumed his sister meant was her and Patricia. Not Lilí!

Talk about a freaking heart-stopping game changer.

Seeing Lilí with Lourdes. Terror stamping their faces. Chests heaving as they gasped for breath. His world had bottomed out.

One look at Lourdes's bloodied lip had his gaze racing to Lilí, afraid the same, or worse, had happened to her. Guilt slammed into him like a Chicago Bears linebacker. He'd *known* something like this would happen if she got mixed up with his sister.

"Is either one of you going to tell me how the two of you wound up here?" He pointed his thumb at the building. "With a crackhead threatening you?"

Palming a baseball bat in front of her—a freaking baseball bat, like it was the weapon of choice in this neighborhood—Lourdes stared him down, a surprising bodyguard between him and Lilí. As if his feisty do-gooder needed one.

Although, he knew Lilí well enough to tell she was rattled. If doing her best to hide it.

Standing tall, her chin in that pugnacious jut, she glared at him over his sister's shoulder. But in the depths of those beautiful eyes he'd gotten lost in last night, he caught the flare of apprehension. The speck of white against her full bottom lip as she worried it with her teeth.

He'd bet the same fear that had seized his chest as he'd strained to catch pieces of the argument through Lourdes's phone had gripped both women in its strong clutch.

This Octavio guy's level of insanity seemed to rival Tito González's, if not exceed it.

The thought of Lourdes *and* Lilí facing a prick like that, of him laying a hand on either one of them, sent dread, rage, fear, and more, mixing and mashing up inside Diego like the colored paint in one of the preschooler artwork displays hanging on the center walls.

"This was supposed to be a quick stop to pick up my stuff." Lourdes hefted the strap of her worn backpack higher on her shoulder. "I told you earlier, I'm working some things out."

"*Pues*, you're doing a great job, apparently."

Lourdes sucked her teeth at his snide remark, her fat lip curling with disdain.

"That attitude doesn't make this situation better," Lilí chimed in, moving to stand alongside his sister.

"That's what I keep telling her, only—" Diego broke off when he realized Lilí had directed her jab at him.

"You talking to me?" He slapped a hand to his chest, floored by Lilí's nod. "Hey, I'm the good guy, remember?"

His gaze flew back and forth between his sister and Lilí standing shoulder to shoulder.

"Look, I called you because I thought we might need the police. Maybe I shoulda called 911. But I didn't want you hearing about this over the radio. Plus, you're my brother and . . ."

"*Sí*, I'm your brother." He jabbed a hand at her, laying the most important card on the table. "So you should listen to me before you get in over your head. Before you make a crappy decision that compounds another crappy decision!"

"Again, not helping," Lilí muttered.

Stevens coughed. More to cover his smirk, the wiseass.

Hands on her hips, Lilí hit Diego with the arched brow, pursed lips face she'd given one of the kids when he'd tried to pull a fast one during the Cubs game.

Next to her, his sister jerked her right wrist, lifting and dropping the bat, tapping it in the palm of her left hand. A menacing scowl wrinkled her brow.

Diego rubbed at the tension knotting his neck.

The two women couldn't be more different. One street smart out of necessity. One too kindhearted for her own good. Yet, together they created the united front he'd yearned to be with, and for, his sister all these years.

That Lourdes continually pushed him away when he only sought to make things right picked at an age-old scab deep inside him. One that never seemed to heal.

Hurt and frustration swelled within him, whooshing in his ears and sucking him back to when he was a twelve-year-old kid, determined to be the man of the house, to protect his family, but having no means to do so.

Joining the army, earning his degree, and getting a decent job to provide for his mom and sister had been his plan. A solid one, too. Only, time hadn't been on his side. Lourdes got in too deep. Mami's heart hadn't been able to take the stress. He'd arrived home too late.

He'd stood over his mom's casket and promised to take care of Lourdes. Accomplish what his *mami* had died trying to do. But he couldn't get his sister healthy if she wouldn't let him!

Hurt and frustration clogged his throat. His eyes burned and Diego turned his head away, pretending to scan the area up and down the street. All he wanted was to ensure no one else he cared about got hurt, or worse, on his watch.

Maybe his sister refused to listen to reason, but he'd thought Lilí at least respected his wishes. This morning, he'd made it clear he didn't want her interfering. For her own good.

He cut his gaze to Lilí, unable to squelch the spurt of betrayal at finding her here. "I warned you that things could get messy. But you can't seem to take my advice either."

"This is my *job*," she answered.

Like that was sufficient explanation.

Diego balled his fists at his side, wishing he could shake some sense into her. "Didn't you learn anything from what happened with Melba and Tito? Didn't that scare you enough to think twice about crossing boundary lines you shouldn't?"

"Don't do that." Lilí shook her head, waggling a finger at him like a nun chastising a disrespectful child. "Don't you dare throw that in my face so you can hide whatever hang-ups or insecurities you've got. I did nothing wrong by coming here with Lourdes."

"I asked you to keep out of it," he growled.

"This had nothing to do with you."

"Are you kidding me?" He scrubbed a hand across his forehead, trying to calm the pounding radiating between his temples.

"This isn't personal," Lilí said.

He scoffed. "It felt pretty personal between us last night."

She flinched.

Diego closed his eyes, regretting his outburst. That was a low blow. He knew it.

When he looked at Lilí again, her lips were pressed together in a grim line. Eyes flashing with anger as she glared at him, her nostrils flared on a huff of breath.

Asshole.

She didn't have to say the word out loud. He felt enough like one already.

"Lilí, I didn't—"

"Look, you wanna act like a prick, throw it my way." Lourdes edged in front of Lilí, as if to say, *Get behind me, I got this.* "I'm the one who went to the clinic looking for her. I'm the one who asked her to swing by here before I check myself into rehab."

Diego jerked in surprise. "You are? *¿En serio?*"

"Yeah, seriously. That's why she came with me."

Like the sun peeking over the horizon, lighting the path on one of his early morning runs, relief poked its cautious head out to whisper hello in Diego's ear.

"Let's go then. I'll radio the station. Let them know we have an emergency drop-off."

He jerked his head toward the squad car, already stepping in that direction. Ready, willing, and able to do this for her. For his mom. For their *familia.*

"I don't want you to take me," Lourdes said.

The relief that had dawned moments ago sank back into the earth, darkening his world again.

She linked her arm with Lilí's. A move that seemed to surprise Lilí as she blinked a few times, her expressive eyes widening.

"I can't keep relying on you to rescue me," Lourdes

went on, the earlier anger in her voice giving way to a sadness he hadn't heard before. It shadowed her face, twisted his gut.

"But I—"

"*Hermanito*, I've messed up my life, and yours, long enough. I gotta take care of me, so you can take care of you."

He reared back as if his sister had slapped him.

What was she talking about? He was good. All he needed was for her to get better.

"Lili's taking me to the treatment center. She's already called and they have an opening."

A spurt of jealousy he wasn't too proud of burned in his belly and his gaze shot to Lili's. He imagined an I-told-you-so danced on the tip of her tongue, though her eyes—those damn eyes that got to him every time—brimmed with . . . with pity?

Anger would have been better. Anger wouldn't have gutted him the way she did now.

"Look, I can take it from here," Lilí told him calmly, measured. Like he needed to be handled with kid gloves or something. "It would be good for you and Stevens to go check on Patricia."

When he didn't respond, she turned to his partner. The one cop here who seemed to have his faculties, because between Lourdes's rehab news and the pity—pity!—Lilí was showering on him, Diego couldn't remember his badge number, much less proper protocol.

¡Coño! He was no longer the little boy woefully unprepared to be the man of the house, in charge of keeping his *mami* and sister safe. No longer the scrawny kid who'd been easily pushed around when he tried standing up for his sister. Nor the unwanted

son conveniently brushed off when he contacted his father begging for financial assistance to put Lourdes in a good facility.

No. He was a problem solver. A man capable of helping others. If they accepted his outstretched hand.

Today, both his sister and Lilí hadn't done that. They'd joined forces to ice him out.

". . . probably. I'm not sure what they took. I could hear Patricia trying to talk some sense into her boyfriend," Lilí was telling Stevens, and Diego realized he'd checked out of the conversation.

"*Sinvergüenza*," Lourdes threw in with a sneer.

"Definitely." Lilí tucked behind her ear a few strands of hair that had come loose from her long braid. "But that guy wasn't listening to anyone. Please, I'd really like to make sure Patricia is safe."

Of course she would. Because she always put others ahead of herself. Except for when it came to his request that she stay out of his family business. Let him do his job, as a brother and a son.

Instead, she'd not only wormed her way in, she'd taken over his responsibility. And while part of him knew he should be grateful his sister was getting the assistance she needed, that Lilí had come through for her—

Betrayal burned deep inside his chest.

"He actually said that?" Brows arched in surprise, Yaz folded her legs tailor style, shifting to face Lilí, who was seated on the couch beside her.

Lilí nodded, hugging her wineglass closer to her chest. She glanced from Yaz, to Rosa, to her cousin

Julia, all three gathered around her in the family living room Sunday afternoon.

Earlier today, she had sent a group text with the signal for an emergency sister-cousin meet-up—four female salsa dancer emojis, followed by four wineglass emojis, ending with four exclamation points.

Rosa had answered right away, letting them all know that Jeremy was taking the kids over to Yazmine and Tomás's house for pizza at six. Julia and Ben had arrived back in town late the night before, so she'd answered with a thumbs-up.

For the past thirty minutes they'd listened to Lilí's tale of woe. And even Rosa, bless her, hadn't stopped to lecture Lilí about the dangerous aspects of her job.

"I'm surprised you didn't break out one of your self-defense moves and kick him in the *cojones*. Just sayin'," Julia added at Rosa's appalled gasp. "A guy throws your intimacy in your face, in front of others? *Lo mato.*"

Bueno, Lilí hadn't quite felt like killing him in that moment, but a kick in the privates might have made her feel better. Maybe.

Probably not.

She sighed. A deep, heavy breath that did nothing to dispel the sadness engulfing her.

"*Ay nena*, I'm so sorry he hurt you." Rosa's brow puckered with concern. Perched on the edge of the coffee table, something she harped on them all *not* to do, she placed a comforting hand on Lilí's knee where it poked through her ripped jeans. "Diego seemed like such a good guy."

He is, a tiny voice inside Lilí complained.

Mutinously she silenced it.

"*Pues*, even though I appreciate him playing the

guitar for the Chicago Youth Association's fundraiser last Christmas, he better hope I don't run into him anywhere now. I mean, what were you supposed to do, ignore his sister when she came to your clinic? *Por favor*, save me from another show of machismo!" Julia combed her fingers through her black hair, tossing her shoulder-length tresses in obvious irritation. "Although, I wouldn't mind siccing one of my brothers on him! *¡Manganzón!*"

Her sisters laughed at Julia's dig, and Lilí tried to force her lips to curve in a smile.

Her cousin's feisty attitude came from being raised with three brothers whose baseball teammates were always around, rough-housing and giving her grief. Plus, a *mami* entrenched in the old-school ways of their culture that unwittingly bred the stereotypical Latino male chauvinism in her sons. It was the reason why, last Christmas, Julia had moved from Puerto Rico to find a job in Chicago, near Lilí and her sisters.

"I agree with Julia. *Manganzón* is right," Yaz said. "Sounds like Diego acted exactly like a man-child, biting off your head because he wasn't getting his way."

"Oh, you should have heard Jeremy before he left with the kids," Rosa threw in.

Lilí gasped, dismay tightening her grip on her wineglass. "You told him? I asked all of you not to say anything."

"*Bueno*, I can't help it if he overheard me talking." Rosa lifted a shoulder in a shrug. "Plus, he saw how upset I was because you'd been crying. I was this close"—she held up a thumb and pointer finger, leaving an inch between them—"to heading into the city to pick you up, because I was nervous about you driving. What's with the secrecy anyway?"

Lilí pressed a knuckle to her temple, applying pressure to the incessant pounding. Her reasoning didn't make any sense, not when you considered what a jerk Diego had been.

And yet.

"I don't know . . . I guess I don't want Jeremy or Tomás, even Ben, to, to . . ."

She trailed off, seesawing between the anger and hurt she'd been struggling to balance since yesterday afternoon. Since Diego had backed away from her, betrayal tightening his chiseled jaw, his dark eyes nearly black with fury.

He'd walked away, following Stevens into Patricia's apartment building without even a good-bye.

She'd known he'd be upset. Before everything had gone to hell in Patricia's apartment, her instincts had been to touch base with him, let him know about Lourdes. But protocol demanded she stay silent.

Ultimately, she'd kept him out of the loop, expecting him to be angry, just not to that degree.

When it came down to it, Lilí knew she'd done nothing wrong. She hadn't deserved his cutting remarks, or the way he'd thrown their night together in her face. Cheapening what they had shared.

"You don't want the guys to what?" Julia tilted her head in question, her brow puckered with confusion.

Lilí ducked her chin. This was ridiculous. Diego didn't deserve her loyalty. If her brothers-in-law thought poorly of him after this, that was his doing. Not hers.

Still.

That tiny voice inside her wanted the guys to like him. Yearned for something she had begun to think might be possible with Diego. Only, not if he couldn't let her in.

How could someone emote through music as beautifully as he could with his guitar, yet not tap in to that depth with those he claimed to care about?

Tears clogged her throat, burning her nose and eyes.

She felt Rosa's hand softly skim along the side of her head. Once, twice. She knew the gesture was meant to soothe, only it made her eyes brim with tears. The moisture overflowed, falling on her lap to leave tiny dark spots on her faded jeans.

"*Ay, no llores,*" Julia crooned. She rubbed tiny circles on Lilí's back. "He's not worth your tears."

"Well, I don't know about that, exactly," Yazmine ventured, drawing out the words.

Lilí sniffed, angling her neck to peek at her sister. Yaz was dangerously close to breaking their sister code: He who hurts one of them, hurts them all.

"I'm not giving the guy a pass or anything," Yaz explained. She leaned over to set her wineglass on the coffee table next to Rosa, then reached for Lili's hand. "Diego definitely has some explaining to do. Sounds like some soul-searching, too. But you know as well as I do that, like a good number of kids at the center, he's got some serious family baggage."

"We all do," Rosa added softly, reminding Lilí of the misplaced guilt her middle sister had carried for years after their *mami*'s death. Thankfully, she'd finally admitted her feelings to her sisters, after some nudging from their priest, and had worked past them.

Wiping the wetness from her cheeks with the back of her hand, Lilí nodded. "I know. That's what makes me so sad. He's a good person. Just hardheaded."

Rosa cleared her throat. Loudly.

Lilí rolled her eyes, at the same time her lips curved in a real smile. The first since she and Lourdes had climbed out of that fourth-floor window onto the fire escape yesterday afternoon. Since Diego had lashed out at her like a cornered animal, then slunk off to lick his wounds.

"I know," she muttered. "Pot, kettle. You don't have to say anything."

Rosa tugged playfully on the end of Lilí's long braid where it hung down the front of her left shoulder. "So what are you going to do, *chiquita*? You're bound to run into him sooner or later."

"Yeah, especially since you're volunteering with the center's dance extravaganza," Yaz added. "Rehearsals start this week, with the show on Saturday two weeks from now. Are you going to be okay with that?"

"Does he really have to be there?" Lilí asked.

"He's playing the music for two solos." Yazmine scrunched her face in apology. "Those are scheduled to rehearse Tuesday and Thursday evenings. What if you come on Monday and Wednesday instead? During the actual show, we can always use more hands in the dressing rooms. Less chance you'll see him that way."

"Plus, I'll be around that second week to run interference if needed," Julia threw in.

Her thoughts a jumbled mix, Lilí stared down at the pinot noir filling her wineglass. The dark liquid matched her dark mood.

What if Diego didn't seek her out? If he was fine with the two of them simply going their separate ways, becoming polite acquaintances when their paths crossed?

A sharp, burning pain flared in her chest, radiating outward.

"Whatever you need from us, *estamos aquí*." Rosa's

softly spoken promise was a gentle balm, soothing Lilí's turmoil.

Mami and Papi had taught them that *familia* was there for you. Always. Even when they weren't physically present, like Mami and Papi couldn't be now, their presence surrounded her. Gave her comfort and strength. Reminded her of what she deserved and what she sought to give others.

Closing her eyes, she took a deep, fortifying breath.

Sí, she'd be disappointed if things with Diego were over just as they'd started to begin. Hugely disappointed.

But she deserved someone who respected her. Who valued her. The *músico* Papi's letter assured her was out there, waiting for her, would make mistakes, like she would, but he'd be man enough to admit them, to work through them alongside her.

If Diego couldn't do that, she didn't need to hear anything else from him.

Taking a sip of her wine, Lilí forced herself to swallow the truth, despite its bitter taste.

Chapter Sixteen

"See you Saturday afternoon, David!"

"Bye, David. Don't forget to email me the attendee list for next week's cyberbullying class."

Diego listened to the good-byes Yaz and Lilí called to David as they walked by the center's front desk Thursday evening. Leaning his guitar case against the counter, he acknowledged Yaz's head tilt in his direction with a vague wave of his hand.

His gaze immediately slid to Lilí, desperate for one last glimpse of her.

She gave him the same polite ghost of a smile she'd given him the few times he'd seen her over the past two weeks. It didn't quite freeze him out. Didn't invite him closer, either. Worse, it never quite reached her beautiful eyes.

When he'd wrapped up Héctor's guitar lesson last Tuesday, then headed into the gym for the dance program's rehearsal, he hadn't known what kind of reception he'd receive.

He'd fully expected Yaz to tell him to buzz off. Had anticipated Lilí laying into him for acting like an ass on Saturday. That would have been ten times better than her freeze-out the previous three days.

His eyes had scanned the gym as soon as he entered, searching the mix of kids sitting on the wooden bleachers and gathering in small groups sprinkled around the basketball court. Yazmine stood in the midst of some teens, all of them, like her, dressed in leotards and tights, her hair up in a sleek bun, her long arms and legs graceful in motion as she demonstrated a move. She easily caught his eye. Still, he only paused briefly before continuing his search of the crowd, looking for the one person he needed to see.

The one person it had taken him too long to realize he owed an apology, if he could only figure out what the hell to say.

But his search had been in vain. Lilí wasn't there.

His spirits sank faster than an unregistered weapon tossed into the Chicago River.

Yaz had excused herself from the group she'd been instructing when she spotted him. Shooting him a pointed look, she jerked her thumb toward a far corner of the gym, then spun on her ballet-shoed heel.

Like a perp about to face the judge, Diego trudged behind her. Fingers gripping his guitar case handle, he'd told himself he deserved whatever she threw at him. Probably worse.

Arms crossed, hip cocked in a move reminiscent of Lilí's feisty attitude, Yaz wasted no time laying into him. "You screwed up. Big time."

"I know. But it's complicated."

Her arched brow told him his answer wasn't going

to cut it. At the time, it was the only answer he'd been capable of giving.

The gym door had banged open and he craned his neck to see who entered, hoping.

"Don't bother," Yaz said, her tone dry. "She's not coming tonight. Or Thursday."

Both nights he was scheduled to play during rehearsal.

"That gives you time to figure your crap out," Yaz went on. "Without my little sister getting hurt any more than she's already been."

Diego winced, hating himself for the pain he had caused Lilí.

Ultimately, with a roomful of dancers waiting for rehearsal to begin, Yaz had laid down the law. Either man up and make things right with Lilí or leave her alone. If not, he would answer to the entire Fernandez *familia*.

Diego hadn't expected anything less.

Familia primero. He and Lilí had shared the family-first motto that day at the Cubby Bear. Although, his way of living by it had become a little skewed over the years.

For Lilí it was different. The bond among her *familia* had been a palpable entity when he'd joined the Fernandez clan for dinner in their childhood home. Like a force field protecting them, linking them together. For the briefest moment, they'd welcomed him inside it.

Then he'd gone and blown everything.

It'd taken the past two weeks of sleepless nights, a heartfelt phone conversation with his sister when she'd called from the treatment center's community phone, and countless miles pounding the city streets in his running shoes to make him realize that truth.

Now Diego watched the center's metal front door clang shut behind Lilí and her sister. The sound reverberated in his head, like a cell door slamming closed, locking him in isolation.

"Dude, I don't know what you did, but it definitely was not good." David's thin face scrunched in disbelief as he muttered his censure.

Diego bit back a resigned sigh. "Yeah, it wasn't."

"Well, if you're smart, you'll figure out how to fix it. Lilí Fernandez is a catch. With a capital C. If I thought I had a chance, I'd ask her out myself."

Diego's head whipped around so fast, a muscle in his neck pinched. A deep burn spread from behind his ear downward.

"Whoa! I said *if*!" David held up his hands in surrender. "All she's given me is the friend vibe, so don't go thinking I'm interested in stepping on your toes."

Diego rubbed the side of his neck until the burn eased. If he didn't watch it, his surly attitude would alienate someone else he usually liked hanging around. Already this week, he'd been called out for playing too rough in a game of two-on-two basketball at one of the outdoor courts.

Yesterday, Stevens warned that if he wasn't in a better mood their next watch, Stevens would make him ride in the back seat of the squad car. Not that he could, but Diego got the point.

Basically, he needed to get his shit together.

"No worries," he told David, leaning down to pick up his guitar case. "It's not like I have any say in who Lilí's spending time with."

If he did, he wouldn't be heading home by himself, feeling adrift, somewhere between relief that Lourdes sounded healthy on the phone and lonely now that he'd experienced Lilí's positive energy. He couldn't sit on his couch without remembering her there beside him. Singing to his music, giving in to temptation along with him.

"If you ask me, I get the sense you'd like to," David said, interrupting Diego's mental brooding. "Guess it's up to you whether you're going to do anything about it."

Two young girls Diego didn't recognize approached the front desk to ask David a question and Diego edged away.

He waved good-bye, nodding his head when the assistant manager reminded him about the 2:30 PM report time for the dance extravaganza on Saturday.

That meant two long days until he'd see Lilí again. Forty-eight hours for him to figure out what he wanted and, more importantly, what was best for her.

"You look like crap," Lourdes said on Saturday morning when he met her in the treatment center's common room for her first family visit.

"Thanks," he grumbled.

She pulled him into a hug, something they hadn't shared enough of in recent years. Caught off guard by the gesture, it took Diego a second to wrap his arms around her, squeezing tightly. Man, it felt good.

He held on a little longer, making up for the hugs he hadn't given her over the years.

When they finally broke apart, Lourdes leaned back, her brows angled in a frown. "*Qué*, no wisecrack back at me?"

He lifted a shoulder in a resigned shrug. "I saw

myself in the bathroom mirror this morning. I know what I look like."

Tired lines around his eyes and mouth, shadows darkening his eyes like a raccoon's, thanks to too many sleepless nights.

"Ah, I get it. You haven't made up with Lilí yet, huh?"

When he didn't respond, Lourdes sucked her teeth at him.

"*Terco*," she grumbled.

Being hardheaded wasn't his problem. More like, being freaked out by how badly he missed Lilí when they hadn't known each other all that long to begin with.

Her sassy grin, the teasing glint in her beautiful eyes, the tropically sweet smell of the lotion she favored. Her vibrant personality and the sense that all could be right in his world, if she was there along with him.

Only, she wasn't.

"Come on." Lourdes grabbed his elbow to lead him over to a laminate-topped round table.

She pulled out a navy vinyl-upholstered chair and plopped onto it. Two women, one older, the other a younger version of her, sat at a similar table about ten feet away, their heads bent together in conversation. The distance allowed for a measure of privacy and with Lourdes seemingly intent on grilling him about Lilí, he appreciated the space.

"Let *me* help *you* for once," Lourdes offered. "Sounds like you need it."

Selecting the chair across from her, he sat down. "What's that supposed to mean?"

"It means, if you keep being so thick-skulled, you might really mess things up."

Like he hadn't already. "She's got a lot going on right now, her sister's in charge of the dance recital at the center and Lilí's doing stuff for that."

Lourdes batted away his lame excuse. "That's a cop-out."

"I didn't come here to talk about me." Uncomfortable being the focus of her attention, he brushed imaginary crumbs off the table. "I want to know about you, how are you doing?"

"Fiiine. I'll go first. But you *are* talking. This goes both ways."

He frowned, but her quirked brow and the don't-mess-with-me twist of her lips told him Lourdes would keep nagging until he agreed. Honestly, this kind of conversation, asking his big sister for girl advice, was something he'd missed out on growing up. Call him crazy for wanting a little of it.

"Deal," he agreed. "You actually look great, by the way. I was relieved to get your call this morning."

Lourdes smiled, the grin rounding her cheeks, reaching her rich chocolate eyes so like their *mamá*'s. Her skin coloring was healthier, highlighted by subdued makeup. She had brushed her curls into smooth waves and she wore a flowy floral top over a pair of navy leggings. Less show-off-the-goods and more I'm-comfortable-with-who-I-am.

"*Gracias.* Coming here was the right move. But it's just the beginning for me. This addiction is something I'll struggle with for the rest of my life." She splayed her hands on the table in front of her. Honest. Open. "I can see that I've made progress. And, when I'm ready, they'll find a halfway house for me to live, so I have a better shot at sticking with the plan. They call it a sober living situation."

"You know you're welcome at home," he offered.

Then maybe it wouldn't be so quiet. Maybe he wouldn't keep seeing Lilí in his kitchen, in his living room. If only he could stop hearing her emotion-rich voice singing when he sat on his couch strumming his guitar.

Even his music hadn't quieted his demons lately.

"I figured you'd say that." Lourdes reached an arm across the table toward him, her palm up.

He grasped her hand, holding it tightly between both of his.

"Talking with the counselors," she continued, "having all this time to think about what I've done, the choices I've made. I'm so sorry, *hermanito.*"

Her voice trembled, evoking an echoing remorse that had Diego sliding over to the empty seat beside her. He placed an arm around her shoulders, hugging her close.

"I know my situation made you put your life on hold. A lot. You took on the responsibility of looking out for me when I wasn't making the best choices."

"You're my big sister, I'd do anything for you."

"*Pues,* now it's my turn to look out for you. To give you some advice."

"Why don't I like the sound of that?" he grumbled.

Her raspy laughter was like a favorite song he hadn't heard enough over the years. It reminded him of when she used to tease him about his lame kid jokes. The warm feeling he'd get when she ruffled his hair.

Too soon she sobered, becoming the taskmaster who used to make him go to bed on time, no matter how hard he pleaded.

"Don't do what I've done," she warned. "Don't push away the people who want to do what's right for you. Those going out of their way to show they care.

The ones who overlook our flaws and see the good that's inside us."

He shook his head. "I think you're reading into things. Lilí and I haven't known each other that long. It's not as serious as you think."

"Are you sure?"

He couldn't answer that. Not on Lilí's behalf anyway. But for him, these last two weeks, especially after pulling his head out of his ass and admitting he'd overreacted, he knew which way he leaned.

Lourdes eyed him with a tender expression that reminded him of their *mami*. Nostalgia filled his chest, rising to knot in his throat.

"All I'm saying is, if you'd like whatever you got going on with Lilí to be more than what it is or was, then maybe you need to stop worrying about me so much, and take a good hard look at what you want. *Who* you want. Figure out what's stopping you and instead of pushing Lilí away, decide what you gotta do to show her that you want more."

Diego stared at their joined hands resting on the tabletop. It'd been a long time since he and Lourdes had sat like this together. Since they'd shared a conversation that didn't end with one or both of them pissed off, disappointed.

"Whatever you decide, I'm here for you, *hermanito*." She squeezed his hand. "I'm determined to do this right. To get my life together. For myself. For you. For our *familia*."

Pride for his sister swelled inside Diego.

As he hugged her to him again, he felt her warm tears wet his neck. Unbidden, a thought whispered through his mind: Lilí would be thrilled to know his sister was doing so well and he couldn't wait to tell her.

Not because of her professional role in getting Lourdes here, but because in the short time since Lilí had come storming into his life, she'd shown him how amazing it felt to connect with someone. To share the good, and the bad.

Only, not just anyone, the *right* one.

Now, he simply had to figure out how to break down the wall of reservation she'd erected between them, before it was too late.

Chapter Seventeen

"Is it almost our turn?" Alicia Rodríguez, a cute four-year-old with enough energy to light up the entire Wrigleyville neighborhood in an emergency blackout bounced on the tips of her toes as she asked the same question she'd asked Lilí barely thirty seconds ago.

Rather than be annoyed at the little dancer's version of *Are we there yet?*, Lilí smiled down at the child and repeated, "Only two more songs, then it'll be your number. Right after the second dance solo, okay?"

"Okay!" Alicia hop-skipped away to join another little girl wearing the same light pink tights, leotard, and ballet slippers. The two girls giggled at something, their excitement adding a flush to their pudgy cheeks.

The show was about three-quarters of the way through, and from Lilí's vantage point as co-chaperone of the Tiny Tot group, the show seemed to be running smoothly. She had even managed to avoid Diego, thanks to keeping herself contained to the classroom they had turned into the Tiny Tot changing room.

She'd purposely stayed here during the first solo, assuring the mom co-chaperoning with her that she was fine covering so the woman could hear Diego play. Apparently many of the moms, especially the single ones, had been looking forward to his performance as much as their kids' numbers.

For her part, she didn't mind skipping it. If she was lucky, she'd only catch him playing the tail end of the second solo while lining up Alicia and the rest of the Tiny Tots in the hallway outside the gym doors.

Over the past two weeks he'd made no move to contact her. Nor had he sought her out at the center this week during the full show rehearsals when it'd been all hands on deck.

She could take a hint as well as the next girl.

He wasn't interested. Or he was simply unable to accept that her intent hadn't been to ignore his request that she stay out of his business, and more about doing her job. Despite the personal connection.

If she was honest, their personal connection had driven her to make the treatment center arrangements herself to ensure everything went smoothly for his sister. All the while, Lilí had anticipated, wrongfully, that Diego would appreciate her extra effort.

"Listen up, dancers." Lilí clapped her hands to get the Tiny Tots' attention. The six girls and one boy between the ages of three and five grew quiet. "*Gracias*, I appreciate you being such great listeners. Let's go ahead and start forming your two lines so we can walk quietly to the gym."

In no time the kids were lined up, some like Alicia bouncing on their toes with excitement. A few had that stage-frightened, wide-eyed nervous stare on their adorable faces. Lilí made sure to give those a friendly pat on the shoulder, stopping to offer them an encouraging smile.

"Everyone's going to do great!" she said, trying to pump up those who needed it.

Moments later, the two lines compressed against the far right wall in the hallway in front of the gym, making room for a group of junior high dancers exiting. With the door open, Lilí heard Yaz introduce the high schooler who would perform a solo flamenco dance, with Diego playing accompaniment.

"He is so talented," the mom chaperoning with her whispered, awe giving the woman's words a breathy quality. "And easy on the eyes, isn't he?"

Yes and most definitely yes.

Lilí kept the opinions to herself, choosing to respond with a noncommittal, "I suppose so."

No need to link herself to his fan club.

The mom took the front of the line while Lilí rounded out the back to keep any kids from wandering off. Of course, had she known the lady planned on propping the right door open slightly, allowing Diego's music to drift into the hallway, Lilí might have suggested swapping places to ensure the door stayed closed.

The moment Lilí heard his first chord, her breath hitched. She steeled herself against the urge to edge closer. Sneak a peek at where she knew from rehearsals he sat off to the right, allowing the dancer to take center stage.

She didn't have to see Diego to picture him though. The image of him playing for her was emblazoned on her mind. His Spanish guitar nestled in his lap, his left hand caressing the guitar's fretboard, the fingers on his right hand strumming and plucking the notes. The same way he'd expertly played for her throughout their night in her apartment. Coaxing a response she'd never felt before.

Annoyed with herself for thinking about their time together, when she'd promised herself she wouldn't pine for him like some lovesick schoolgirl, Lilí forced her attention back to the kids. One girl had that pale, I-think-I'm-going-to-puke expression Lilí had seen from others when she'd volunteered in the past, moments before they changed their mind about performing.

She hunkered down beside the child so they were eye-level. "*Hola, mamita*, you holding up okay? I saw your *abuela* sitting out there. Super excited to see how beautiful you look in your ballerina clothes. Everyone knows how hard you've been practicing and they're ready to cheer you on."

Her dark brown eyes wide, the girl stared back, lower lip protruding in a pout that said she was not convinced.

"You know Ms. Yazmine's my sister, right? *Bueno*, she told me what an amazing dancer you are."

"She did?" The child's tentative question had Lilí nodding in answer.

"Uh-huh, and believe me, she knows a good dancer when she sees one. You're gonna be amazing!" Lilí winked at the little girl, pleased when the child smiled in response.

Seconds later, clapping sounded from inside the gym. The solo was finished. The Tiny Tots were up.

The mom pushed the door open, holding it with one hand. She gestured for the two lines to move inside, stopping at the edge of the basketball court like they'd rehearsed. Yazmine would introduce the group, then they'd gracefully, well, Tiny Tot gracefully anyway, move to their spots in the center of the court and wait for their music to start.

As she brought up the rear, Lilí heard the crowd

rustling in the wooden bleachers. She looked up to see what the chatter might be about and noticed Yazmine and Diego talking near the court sideline at what would be considered front center stage.

Yaz frowned at whatever Diego said. Her gaze cut to Lilí, but before Lilí could decipher her sister's expression, Yaz turned back to Diego.

It was the first time Lilí had seen him tonight and she drank him in as if she were a card-carrying member of the moms' newly formed Diego Reyes fan club.

Dressed in black slacks and a form-fitting maroon button-down that stretched taut over his broad shoulders and muscular biceps, he looked absolutely delectable. Despite the shadows under his eyes, which left her wondering if he'd been working long hours or extra watches over the past two weeks, his chiseled jaw and angular features made her long to caress his tiredness away.

She strained to read his lips, but his rushed speech made it impossible. It wasn't until he paused, took a deep breath that expanded his chest, straining the top buttons of his shirt, that Lilí made out his, "Please."

Yaz's rigid posture relaxed. She leaned closer, and whatever she said had him nodding quickly as he drew a quick cross over his heart with a finger. Then he was striding back onto their "stage" where he slid his chair and step stool to the center of the floor.

Yaz spun around to face the audience. She flicked the button to activate the cordless mic, then shot a quick glance at Lilí, her expression a mix of anxious anticipation that had Lilí clutching her stomach to calm the butterflies suddenly taking flight there.

"It seems we're in for a treat this afternoon," Yaz told the crowd. "A surprise you won't find mentioned in our program. However, Diego Reyes has asked to play a special song for us. I hope *everyone*"—her gaze slid over to Lilí briefly—"will give him your consideration. So, without further ado, Diego, take it away."

Grabbing the microphone stand, Yaz carried it out to him. She held the mic out with a stiff arm. Diego swallowed, almost uncomfortably, before taking it.

He cleared his throat, the sound scratchy over the speakers.

"*Perdón,*" he muttered, repeating the apology in English.

He wiped the back of a hand over his brow, his complexion a little pale. For someone with as much experience playing in front of small groups like this one, he acted strangely nervous to Lilí.

She wanted to leave before he started. Distance herself from the pull she felt whenever he played. Torn, she stepped closer to the mom, on the verge of excusing herself and letting the other woman know she'd meet them in the designated area in the stands where the kids would sit after their number so they could watch the rest of the show.

Then Diego started talking, his deep timbre and humility gluing her feet to their spot.

"I took my first guitar lesson in this youth center many years ago. I learned from a man whose patience and kindness infused me with a love of music that kept me off the streets. At first, I only played for my *mami*, who encouraged me, even when the chords I struggled with sounded more like cats screeching."

The audience laughed. Diego flashed his smile, but she spotted his lingering unease.

"My *mami* asked me to learn one song. And once I did, she made me play it every day before I finished practicing. Without fail."

Lilí sucked in a painful breath. No. She shook her head. No way was he going to play "Somos Novios."

He knew what that song meant to her. To her *familia*. What it would forever mean to her now that they'd performed it together.

Her gaze sought Yazmine, only to find her sister's hopeful expression. Yaz bent her elbows, palms up at her sides, as if to say it was out of her hands.

"Now there's another special someone," Diego continued. "Someone whose positivity, caring heart, and passionate nature have brought new meaning to the lyrics of this song for me. So I'd like to play it today for you, but especially for her, in the hopes that she'll accept my apology."

A palm pressed over her mouth to silence her shocked gasp, Lilí watched as Diego sank into the wooden chair. His left hand caressed the guitar's neck while he flexed the fingers on his right. Her skin warmed as if he'd touched her, tiny pinpricks of awareness shimmering through her.

He took a deep breath. Blew it out with puffed cheeks. Then, eyes closed, he brought Mami and Papi's wedding song to life.

Though he played it as an instrumental, she knew the words from memory. They were an homage to desire and commitment. Of lovers' spats and stolen kisses. Pure emotion and profound love.

The rise and fall of the music's swell called to her wounded soul. Diego occasionally ad-libbed, as if he felt the music so intensely it drove him to give more. Feel more.

Heart in her throat, Lilí couldn't tear her gaze away from him. Admiring the way his fingers masterfully strummed and pressed the strings. Eyes closed, his face taut with emotion. A man and his music, one and the same.

When his voice joined in on the last chorus, smooth and rich, crooning about love and passion, finishing with the promise of *siempre novios*, a warm tear slipped down her cheek.

He wasn't playing fair.

Diego knew his music would get to her like nothing else he might try. She wanted to be angry with him for using that weakness against her. And yet, the fact that he knew her well enough to understand how their mutual appreciation and love for the language of music might bond them, made her heart race with hope.

The last strains of the song faded away and the audience rose to their feet with thunderous applause. Overwhelmed with emotion, Lilí spun around and fled the gym.

Out in the hall she pivoted to the right, heading down the row of classrooms. With most of the routines completed and the dancers in the stands, only a few remaining dance groups milled about, waiting their turn. She ignored them, desperately searching for an empty place where she could hide and pull herself together.

"Lilí!"

Hearing Diego's call, she ducked into a room nearby. Only one row of its fluorescent lights was on and she was relieved to find it free of the dance bags, makeup and hair products, and other items indicating it was being used as a changing space.

Footsteps pounded in the hall.

Leaving the rest of the lights off, Lilí sat down at a desk in the back corner.

Part of her wanted him to bypass the darkened

space, expecting it to be empty, giving her time to wrap her head around his apology, decide what to make of his use of that particular song.

A larger part yearned for him to find her. For them to be able to work through this. And yet, after his horrible behavior the other weekend, the first move to make amends had to come from him.

"Lilí!" His voice echoed down the hall, his footsteps drawing nearer.

She held her breath, waiting. Wanting. Hoping.

"Hey."

His soft greeting had her glancing up to find him hovering in the doorway. "Hi."

"I'm glad I found you," he said, the eager, yet tentative note in his husky voice raising goose bumps on her flesh.

He leaned a shoulder on the door frame, his figure partially shadowed thanks to the room's dim fluorescent lighting and the hallway's brightness, reaching around him to cast a long beam along the floor.

"Man, I didn't think my rendition of the song was that bad," he teased. His hesitant smile nearly coaxing one from her.

But the disillusion that had grown with each day that had come and gone without him seeking her out, wouldn't allow her to forgive him that easily.

"I guess it could have been better," she deadpanned.

His soft chuckle brushed up against her like a caress. He stepped into the room and her stomach clenched, anticipation building.

"I think it would have been better, perfect actually, as a duet," he said.

Her heart skipped, then kicked into double-time. "That depends."

Head angled to the side, he dug his hands in his pants pockets and peered at her intently. "On what?"

"On what else you have to say to me. Without your guitar. Because I'm pretty sure you know you're practically irresistible when you play."

"Irresistible, huh?"

She rolled her eyes at the flash of his white teeth in the play of shadows.

"May I?" he gestured toward the desk next to hers.

"It's a free country."

Diego sat down, swiveling in the seat to face her. Right arm crooked on the laminate desktop, his big body filled the space. The subtle scent of his musky cologne teased her senses.

"You're not going to make this easy for me, are you?" he asked.

"Not really, but I don't think you expected me to. Did you?"

"No, I didn't," he answered truthfully. "Because you deserve more. Better."

She'd left her hair loose today and now he gently tucked a little behind her left ear, his fingers lingering to softly brush the side of her neck. She yearned to lean into his touch. Instead, she remained firm in her resolve.

They had started something good together. She honestly believed that. Something beyond mere sexual attraction, rooted in their love of *familia* and commitment to making a difference for others.

Sure, the moms in the gym audience looked at Diego and saw a man who was simply too delicious for his own good. Yet Lilí knew from glorious personal experience the strength, the gentleness, the compassion that lay beneath his handsome surface. She wanted more of that, and so much more than one memorable night together.

"My sister says hello," he said.

The unexpected change of subject took her by surprise, but it pulled her wandering thoughts back on track.

"I heard she's doing well. I mean, I haven't seen or spoken to her, but I've called to check on her progress. As a professional," she qualified, holding up a hand to stall his concern that she might have overstepped. "I promise, I've kept my distance, respecting her privacy. And yours. Careful not to interfere or pry."

Diego grasped her fingers, the warmth from his seeping up her arm. His thumb brushed the back of her hand, setting off gentle waves of desire lapping against her wall of reservations.

"It's never interference when it comes from you," Diego said. "Not in a negative way, and only with good intent. I realize that now."

The earnestness in his dark eyes begged her to believe him.

"I probably did all along," he continued. "But I was too wrapped up in my own issues to be objective. I'm sorry, Lilí."

A pained look pinched his handsome face. The urge to comfort him was swift, instinctive. And yet, she needed more from him.

"Go on."

"Those words sound so lame. I know that. My *mami* used to tell me 'I'm sorry' could be easily said, but it was the actions behind them that made the difference."

"Smart woman," Lilí murmured.

"Yeah, she was. A lot like you."

A knot of emotion welled in Lilí's throat. She ducked her head, swallowing around the tightness.

Ay, how she would have loved meeting Alma Reyes. The woman had raised an incredible son, and she would be relieved to know that the daughter she loved might finally be on the right path.

"I messed up, Lilí. In many ways." Gently, with a finger crooked beneath her chin, Diego bade her to look at him. "I complained about Lourdes shutting me out, not giving me a chance to help her make things right. Then I went and did the same to you. I've been afraid of losing her for so long, hating being alone, and then you barged into my life."

"*Bueno*, if I had to do any barging, it's because you were doing your immovable oak impersonation on Melba's front stoop."

He laughed, his sexy smile finally tugging one from her.

His thumb traced the edge of her bottom lip, his gaze dropping to her mouth. Subconsciously she licked her lips. Desire flared in his eyes, fanning the flame she hadn't been able to extinguish when it came to him.

"This immovable oak's been moved by you, Lilí Fernandez."

Ay, she liked the sound of that. "*¿De veras?*"

"Yes, really." Softly he brushed her wispy bangs out of her eyes. "Here's the thing: I've been keeping people an arm's distance away for a long time now. But I don't want to do that with you. I want to soak up your positivity, and do what I can to keep yours alive. For the first time in a long time, I feel like I belong. With you, with my sister, with your *familia*. Maybe it's too soon, and I'm jumping the gun here, but I know where I'd like whatever we've started to be headed. And that's in whatever direction you're going."

He rose, pulling her to stand.

Her legs wobbly, she leaned her thigh against the chair's backrest, completely stunned by his admission.

"The past two weeks have felt empty, even my music hasn't been as soothing to me. Something's missing without you. So I'm asking, please forgive me. Give me a chance to make things right between us. Let's see where our musical duo can go. Together."

He stepped around the back of her chair, moving to the aisle with her, so nothing stood between them.

She gazed up at his handsome face, the tiny V between his brows telegraphing his anguish.

"What do you say? Will you forgive me?" Desperation hung on his request.

Overwhelmed by his honest sincerity, afraid if she tried to find the right words she'd end up a blubbering mess, Lilí did what she'd wanted to do from the moment she'd stepped into the gym and caught sight of him.

Cupping his face in her hands, she rose up onto her tiptoes and pressed her lips to his.

She felt the tension ease from his body, then his arms came around her, pulling her closer. Holding her tightly in his embrace.

"Is that a yes?" he murmured against her lips. "Please tell me that's a yes."

She grinned. "Most definitely yes."

It was all the answer he apparently needed as he covered her mouth with a deep, toe-curling kiss. She opened for him, savoring the sensual brush of his tongue along hers.

Desire whooshed through her, a wildfire of heat and passion he stoked with each caress of her back, hips, butt. His fingers found the hem of her sundress, the calluses from his guitar playing rough as he traced a sensual trail along her lower thighs, drawing shivers of heat that shot straight to her core.

She crooked a knee up on his hip, desperate to be closer.

Diego broke their kiss on a muffled groan. He dropped his head to her shoulder, burrowing his nose in the crook of her neck.

"Man, I've missed the smell of your lotion. Makes you even more . . . delicious." The tip of his tongue laved her neck, and she moaned with pleasure.

He chuckled. Not exactly the response she expected and she drew back to peer up at him in the shadows. "What's so funny?"

"I've been dreaming about getting a hot girl to come make out with me in one of these classrooms since I was a horny teen."

His satisfied smirk had her throwing back her head with laughter.

"I'm happy to assist in checking that item off your bucket list," she teased.

"More like starred with a red permanent marker." He winked, leaning down to rest his forehead against hers.

She held on to the back of his neck, her fingers splaying at his nape.

"I'm all in, Lilí. I mean, I know I'll make mistakes, but I want this to work. I want *us*. What do you say?"

Gazing up into his dark eyes, Lilí saw the truth, the hope, the desire he didn't bother trying to hide.

Papi had been right. Like always. Her *músico* had been out there, waiting for her. Searching for her.

Now, she was certain she'd found him, and she didn't plan on letting him go.

"I say, you had me at the first chords of 'Somos Novios,'" she answered.

On that note, Diego swooped in to seal her words with a soul-searing kiss, a promise of the gloriously perfect music and melodies they were ready to create. Together.

If you enjoyed *Their Perfect Melody*,
be sure not to miss all of Priscilla Oliveras's
Matched to Perfection series, including

HER PERFECT AFFAIR

Rosa Fernandez doesn't act on impulse—she's the responsible one, planning her career with precision, finally landing a job as the librarian at conservative Queen of Peace Academy, confining her strongest emotions to her secret poetry journal. But she's been harboring a secret crush on dreamy Jeremy Taylor, and after one dance with him at her sister's wedding, Rosa longs to let loose for the first time. She deserves some fun, after all. So what if she doesn't have a shot with Jeremy, not with his wealthy pedigree and high profile lifestyle. But one dance leads to one kiss, and soon Rosa is head-over-heels . . .

The adopted son of a prominent Chicago lawyer, Jeremy has a lot to live up to—especially with his birth father in prison—the perfect example of a bad example. With a big promotion and a move to Japan in the works, Jeremy is worlds away from settling down. But sweet, steady Rosa is a temptation he doesn't want to deny himself, at least for now. Yet when their simple fling turns complicated, everything they've both worked for is threatened— except the red-hot intimacy they've found together. Can forever really grow from just-for-now?

Keep reading for a special look!

*A Zebra Shout mass-market paperback
and eBook on sale now.*

Rosa Fernandez stared at the sea of wedding guests whirling on the dance floor. Her toe tapped to the beat of the salsa music, but she didn't join in the revelry. Not when it was her responsibility to make sure everything was running smoothly.

Scooting around a potted palm, she made a beeline for the buffet tables and wedding planner, relieved that so far all had gone according to schedule. Her big sister and her new husband had departed over an hour ago amidst kisses and well wishes. With huge grins on their faces and love for each other in their eyes, they'd headed upstairs to one of the finest suites the downtown historic Chicago hotel boasted.

Now, with the clock close to striking 1 AM, the party would be ending soon.

Without Rosa having worked up the nerve to ask a particular someone to dance. Her gaze scanned the crowd, looking for—

"It was a beautiful September wedding, *mija*."

Rosa turned her attention to her neighbor, bending to accept the elderly woman's hug. "*Gracias*, Señora Vega."

Señora Vega smiled, the wrinkles on her face deepening. "You did a fabulous job. Just like the church senior social you organized last month."

"I'm glad you enjoyed them."

"*Bueno*, no one doubted tonight would come together beautifully in your capable hands," Señora Vega said. "You're always on top of things. That's your specialty, *verdad, nena*?"

Right.

Or maybe it was her affliction.

Rosa kept the errant thought to herself, returning Señora Vega's smile with a tremulous one of her own. "Yazmine and Tomás deserve the best."

"*Que nena buena eres.*" The older woman patted Rosa's cheek, a wistful sheen in her eyes. "Your parents would have loved this," she said, leaning in for a good-bye hug.

Rosa nodded mutely, melancholy wrapping around her heart at the thought of her parents and how much she missed them. They should have been here. Sure, there was nothing any of them could have done to stop Papi's cancer, but her mother's car accident all those years ago . . . that should never have happened.

For now, Rosa pushed aside the memories and guilt. Today was her big sister's special day, so Rosa would do her best to channel their mom and her knack for organizing the best parties anyone could throw.

As Rosa wove through guests, the reception music changed to the heavy bass of a popular reggaeton song and the crowd on the dance floor let out a cheer.

"Hey, Rosa, come join us!" Arms raised overhead, her younger sister waved at her.

Surrounded by a crowd of her old high school friends, Lilí shimmied her hips and shoulders in reckless abandon to the Spanish rap music. Thanks to her sweaty gyrations throughout the night, her pixie haircut had lost some of its spike, but Lilí's playful grin had only grown bigger.

One of the guys snaked his arm around her lower back, and Lilí plastered her lithe body against his. They moved to the music as one, simulating an act that more likely belonged in the bedroom than on the dance floor.

Rosa shook her head in bemusement. Lilí puckered up and made a show of blowing her a kiss.

Ay, the little brat. A cocktail dress and heels could not a properly behaved young lady make.

Lilí yelled another catcall in her direction.

Rosa waved her off. Mosh-pit-style dancing wasn't really her cup of *café con leche*. Lilí knew that.

Lilí stuck out her tongue, then went back to her fun.

With a resigned sigh, Rosa turned away. Lilí might not understand that there were responsibilities to attend to, but *she* certainly did. With Papi's passing earlier this year, Rosa felt compelled to take charge. Even more so than after Mami's death almost ten years ago, when Rosa and Yaz had been in high school.

Be responsible. Do the right thing. It was what she did best. Even if the "good girl" reputation Señora Vega had referred to sometimes made Rosa itch to break out of the mold.

Shaking off the lingering melancholy, she continued moving through the crowd, stopping now and then to chat with friends and guests, thanking them for their attendance, reminiscing about her parents.

She was halfway across the ballroom when a thick arm encircled her waist from behind.

"Red Rosie, you've been avoiding me."

Recognizing her former classmate's voice, Rosa bit back a groan.

"Héctor!" She turned, leaning away from him, barely stopping herself from stomping on his foot with her heel. It would serve him right after grabbing her butt earlier in the buffet line!

"*No seas mala!*" he complained.

"I'm not being mean. I'm busy."

"One dance. A slow one. Come on, Red Rosie."

The embarrassing high school nickname grated on her already frayed nerves.

"Héctor, I have to check in with the wedding planner."

"All work and no play—"

"I know, I know. But this party is all about Yaz and Tomás. How about you go play a little harder for the both of us, okay?" Rosa schooled her face into her understanding-yet-I'm-not-giving-in expression. She might only be seven weeks into her job as the librarian at Queen of Peace Academy, but she'd been practicing this look in the mirror for months. "Marisol is sitting by herself. I'm sure she'd love to dance with you."

Rosa pointed at their mutual friend.

When Héctor gave her a sad-eyed pout, Rosa arched a brow to make her point, but softened it with a teasing smile.

"*Está bien,*" he finally moaned.

She watched him trudge away, part of her wanting to join him and the crowd having fun. Yet, she held back. Her job wasn't done.

Moments later, after a short discussion with the wedding planner, Rosa learned all was in order. She wasn't needed anymore. Just like at home now that Papi was gone and Lilí was off to college.

Uncertainty weighed heavy in her chest.

She glanced from her peers, excitedly dancing, to the older couples chatting at the circular tables. Most people here would say she fit in better with the older, more reserved crowd. Not that she could blame them. It's where she typically gravitated. She heaved a sigh weighty with resignation.

No one knew about the increasing number of times lately that she wondered how it might feel to shake up the status quo. Do something just because it felt good, without worrying about the consequences.

Although, shaking things up might not be what the Catholic diocesan school board at Queen of Peace Academy in their quiet Chicago suburb of Oakton, Illinois, wanted from their new librarian. She'd worked hard to finish her MLS on time so she could take over when Mrs. Patterson had retired this past summer. Now was Rosa's chance to carve her own niche amongst the staff, moving from former student to colleague. Allowing her to work on becoming a mentor to her students.

So what if she felt something was missing. It would pass.

Feeling out of sorts, Rosa edged her way toward the back of the ballroom near one of the portable drink stations.

"One ginger ale with a lime twist for the *señorita*, coming right up," the bartender said as she approached.

"You remembered!"

The gray-haired man filled a cup with ice and smiled at her. "Why aren't you enjoying yourself with the other young people?"

"I was just about to ask her the same question."

Rosa started at the deep voice coming from behind her.

She glanced over her shoulder, thrilled to find Jeremy Taylor standing close by. His broad shoulders and football-player physique filled out his navy pin-striped suit to perfection. Even though her heels added a good four inches to her five-foot-six height, Jeremy still towered over her. He smiled, his blue eyes crinkling at the corners. A thrill shivered down her spine.

"I'll have what she's having, please," Jeremy said.

"Ginger ale?" the old bartender asked.

Jeremy blinked in surprise before he slowly shook his head. "Rosa, Rosa, Rosa. How can you celebrate your sister's marriage without enjoying some champagne? C'mon, share a glass with me?"

Longing seared through her, fast and hot. *Ay*, little did he know that she'd share pretty much *anything* with him.

Jeremy tilted his head toward her, urging her to say yes. But not pushing.

Ever since Yaz had introduced the two of them almost four years ago, Jeremy had been nothing but friendly, almost brotherly. After Papi's death back in January, Jeremy had been amazingly supportive. A perfect gentleman.

Just not *her* perfect gentleman.

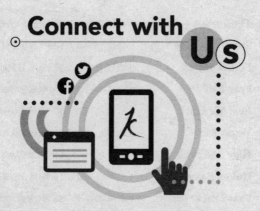

Books by Bestselling Author
Fern Michaels

___	The Jury	0-8217-7878-1	$6.99US/$9.99CAN
___	Sweet Revenge	0-8217-7879-X	$6.99US/$9.99CAN
___	Lethal Justice	0-8217-7880-3	$6.99US/$9.99CAN
___	Free Fall	0-8217-7881-1	$6.99US/$9.99CAN
___	Fool Me Once	0-8217-8071-9	$7.99US/$10.99CAN
___	Vegas Rich	0-8217-8112-X	$7.99US/$10.99CAN
___	Hide and Seek	1-4201-0184-6	$6.99US/$9.99CAN
___	Hokus Pokus	1-4201-0185-4	$6.99US/$9.99CAN
___	Fast Track	1-4201-0186-2	$6.99US/$9.99CAN
___	Collateral Damage	1-4201-0187-0	$6.99US/$9.99CAN
___	Final Justice	1-4201-0188-9	$6.99US/$9.99CAN
___	Up Close and Personal	0-8217-7956-7	$7.99US/$9.99CAN
___	Under the Radar	1-4201-0683-X	$6.99US/$9.99CAN
___	Razor Sharp	1-4201-0684-8	$7.99US/$10.99CAN
___	Yesterday	1-4201-1494-8	$5.99US/$6.99CAN
___	Vanishing Act	1-4201-0685-6	$7.99US/$10.99CAN
___	Sara's Song	1-4201-1493-X	$5.99US/$6.99CAN
___	Deadly Deals	1-4201-0686-4	$7.99US/$10.99CAN
___	Game Over	1-4201-0687-2	$7.99US/$10.99CAN
___	Sins of Omission	1-4201-1153-1	$7.99US/$10.99CAN
___	Sins of the Flesh	1-4201-1154-X	$7.99US/$10.99CAN
___	Cross Roads	1-4201-1192-2	$7.99US/$10.99CAN

Available Wherever Books Are Sold!
Check out our website at www.kensingtonbooks.com